Praise for

In The Blood: Book One of The Blood Royal Saga

"...reminded me of the movie, **The Hunger** and there's a real sense of authenticity to the vampires. That's hard to pull off when you're writing about (presumably) imaginary creatures. Definitely one to check out if you like your vampires sans-sparkles, particularly if you're a fan of Anne Rice's **Vampire Chronicles**."

– **Phillip Harris**, Author of **The Leah King Trilogy** and **Serial Killer Z**

ALSO BY DELIA REMINGTON

In The Blood: Book One of The Blood Royal Saga

Out For Blood

BOOK TWO OF THE BLOOD ROYAL SAGA

Delia Remington

EAGLE HEIGHTS PRESS

Fayette, MO

To Keith who taught me everything I know about forensics.
I'm forever grateful.

To my parents for supporting my vision.

To my Twitter peeps who give me courage and joy on the daily.

And especially to my hero. You know who you are.

PART I

City of Lights

Marie Antoinette

I awoke as the flight began to descend over the Venice airport, or Venezia as the Italians call it. Only a sliver of moon showed in the black sky. I remained silent despite Wolfie's efforts to engage me in conversation. My mind was far too occupied with all that had happened. I felt as if my life had taken a sudden turn and now hurtled me toward a future that frightened me more than I ever wanted to admit.

I had lost Raul, my shop, our home, and the identity I had been so careful to create. How could I go back to being Claire Marie now I was exposed? Moreover, any chance of a safe haven with Vincent in Chicago had just disappeared now that Sybill's father was looking for her. My peace of mind had gone for good.

My fears for Raul were ever present. If I started thinking about it too much, I began to panic. Who had taken him? What did they want with him? Where were they keeping him? What did they do to him? Was he even still alive? I had to believe he was.

Vincent had said Sybill's father was a dangerous man when pressed, and certainly, if the man thought his daughter had been kidnapped, he would never rest until he found her. I hoped I had not inadvertently brought trouble to Vince's door. He might care for me, but he would not forgive or forget any problems I caused him. Not again. I remembered enough of our past to know just what he was capable of, and sentimental notions would be tossed aside if someone crossed him, even me.

To my shame, however, my deepest concern was for Sybill, Wolfie, and myself. How could we avoid capture without knowing who to trust? We could not fight back if we had nowhere to go. Most of all, how could I live with myself if something happened to either of them, knowing I was the one our pursuers were after? Yet my survival instinct prevented me from turning myself in. I felt self-serving and cowardly, though I could hardly help it. We would all like to believe we are noble, but at the end of the day, how many of us deserve that description?

All of these concerns had to wait until I addressed the more immediate situation at hand, however. As the plane touched down, I chewed my lip, internally praying we would find what we had come for – my progeny, lost so many years ago I had given up hope of ever reuniting with him again. I could not anticipate what sort of reception we might find, and whether he would be able or willing to assist us I could not foresee. If this effort failed, I didn't know where to turn next.

We taxied to a stop in front of a small hangar and a few minutes later, a customs agent came aboard. She checked our passports, stamped them, and then told us to enjoy our stay. Sybill seemed amazed at the simple process, but I explained men like Vincent could afford to avoid annoyances like long lines in airports. The flight crew helped carry our bags down the steps to the tarmac where a black limousine stood waiting. The door opened, and the driver stepped out to greet us.

As we approached, he looked down, taking our bags. He had obviously been carefully coached to avoid vampire influence. "Madam, Sir, Miss," he said with a heavy Italian accent. "Please, you come, yes?"

"Did Mister DeLuca send you here to meet us?" Wolfie said, stepping forward and putting a hand on the man's arm to halt him.

The man paused and nodded, and I knew if his hands were not full, he would be gesturing just as emphatically. "Signore DeLuca, yes. He send me. Come. We go now. Boat waiting. I take you, yes? Come."

"Why do we need a boat?" Sybill said warily, still hesitating behind me.

Her question made the man glance up at her, though he quickly lowered his gaze once more as he replied, "Is Venice." As if that explained everything. "You come. Please."

He loaded our bags inside the trunk, then opened the back door of the car and stood waiting for us to get in. Sybill turned to me with uncertainty in her eyes. "How do we know he's telling the truth?" she whispered.

"We don't," Wolfie said, leaning in close and taking my hand.

"True," I said. "But this man is human and knows we could kill him in seconds if we thought he deceived us. Leave this to me." I pulled my hand away from Wolfie's, stepped forward, and looked the driver in the eyes, exerting my influence on him to get to the truth. "Have you come here in good faith? Are we safe with you?"

The man nodded slowly, eyes reflecting the scant moonlight. "Si, madame. I have tell you only truth."

"There," I said, releasing my gaze and smiling at Sybill. "Satisfied?"

"I suppose so," she said with a shrug, some of the tension in her shoulders visibly easing, though I could tell she still did not entirely trust the situation. That wary nature of hers would serve her well, I knew, but though I would rather not admit it, we had no choice but to go where we were bid. The price of needing help is trust.

"You are welcome to stay here alone if you do not believe it is safe," I said. "As for me, I would rather not be rude to the local coven."

With that, I got into the car, not looking back to see if she followed. Wolfie climbed in behind me, and Sybill hesitated stubbornly for a few seconds before giving in. As the door closed, I saw her begin chewing her thumbnail out of the corner of my eye.

"That is a nasty habit, dear."

She glared across at me, but stopped, and all three of us were silent as we drove away in the darkness.

We were soon brought to the harbor, just as he'd said, and transferred to a gondola, steered by a man who spoke almost no English. Wolfie tried to engage him in conversation in Italian, but the man simply told him he had been hired anonymously to take us to our destination. Wolfie gazed up at the sky. "Well, my dear, these associates of Vincent's seem to have us well in hand."

Though I again felt a stab of apprehension, wondering if this would turn out to be another choice I would regret, I knew any outward show of fear would undermine my authority and position. Instead, I laughed as though I had never known a day's care in all my years. "Oh, Wolfie, how you do go on. Vincent would never do anything to hurt me. The man is devoted to me. You could see that. He has brought us this far, has he not? If he wanted us dead, why not do it there in Chicago and be done? No, this is too much trouble if he meant us harm."

"You've got to be kidding me," Sybill said, looking down at the gondola, scowling. "That's like an oversized canoe. I'm not getting on that thing."

"Come, come, my dear. Where is your sense of adventure?" Wolfie said.

Sybill stared wide-eyed at the narrow boat, shaking her head insistently. "No way. That thing is a death trap."

"Ridiculous," I scoffed. Wolfie stepped onto the deck, then turned and held my hand as I climbed aboard the gondola after him. "Get in. You cannot stay here."

"Where are we going?" she said, still eyeing the craft, one eyebrow raised.

Wolfie turned to the man and asked him where we were going in Italian, but the man just waved at Sybill to follow us on board, repeating, "You come. We hurry, please."

"That doesn't answer the question," she insisted, crossing her arms over her chest. "I want to know where we are going."

Taking a seat, I rolled my eyes and sighed heavily. "Oh honestly, darling, just get on the boat. We do not have time for this."

Her eyes narrowed and her expression darkened, but she did as I bid her. I knew she would dislike it, but nothing more could be said. I was going, and she could not remain behind. I knew if anything went wrong, she would never let me forget it. Silently seething, she crossed her arms over her chest, watching the man's every move as he let loose the lines and began propelling us forward.

Wolfie settled beside me and placed his arm behind my back protectively. We gazed out over the water as the lights of the city glittered and glinted on the waves. I tried to project an aura of easy confidence, but inside, I shared Sybill's curiosity and uncertainty about our destination. As we were borne across the dark waters, I trained my eyes on the shoreline, and when we entered the Grande Canale, I told myself I would pay attention to the passing palazzos in case a hasty escape became necessary. However, once we entered the maze of smaller canals which fed off the main route, crumbling ancient walls crowding in on all sides and set together at jaunty and unexpected angles, I soon lost all sense of direction. We were truly at the mercy of the City of Lights and the coven who controlled it.

Our gondolier seemed to have the devil's own sense of direction, however. He navigated narrow passageways without hesitation, and at last he pulled to the side of a set of steps carved into a bare wall. A woman wearing black leather pants and boots with a black turtleneck stepped from the darkness to greet us. Her hair had been pulled tight into a bun at the nape of her neck. The woman gestured for us to disembark. "This way, please."

"But our bags," said Sybill, hesitating, her eyes full of trepidation.

"They will be seen to," said the woman with an enigmatic smile that didn't give any sort of comfort. "Come."

A door at the top of the steps opened slightly, a pale light gleaming from inside giving the barest illumination to the way we were meant to go. We stepped out onto the cold stone, our feet making quiet echoes in the darkness. As we followed up the steps and found ourselves in a narrow corridor, a man passed us and went down to the gondola, presumably to gather our belongings.

By this point, Sybill started to balk. She scurried up close behind me and whispered as loud as she dared. "What's with all the cloak and dagger? Are they taking us to a palace or a prison?"

Turning my head, but not faltering in my step, I kept my voice low as I said, "It is for our safety as much as their own. They cannot exactly bring me in through the front doors and announce my presence, now can they?"

"Right. Everyone is out to get you. How could I forget?" She fell back into sulking silence again.

Wolfie took my hand to comfort me, but his touch only heightened my sense of being trapped. Though I felt he needed reassurance, I pulled away from him and quickened my pace, forcing myself to walk, back straight and head high, as though I had all the confidence in the world and held all the cards in this game. I knew I had to avoid seeming weak or uncertain. They must see me as a queen, even if I did not feel like one. I must show a strength I did not feel if I ever hoped to get help to accomplish my goals— finding my lost child, rescuing Raul, and defeating our enemies.

I followed the woman up a winding back stair and down a corridor, Wolfie and Sybill trailing in my wake. At last, we stopped in front of a pair of large wooden doors. The woman turned and said, "Signore Mozart, if you would kindly wait outside until you are called." He tried to protest, but the woman simply waved her hand toward a chair on the other side of the corridor. "Please, wait here, maestro."

Wolfie looked at me with a furrowed brow.

"Do not worry," I said, hoping my voice sounded steady. "I will see you soon."

He walked over and sat, fidgeting with obvious concern. I, however, gave the woman a benign smile as though I expected this. She bowed her head to me again and said, "The council will see you now. They have been waiting for your arrival."

She reached for the handle and turned it, then pushed the door open wide. Several vampires sat at a long trestle table with one at the far end facing me. I tried not to let my reaction show on my face as I walked into the room. I recognized the handsome face of the man at the head of the table. His striking blue eyes and shoulder length hair, paired with a grace and ease of bearing made him memorable. I also remembered how I had slighted him when our roles had been reversed. He had begged my help when I still held court in Versailles, but I had never answered any of his entreaties. Inwardly, I hoped he would not hold a grudge after all these years, yet I felt my heart sink with despair.

Determined not to show my anxiety, however, I smiled as they all rose from their seats upon our approach.

The woman paused before the assemblage and gestured toward us sweepingly. "I brought them here directly, your excellencies."

"Thank you, my dear. That will be all," said the leader of the coven, and he gave her a smile before she turned and walked away. The door shut behind her with a loud sound of steel and wood. He turned to look at the group. His smile disappeared. "Please be seated."

All of them sat. There were no chairs for us. "I trust you found your journey uneventful?" he said by way of opening conversation, settling back in his seat to look over at me with an inscrutable expression.

"Indeed, yes. I thank you."

"I suppose you know why we are all here to greet you?" His tone light, he gazed at me impassively, one eyebrow raised.

"No, Signore Casanova, I have not the slightest idea, though I hope the motive is not for gossip mongering. I do so enjoy my privacy nowadays."

Sybill gasped behind me, and I heard her say, "Casanova?"

He sat forward and gave a soft chuckle. "Even after all these years, my reputation precedes me, I see? Please, won't you introduce us to your charming companion, my lady?"

My lady, not *my Queen*. I could not tell if he intended a slight or wanted keep my true identity secret. Were there any yet among those assembled here who did not know my name? I suddenly felt surrounded by a pit of vipers waiting to strike. I decided to use our pseudonyms for fear spies might have infiltrated the gathering.

"Evangeline Mars. My protégé."

"Miss Mars. You are welcome here." Yet I saw the hint of fang as he said these words, his greeting also a warning.

"Um, thank you," she said, giving an awkward curtsey and waving to the assembly in that absurd modern way that is so distinctly American.

I wanted to roll my eyes, but instead, I gave a tight-lipped smile and looked back at Casanova steadily. He met my gaze for a few long moments, and then he gripped the arms of his chair tightly and said. "Let us get right to the crux of the matter. Vincent DeLuca has been murdered. Kindly divulge whatever you know about this matter immediately. We would like to avoid any unpleasantness."

The shock on my face must have been answer enough.

"I take it this information is news to you, my lady?" His eyebrow raised, he kept his voice calm, but firm. "Give the lady your seat, Signore Barbaro. She seems a bit faint."

The gentleman stood and offered me his chair. Bewildered, I sank into it heavily, fighting back tears, covering my face with my hands. Sybill moved to stand behind me, one hand on the back of my seat.

He watched me for a moment, then Casanova looked down the long table at the group and said, "Thank you, everyone. I believe that will be all for now. We will reassemble here tomorrow."

Chairs scraped the floor as the entire coven rose and left without another word, though I saw a couple glancing back over their shoulders to stare at me before exiting the room. My hand trembled, and Sybill took the seat beside me, reaching for my arm to touch me consolingly.

"I apologize for my bluntness of manner, your majesty," he said, his voice suddenly changed and full of concern. "You will understand, of course, my reason for caution. We had to know if you were behind his assassination."

"Assassination?" I said, barely able to speak the word. "H-how?"

"A bomb. The entire hotel was leveled. Do you know any reason someone might have targeted him? Of course, he has enemies. If one lives long enough, one is bound to make a few. But this action went beyond what we might have expected from any of them."

"My Vincent...gone?" I sat there stunned, my vision blurring with tears, clasping the table in both hands to keep from swaying.

"Ah. I see." Casanova tilted his head in curiosity, eyebrows lifted in surprise. "I had not anticipated such a thing."

Sybill shook her head, and I could feel her sadness turn to anger as she sat beside me. "He was kind to her. That's all. He didn't ask or expect anything in return. They weren't a couple. He cared about her."

"Oh my dear, you are so young," he said with a grin. "It is refreshing to have such faith in the selflessness of others."

"Can't you see she's overwhelmed?" I could hear the tension in her voice as her anger rose, and she glared back at him with defensive rage burning in her eyes. "She doesn't know anything about what happened to him. All she knows is a good man is dead. You are mocking her pain."

Casanova rose from his seat and crossed over to her, looking down his nose seriously. "Let no one ever say I am heartless. Though others may have treated me thus."

I felt his words like a little stab, and all my attempted self-control slid away. Suddenly, I began to cry, covering my face in my hands. "Oh god. He is gone!"

With a sigh, he handed me a handkerchief, and I wiped my bloody tears. "There, there, dear lady. If you knew half of what he had done in his life, you would not grieve so over his passing. Still, you are right, Miss Mars. You both need time to accept this news before our conversation can continue."

"Conversation? Is that what you call this?" said Sybill. "Looked more like a trial to me."

"Come, let us be friends, Miss Mars. I will take you to a place where you can rest. Tomorrow, after you have recovered, we will reconvene."

He helped me from my seat, then led us toward a tapestry hanging on the wall in the corner. Pulling back the fabric, he revealed a door, which opened onto a hidden bedroom chamber full of antiques and draped in heavy fabrics. He led me across to the large wooden four poster bed and sat me down on the edge of it before backing away. "I am afraid the two of you will have to share for the night. I want to ensure you are kept safe during your stay with me, and I alone hold the key. The others have no knowledge of it. Please, rest. I will ensure no one disturbs your slumber."

"Wait…" Sybill said, but before she could say any more, he walked back out the way he'd come, and I heard the lock slide in the door. We were safe, but we were also imprisoned. "What about Mozart?"

I looked up at her in desperate horror. "We are trapped."

Ripple Effect

Raul

Being a star when you're a kid starts out like a dream. People pay attention to you. They send you nice letters and cards and tell you how wonderful you are. You meet celebrities. You get to be on TV. People pay you lots of money. More money than I'd dreamed possible.

But fame can turn into something frightening too. Girls threatening to kill themselves if they can't marry you. People staring wherever you go like you're some sort of creature in a zoo. Paparazzi going through your trash or using long lenses to photograph you in compromising situations. Blackmail. Threats. Deluded fans who turn dangerous. Business people who think they own your soul. Everyone wants a piece of you.

Before Marie turned me, I'd just started to garner enough attention on-screen to make my off-screen life become a matter of interest to the public. My face appeared on the cover of teen magazines, and I had begun to stretch myself into adult roles, on the verge of emerging as the next mega-star of the silver screen. That kind of attention is flattering, but at the same time, it's intensely weird and intimidating.

In the early days, I enjoyed pretending to be someone else. Acting seemed like a game. But before long, I strained under an extreme amount of pressure on all sides — my costars afraid I might steal the limelight, the studio and the directors and producers wanting me to make them rich, and most of all my parents pushing me to perform in order to pay for all the things the rest of the family needed. It stopped being fun. All those adults turned out to only be thinking of themselves. I felt lost, betrayed, and overwhelmed with the burden to be the best, whatever the cost.

Even my life off-set was alienating. Out of step with my same age peers, never really having a formal education, parents carting me from place to place and never being settled anywhere, I couldn't relate to other kids' talk about home room teachers and recess and which teachers they liked. I taught myself, mostly, and my learning became haphazard at best. I read whatever caught my interest at the moment without an organized plan of any sort. There were gaps in my knowledge you could drive a truck through, and I never knew when I'd be blindsided with some fact everyone seemed to know except me. Home always seemed like a temporary construct. I never let myself get too attached to any place since my parents might, at any moment, decide to move on a whim, uprooting us all once more. I felt as though no one, not one person, really knew me at all.

Being in front of the camera with rehearsed words to say felt easy. Acting never felt like work. I just let the director and the writer tell me who to be.

When the cameras were off and I had to be myself, however, I never knew the rules. My early life didn't teach me normality. I didn't know how to be comfortable with people. It seemed easier dating girls who were actresses, but none of them knew how odd I felt around them, yearning to be ordinary. Each moment with them felt like a lie. I acted for them too, trying to please.

My last girlfriend had played opposite me in a movie, and she was the first person who didn't seem to have an agenda. She just wanted to be with me. But when I tried to explain to her how lonely and lost I felt, she didn't understand. My inability to connect made her feel hurt and disappointed. She couldn't help me the night I died and became someone else.

Living with Marie was like taking on another role. She gave me a name and told me what part to play. I hit my marks. I did what she expected. I hated the hunger. I will never stop hating it. But I had learned early never to complain. I'd been trained from birth to do as instructed, to accept whatever restrictions life gave me and make the best of things. For years after my turning, that was what I did. I immersed myself in her library and in playing my guitar. Marie may have kept me all to herself, but at least she never made me feel like a weirdo for my differences. She had been an outsider too. In that, we bonded. She understood better than anyone what it felt like to be different, to have strange childhoods where we were never really children at all, to have huge holes in our understanding of history or mathematics because no one decided to teach us in a systematic way. She understood the fear of disappointing the hopes of parents who put us under the yoke and made us work the soil of their own dreams, not allowing room for any we might have had for ourselves. With Marie, I did not feel happy, but I found a measure of contentment, and I thought those two words were synonymous until I met Sybill. We knew each other for such a short time, but the impact on my life and psyche was profound.

There in my ancient cell, I had time to think over all these things. I regretted the childhood I'd been denied. Though I cursed the night she changed me, I worried for Marie all the same. Thinking of Sybill left me in such depths of despair, I could hardly bear to say her name. I feared to articulate, even to myself, my questions about her, as if giving them form might make my worst fears prove true.

I wanted to believe she remained back in her apartment, safe and sound. In my thoughts, time had stopped for her the moment I walked out her door. I imagined if I should somehow make it out of this place and return to her, she would be waiting for me, taking me in her arms as though I'd only been gone a few minutes.

Each time I remembered that horrible woman, though, I knew Sybill couldn't be safe at all. That woman knew her name. What she meant to me. Since she had never shown her to me the way she had with Crystal, I knew there were only two alternatives — either they held Sybill prisoner like me, perhaps in this same place, or she had already died. If they'd killed her, though I'd never see her again, at least she wouldn't be hurt or starved or frightened. Her pain would be over. Yet, if she lived, I had the smallest glimmer of hope, however slight, one day I could escape and save her. Though that remote possibility chafed and tormented me, it became the only thing keeping me from giving up altogether.

I made myself survive for her, drinking the blood of mice, rats, and even eating insects though they made me sick. Ignoring my own discomfort, I was determined to make it back to her. My Sybill. I would do whatever it took to be with her again.

My hunger overpowered me. I found myself falling asleep without realizing it, and my dreams were dark and full of visceral, ravenous, bloody thoughts which seemed increasingly appealing until my awakening brought me back to a horrified self-awareness. I could feel that bloodthirsty dream state taking over my mind, my consciousness sliding, until I had trouble recognizing reality, and only with a supreme effort of will could I pull myself out of the nightmare my life became. In my lucid moments, I began talking aloud, repeating my name like a mantra into the dark to keep from forgetting it.

"Raul Griffin. My name is Raul Griffin. Marie will come for me. My name is Raul Griffin, and she will make you pay."

Pick Your Battles

Sybill

As soon as I heard the door lock, my eyes darted around the room looking for ways to escape. There were no windows or doors other than the one we'd just come through. I ran over and shook the handle, then got down on my knees to examine the lock.

"What are you doing?" Marie said, still sitting on the edge of the bed.

"Trying to see if I can pick this lock."

"Another skill in your repertoire?"

At her mocking tone, my cheeks flushed with annoyance. "No," I said, "but I figure there's a first time for everything." Since I didn't have any hair pins, I began searching the room, opening drawers to look for something I could use as a lock pick. "At least I'm doing something."

She laughed bitterly, leaning back on her hands and watching as I grew more frustrated by finding nothing to help me. "Well, you certainly are an optimistic soul, I must say. It is useless, my dear. Even if you could get us out of this room, the palazzo is well-guarded and large. Escaping would be highly improbable. Even should you succeed in that, where would we go? The city is a labyrinthine maze of waterways and narrow passages in which we are likely to be lost or recaptured by those who know their way in this place. No, my dear. I am afraid we must accept our captivity until Casanova releases us."

"You're giving up? Just like that?" I couldn't believe she would not fight back with me. Walking over to a dresser on one side of the room, I opened a large, antique, mahogany inlay jewelry box which sat on the polished wooden surface. Empty. I frowned and shut the lid with a snap.

"No," she said. "I am merely calculating the odds and waiting for a better moment in which to make my move. We need Casanova's help. Do you think he will be more inclined to give it if we defy him?"

Her reply sounded logical, but it filled me with a righteous indignation. "This is just slowing us down. We have to find Raul. We need to save him. Who knows what they're doing to him?"

Marie rose and, crossing the room toward me, placed her hand on my arm. "I have not forgotten. I love him too. But we cannot save him if we cannot help ourselves first."

Turning to face her, I forced myself to ask the question I'd been dreading to even contemplate. "What if he's already dead?"

She paused for a moment, and I thought she might cry, but then her expression hardened like steel. "Then he shall be avenged."

Those words broke something inside me, and I felt my knees begin to buckle. I threw my arms around her to keep from falling. All my strength and inner resolve melted away. Within the span of a few moments, we had traded roles of comforter and comforted. My voice cracked as I said, "I'm sorry about Vincent."

She held me close and stroked my hair. "I will miss him. He was not a good man, but he was good to me, and that is enough."

"Who do you think killed him?" I said, pulling back to look into her eyes.

Taking my hand, she led me over to the bed and we sat down side-by-side. "Vincent had many enemies."

"Yes, but if you were to bet?" I looked down at my hands thoughtfully, trying to puzzle it out. "None of us set the bombs. Do you think someone on his staff might have done it?"

"His servants and soldiers were all too loyal and too frightened by him to ever attempt to destroy him." The serious tone in her voice made me look up as she spoke.

"Sounds like you were afraid of him too."

She glanced away across the room for a moment as if thinking about her response, then her eyes turned back toward me. "A man like Vincent, when he loves you, he would give you the world. But his means of acquiring it would leave everything drenched in blood. If he felt you betrayed him, you would find that same violent ruthlessness turned upon you with terrifying speed."

As she spoke, I thought of my father, and of what he would do to anyone he held responsible for hurting me, his princess. My eyes grew wide with horror as I came to a sudden conclusion that made the pit of my stomach clench in fear. "What if my father did it?"

"Darling, that is impossible."

"No, it isn't. You don't know him. He's just like Vincent. They're so alike, it's almost terrifying. If my father figured out we were up there, if he thought Vincent had kidnapped me? He wouldn't have stopped at anything to get me back, and there would be hell to pay if he thought me dead."

"You don't know that. Be reasonable. How would he have even dreamed of finding us there?" Her words were meant to calm me, but I jumped up and began pacing with agitation.

"I don't know. But if he did...that makes it my fault." I chewed my lip to bite back the fear. "What would they do to him?"

"Sybill," she said, her voice stern and full of warning. "Stop this right now. If you want to keep your father and the rest of your family safe, you will not breathe another word of these ramblings. Do not set these bloodhounds on the wrong scent. If any one of these people believed in any possibility of what you suggest, the punishment your family would face would be on your conscience for centuries. Suspicion is a demon that once started will never die. Do not give it life, or it will destroy everything you love. Tomorrow, Casanova will give us information, and he will see to it Vincent's death is given a thorough investigation. Let that be an end to it."

I sensed from her demeanor she spoke from her own experience. A deep sorrow in her eyes hinted at unfathomable loss. "Just tell me...do you think it's possible?"

"No." Her voice sounded firm. "If I had to venture a guess, I would say my enemies were responsible for what happened to Vincent. Perhaps they never even targeted him at all. He may have been simple collateral damage, and the bomb might have been meant for me."

I hadn't considered that possibility at all. "Does that mean you think we're in danger here too?"

"Will it help in any way or put your mind at ease for me to answer that question?"

Our eyes met, and I pondered for a few moments before I finally said, "No, I guess not."

"Then let us rest until they come for us tomorrow evening. There is nothing to be gained by talking except further agitation and the discovery of even more unknown fears. Come. Lie down and sleep a while beside me. Whatever happens, we will be better able to face it afterward."

Knowing she was right again, I did as she said. Though I knew my fears would keep me wide awake for hours, I drifted off to sleep almost immediately once my head hit the pillow, and if I had dreams, I did not remember them.

THE FOOL

Mozart

The moment we stepped off the gondola, I knew things were not going to be as easy for my dear Marie as she had anticipated. Then again, when had anything ever gone simply for her since the Revolution? Though I hadn't been a part of her life up to this moment, it clearly had been difficult for her, always having to be one step ahead of her pursuers, never knowing who to trust or when she might be captured. Indeed, the fact that she had found anyone to trust in all that time was amazing to me, given her situation and who she was. Coming here meant putting her faith in Vince's word and in these Venetian vampires who she had no reason to believe would live up to what she'd been promised.

As soon as Marie and Sybil were led away, leaving me in the custody of servants of the coven, my suspicions were confirmed. The officious woman who seemed in charge of managing us did her best to put on a smile and try to convince me that this was all routine, but I saw right through her. "Marie will need me with her," I said. "I am her chosen companion."

"I am terribly sorry, signore," she said, "but we were not expecting you. Our list from Mister DeLuca was explicit. The great lady herself and a female companion. That is all, I am afraid. I understand your concern and annoyance, but you will have to be patient with us. We have our own concerns for the safety of this place and our members. You are an additional security risk, for obvious reasons, and you will surely understand our need to be cautious with such a guest in our midst. I am sure it is a simple misunderstanding that will be cleared up in no time. In the meantime, please allow me to escort you to a more private set of rooms where you can make yourself comfortable."

Though she smiled brightly as she gestured toward the door, her message was clear enough. I was a prisoner not to be trusted, and I had no way of escape or ability to refuse. If I did not cooperate, there was a vague threat lingering in her eyes, unspoken but palpable nonetheless. My option was to either attempt escape, an effort which would clearly be futile, or allow myself to be held indefinitely on the hope that Marie and Sybill would be allowed to claim me once the coven business was resolved. Though my every instinct screamed at me to fight and run, I knew doing so would only result in disaster, not only for me but for all of us. How would it look for Marie if I appeared nervous or untrusting? These people already did not trust her intentions. Demonstrating fear or anxiety at what they might discover about me or her would only make us all seem to have something to hide. I could not risk that. If it were me alone, I might behave differently, but under the circumstances, the only path I saw before me was compliance.

Forcing a smile, I followed along obediently, playing the fool as a matter of survival. It was a role I had taken on and learned to perfect in order to save my own skin more times than I cared to count. People had come to expect me to be the puckish prankster, and I did not correct their misunderstanding of my motives or character. With a wink and a smile, I had carried myself in and out of danger with great success all these long years. I had neither great height nor strength or beauty to move people's opinions or persuade them to do as I wished. The only way I could fight for myself was with humor and charm.

As though I had no concerns at all regarding this incarceration, I distracted the woman with boundless idle chatter about my hopes for a good meal and the possibility of gaining access to a piano, explaining that I was in the midst of a new composition. To press the point further, I began humming a new extemporaneous piece on the spot, hoping my antics would make her lower her guard, perhaps even ensure me an indulgent freedom of movement so I could explore and find where Marie and Sybill were being held. I held no illusions that they were not also being held prisoner here somewhere, and to what end, I could not be certain.

The woman led me to a small set of rooms high in one corner of the palazzo. Throughout my endless banter, she had politely smiled, but once I stepped inside, it was clear all my hopes would be for naught. "I regret that a piano is not available for your use, Maestro," she said. "Had we been informed of your arrival, I am sure your needs would have been anticipated. However, I hope you will find these rooms comfortable during your stay."

Ignoring any further attempts to draw her into my confidence and thereby gain her trust and my own freedom, she stepped out, and I heard the door look behind her. I was trapped, and as I stood there trying to squelch my despair, I overheard her telling someone to remain behind and guard the door. All my fears were substantiated in that moment. I really was a prisoner, and for how long or to what end I had no way of knowing. My heart sank, and though the rooms were opulent, befitting a palace, I was filled with dread, where only a few hours before I had been excited at the prospect of enjoying all the city had to offer, a queen at my side.

I had seen what people were willing to do to her all those years ago. What might they do to her now? What chance did she or any of us have of escape? Was there anyone here we could trust? Or had we walked into a trap? Was this night going to be the last for Marie Antoinette and all who stood beside her? It was hard not to lose hope under these circumstances.

As I sat down on the bed in the room I'd been given, I couldn't help wondering how long I would be left there to wait. They had not, however, taken away my cell phone, and so I pulled it from my pocket and sat gazing at the screen for several long moments. I had no new messages, which did not surprise me. I could think of very few people to contact, and none of them would be able to help in this circumstance.

No one back in Chicago would want to hear that Vince's plans had not quite gone the way he expected. Indeed, I was certain he would not want to hear about any trouble we had encountered. Such a report might bring down disaster on the few people here who might have been inclined to give Marie assistance. No. Better to stay quiet on that front unless things began to seem more dire. Until we knew the reason for her treatment and the intent of the coven, there was no profit in creating a fuss that might turn out to be completely unnecessary.

All this technology and none of it any use. It was enough to make me laugh out loud, though there was no one to hear me.

Cursing under my breath, I tried to calm my anxious mind, pondering whether I could charm my way out of the place and go for help. Such thoughts were futile, I knew. No one could help us against the Venice coven. We were not getting out of that place unless they allowed it, and the chances of such benevolence seemed dim.

My mind spiraling into despair, I did not look up as the lock clicked and the door opened. Keeping my eyes fixed on the pattern in the carpet, I sighed in defeat. "If you are here to interrogate me, you may as well give up now. I have nothing to tell you and no information you will find useful."

"My dear Wolfgang, have you no words of greeting for an old friend?"

Eyes snapping upward, they flew open wide as they lit on a face I hadn't seen in years beyond count. "Gio? What...how are you here?"

He laughed and strode quickly over to me, and as I stood, he held out his arms to embrace me. "I live here, of course. Sweet Madonna, it is good to see you, my friend."

Tearing up, I held him tight, laughing and slapping him on the back heartily. "I thought you died. I put you in that crypt myself. I was sure..."

"I was only wounded in that duel, as it turned out. Apparently, the bullet missed my heart, and after time and a great deal of blood, I made a full recovery, as you see."

Pulling back to look up into his eyes earnestly, I held the lapels of his suit jacket. "You must believe me. I had no idea. I would never have left you there. God, all this time I thought you were gone, and now here you are."

"Be calm, dear friend. I knew the risks. I told you to leave if the worst happened. I knew you must have done just as I asked."

"If you knew, why did you not come looking for me? You let me think you were gone all this time."

"I kept tabs on you from a distance. You did not need me anymore."

"The hell you say!" I shook as I released his jacket, pushing him away from me and backing up to glare at him, a sudden rage rising from deep within and engulfing all my other emotions. "You were like a father to me. We were partners. Hell, you made me what I am. And now you're telling me you knew I was still alive and alone and you just abandoned me? Let me think you were dead all this time? I mourned you, goddamn it."

He took a half step back, looking down and straightening his jacket. "This is a shock to you. I see that. I apologize for upsetting you so. Such was not my intention. I thought you would be pleased. It seems fate is not done with us yet."

"A shock?"I scoffed, running a hand through my hair. "A shock, he says. Finding a lost puppy is a shock, Gio. This is much bigger than that. There is not a word for what this is. For years, I longed to see you again. To hear that laugh of yours and tell jokes together as we once did. What a pair we were, eh? Tell me I wasn't the only one missing our companionship."

His expression softened as he looked back at me, shaking his head. "Of course, I missed you. It took me a long time to find you, and by the time I did, you were in the New World and I had my responsibilities here. I could not simply abandon the people here. They needed me. I knew you were well looked-after. Your associates in Chicago were well known to me."

"Vincent knew and kept it from me?"

"I asked him not to say anything. You must not blame him. Especially not after..."

His voice trailed off ominously, and I stared at him in alarm. "After what? Has something happened to him? Tell me. He was not my friend, but the bastard gave me work and a safe place to be. He kept his bargain with me, which is more than I can say for you."

"You really did not know," he said softly as if confirming something to himself. "I thought not, but this only confirms what Marie told us. Wolfgang, after you left Vincent's hotel, someone found their way down into the basement, set charges, and blew the whole place down. Vincent is presumed dead. If the explosion did not kill him, he was crushed under the rubble and then incinerated by the flames."

"Wha...what?" I sank to the bed, incredulous. "Vincent is dead? Holy shit, Gio. You know what this means, right? Who they were really trying to kill? Jesus."

He laughed then, though it was without mirth. "I am afraid our Lord had no hand in these events, but yes, I have my suspicions as to who might be responsible. However, you and I need to keep that name quiet. The coven is already on alert, suspicious and wary of Marie's presence here. If they get it in their heads that such retribution will fall on us here next, there is no telling what they might do. Several of the key members already want to hand her over to her enemies. Unless you want them to follow through with their witch hunt, you will keep silent about your suspicions. After all, they may take you and me and the girl, for that matter, to be sure there is no possibility of invoking his anger for being complicit. Does Marie know of the connection between you and I?"

I shook my head. "No. It never came up. Why?"

"Keep it that way for now," he said. "The fewer who are aware of our past together the better for now. We do not need to draw suspicion in our direction either."

Leaning forward, I covered my face with my hands and murmured. "What are we going to do, Gio? For fuck's sake, tell me you have a plan."

"Of course I do." His forehead furrowed, and for a moment I saw a glimpse of frustration and fear peek from behind his mask of calm, though it quickly disappeared once more. "Trust me. Say nothing unless asked a direct question, and tell them nothing except the certain facts. You were not there when the building was destroyed. You are as shocked as they are at his passing. Let me handle the rest. Understood?"

I nodded, heaving a heavy sigh.

"Good. Now I must leave you. When it is safe to do so, you and I will talk. Nothing would give me greater pleasure than renewing our friendship, Wolfgang."

He turned to go, and as he reached the door, he turned back and smiled at me. "It is good to see you again, Wolfgang. Truly. It has been too long."

Without waiting for my reply, he left me then, locking the door behind him. I felt foolish and out of my depth for the first time in ages. Shoulders sagging, I heaved a sigh, then lay back, still fully dressed, on the bed, and quietly, I began to sing my Requiem under my breath, the music swelling in my memory. Moving my fingers as if playing the notes on phantom keys, I sang myself to sleep. "Requiem aeternam dona ets Domine..."

A Palace or a Prison

Sybill

The sound of a key turning in the door lock woke me next evening. I sat upright, shaking Marie to rouse her. My eyes flew open just as Casanova walked in the door. "Good evening, ladies. I trust you were comfortable here?"

I was making ready with a tirade of complaint, but Marie elbowed me into silence, giving Casanova a smile. "We were, thank you. Your hospitality is very generous."

He bowed then stood again with his eyes on mine, a smirk playing on his lips. "I apologize for the locked door, but I assure you my thoughts were only of your safety, your majesty."

"Of course," she said, and I balked, knowing he had other reasons he clearly didn't want to divulge just yet. A silent acknowledgment passed between the two of them, one I didn't understand fully, and it irritated me. I felt oddly out of place and almost as though I were in the way. I knew nothing about this world, and the helplessness of my situation fell in on me. In this place, I was like a child, expected to be silent, not to speak unless spoken to. There were too many similarities to the way my father had treated me, and the comparison made me unsettled and anxious. Though Casanova had been nothing but polite to us both, life with my father had taught me appearances couldn't be trusted. I scowled between them like a sullen child, angry and frustrated but powerless to do anything about it.

"I took the liberty of having your belongings brought up to you as well as some refreshment with my compliments. The coven will reconvene an hour from now. We request your company, if you please, for there are important matters to discuss." Casanova had couched his demand in the form of a request as a courtesy, a game of subtlety he had clearly played for years.

Marie, however, seemed unfazed by his words. "We would be glad to join you, Signore. Thank you for your thoughtfulness."

As she spoke, two servants entered, one carrying our bags, the other carrying a tray with a carafe of blood and two glasses. They set down their burdens and withdrew without a word.

I opened my mouth, and before Marie could stop me, I blurted, "Where is Mozart?"

With a tight smile, Marie glanced over at me with a warning in her eyes, then cleared her throat. "Forgive my young companion, Signore. She does not mean to be impertinent. We are simply anxious for the welfare of our friend."

Casanova made another bow. "I apologize for any anxiety you might have felt on behalf of Herr Mozart. Rest assured, the gentleman is perfectly well. We made sufficient accommodation for his comfort and security as well, and he will rejoin your company this evening."

In other words, they were holding Mozart prisoner elsewhere in the palazzo. I gasped, making ready to say something more, but Marie cut me off. "I understand," she said. "I thank you for your pains."

"My pleasure. I will leave you now to prepare yourself, madame." He bowed and then withdrew, locking the door once more upon his exit.

"Are you going to kiss his ass the whole time we're here?" I said. "I don't trust him."

She laughed as she threw back the covers and climbed out of bed. "I do not trust him either, but the feeling is mutual, and as long as he and I understand one another and can come to an equally beneficial arrangement, then I will continue to play his game. Now do get up, dear. We do not want to keep our hosts waiting. And from now on, let me do the talking. You are determined, and that is an honorable quality, but you have not yet learned diplomacy."

Though I hated it, I had to concede her point in this situation. Much as it bothered me to admit, I was out of my depth. Rather than continue to argue, I gave in and reluctantly did as I was asked.

An hour or so later, a knock came at the door. "Come," Marie said, as though she were in the position of giving permission rather than at the mercy of these strangers. As if she was still the queen granting favors rather than a prisoner in this place.

Unlocking the door, Casanova once more made his entry. "If you ladies are both ready, the company awaits."

We followed him back out into the large hall, Marie walking a few steps ahead of me and keeping her head erect, behaving for all the world as though she were in charge. This time, there were extra chairs, and Wolfie sat among those waiting for us around that long table. He looked at Marie like he wanted to leap up and throw his arms around her, but he remained seated, as if he knew such a display of personal emotion would only hinder our mission. All the men of the company stood as we approached while the women stayed in their chairs, and Casanova himself seated us before taking his place. "Please, gentlemen, sit. We have much business to discuss."

Beneath the table, Wolfie reached over to place his hand on Marie's thigh, his way of telling her he had missed her. Though Marie did not take his hand in hers or give any outward reaction to his touch, she also did not pull away, and I took it as a signal to him she understood and had felt the same. I wanted to lean over and ask him questions about where they'd kept him and what he knew, but there would be time enough for talk between all of us once we were out of this place.

"It is clear to me our guests had no foreknowledge of Mister DeLuca's demise. Indeed, the news shocked all three of them. I, therefore, humbly apologize for my abruptness of manner in being the bearer of such sad tidings. This puts an end to any suspicions we might have entertained against your person, my lady." This last he said to Marie, and she nodded her silent thanks. "Our investigation will continue, but I believe we must focus on other parties in order to come to the truth of the matter."

As evidenced by the low murmur at the far end of the table, clearly someone objected to Casanova's dismissal of the case against us. With steely eyes, he gave a sharp glance toward the dissenters, and silence fell once more. He began to speak again as though the disruption had never happened, but I had a feeling after our meeting ended, there would be consequences for the interruption.

"This brings us to the next order of business. Mister DeLuca's last message contained a request that we help these three companions in their quest to locate a missing person of some note. I believe the coven should honor this last request of the deceased. However, doing so may put us at risk from certain parties who would perhaps not be so understanding of any connection to the great lady seated here before us. My apologies, Madame, for putting the situation before you so indelicately, but you understand the predicament in which you have placed us, do you not?"

Taking a deep and unnecessary breath, Marie nodded. "I do. I understand your concerns." She pushed back her chair and stood, looking down the table to address the other members of the coven. "Ladies and gentlemen, I would not wish to bring dishonor or calamity to your door. However, my dear friend Vincent DeLuca assured me there are those among you who have the power to lead me and my companions to a man I have sought for many years. A man who is dear to me. I would not wish to trespass upon your kindness further, for I know my presence here is a danger for all who give me aid. Therefore, I only ask you to provide the information I so desperately need, and I will trouble you no more. I will never speak of the source of my information. Any among you who knows my history can attest to my sincerity in this. Once I give my word, I never break it."

And with that, she sat again to await their response.

Casanova kept his face impassive, looking away as he said, "What say you, my brothers and sisters? By a show of hands, how many would give the lady here before us the aid which she requires?"

The muttering few at the end of the table scowled, but the rest raised their hands in agreement. Not an unanimous vote, but it sufficed. I felt my hands relax then, and realized I'd been clenching them tight without being aware of it until that moment.

"It appears your request is granted, my lady." Casanova turned and handed Marie an envelope closed with a wax seal. "I believe this will give you all the information you require. Once you have read the contents, we can discuss the particulars."

She stared at the envelope, turning it over in her hands, her expression full of both anticipation and anxiety. "Thank you, Signore."

He smiled and then rose from his chair. "Ladies and gentlemen, I thank you for your attention in this matter and request your silence regarding our guests and the nature and content of this proceeding. Our work here is done. You are now free to go."

One by one, the assembled coven members rose and departed, whispering amongst themselves as they left. After the room emptied at last, Casanova sat and leaned forward eagerly, a kindly smile at last breaking across his face. "Will you not open the letter, your majesty? You seem hesitant. Did you not get what you desired?"

"Oh yes," she said. "It is only…I have waited so long, and I barely allowed myself to believe I would find him."

"I understand," he said softly. "But do not be afraid. This information is genuine. I would not lead you astray."

Her eyes filled with tears, though they did not fall, and she looked back at him with sincere emotion. "Why are you so kind to me, Signore? When I have given you no reason to be?"

"Because I know I did not deserve your notice those many years ago, my lady, and I do not blame you for ignoring my entreaties. Were I in your shoes, I cannot imagine my own response to someone like myself would have been any different. And because I hate to see you brought so low, madame. I hope you will not find me impertinent to say so. Truly, I mean no disrespect. I have always admired you. Though my duties require me to keep my personal feelings on this matter in check, I assure you if it were in my power to put an end to the injustice you endure, I would do so without question. You have a friend in me, your majesty."

His reply clearly overwhelmed her, and I was surprised to see her brush back tears of gratitude, though whether they were real or fake was unclear to me. For a moment, I wondered how much of this behavior was an act, intended to manipulate him, but I got the impression Casanova wasn't the type to fall for a ploy like that, so I was forced to conclude her tears were genuine. With a demure nod, she said simply, "Thank you, Signore Casanova."

Shaking his head, he handed her his handkerchief. "There is no need, my lady. I only hope one day, our common enemy will be defeated."

She dried her eyes, and with a smile, opened the letter. Wolfie and I crowded in close to look over her shoulder. Only two words were written on the paper — San Lazzaro. The rest of the page was blank.

Marie turned the letter this way and that to be sure there nothing more remained, then looked up at Casanova with her brow furrowed. "I do not understand."

Casanova took the paper from her hands and read the words, then he smiled broadly and handed it back. "It is an island, your majesty."

My heart sank as I began imagining another long journey. "You've got to be kidding me," I muttered.

Marie reached out and took Wolfie's hand, giving it a squeeze for comfort. Casanova saw the worry on her face, for he leaned forward and took her other hand, laughing good-naturedly. "Not at all, my lady. San Lazzaro is but a short boat ride from the city. My men can take you as soon as you are ready."

I breathed a loud sigh of relief. Wolfie reached out to touch Marie's shoulder. "You see? We are close now."

Looking up at me, Marie smiled and said, "Please, gather our belongings if you don't mind, my dear. Let Wolfie help you. I have a few last private things to say to Signore Casanova."

Though I didn't want to leave them alone, I nodded and smiled. "Sure. I can do that. Back in a jiffy."

I could see the hurt on Wolfie's face, but he went with me as Marie asked.

As soon as we were alone, I turned to Mozart, leaning in to whisper. "Do you trust him? Because I don't. How do we know this isn't sending us into a trap?"

Mozart narrowed his gaze at me, and for a moment, I thought he was going to speak, but then he glanced toward the door as if afraid we might be overheard. When he turned back to look at me, it was with a mask of amusement, and he gave one of those characteristically annoying laughs of his, high and almost childish. "You've been watching too many movies, dear girl. Goodness, but you are serious and suspicious. Come now.

Don't be so dramatic. Let's gather those bags of yours, shall we? No more of this morbid talk."

His tone was so dismissive, I wanted to hit the little man, but then I had to wonder if maybe he was forcing it. If so, he was a good actor, but maybe he'd had to be. After all, how much did I know about him? I'd never cared about history much, and even if I had, there was enough of his past no one knew about, it probably wouldn't have done me much good anyway. I was just going to have to shut up and do as I was told, no matter what my instincts told me. I didn't know who to trust anymore, but I wasn't in the position to argue.

Leaving the New World

Ernestine

As I gathered important items from my office in the New World headquarters in New York City, the cell phone in my pocket began to ring. I nearly didn't reach for it, afraid my act in Chicago would not have quite the positive reaction I hoped for with the Master, but I knew not answering him would cause more wrath than an acceptance of consequences.

Imagine my surprise when I saw the call instead had come from an informant. I put on my Bluetooth earpiece and answered, not pausing as I gathered folders and placed them into a briefcase. "Talk to me."

The voice on the other end told me my quarry had arrived in Venice. This news made me frown. "Then they are under Giacomo's protection. The Master won't like this new development."

Snapping the briefcase closed, I lifted it from the desktop. "Separate her from the others. I don't care how you do it, just see to it. Once she is securely under lock and key and in your power, contact me. You have one week. If you want your money, you will do things my way."

Though I could hear the voice begin to protest, I hung up. Making another call as I strode out of the office, briefcase in hand, I said, "Get the plane ready. I will be there in twenty minutes."

My trip across the Atlantic was uneventful, and a second call came just as my private jet rolled to a stop at the Paris airport. My informant again. While the flight crew began transferring my luggage to the waiting limousine, I answered the phone. "You move quickly. She is alone and under your control already?"

What I heard did not make me happy at all.

"I told you not to contact me until you've completed the job. Do not give me excuses," I said, making my way down the steps to the tarmac. "I don't have time for incompetence. Either do the job as instructed, or I will come and do it myself."

Before the pleading began, I hung up, then walked over to the chauffeur putting my bags into the cargo area. I directed the driver to take me to my favorite local hotel, and then I climbed into the back of the car, settling into my seat.

Dawn was approaching, which meant I could not continue on to Avignon until the next night. I couldn't avoid the delay, but being forced to wait vexed me all the same. There would be many questions for me to answer upon my arrival at headquarters. I only hoped the Master would be pleased with the prisoner I had sent on ahead of me and we could use him to our advantage against the fugitive queen.

Reunion

Marie

When we were alone, I turned again to give Casanova's hand a squeeze. "Signore, I will not forget what you have done for me. Though I hope you are never in need, if it is in my power in the future to return the favor, I will be happy to do so."

"Dear lady, you honor me." He kissed my hand tenderly.

"You are so kind. I am sorry I misjudged you."

Shaking his head, he got down on his knee before me. "Never apologize, majesty. You are the queen. You owe me nothing."

"I am not a queen anymore, Signore." These words were bittersweet as they fell from my lips.

"You will always be the queen, your majesty." He looked up into my eyes. "You have only forgotten it for a while. One day, however, you will be free of the tyrant. Of this I am certain. His reign of terror cannot last forever."

I could not help but laugh. "I have lost count of the years I have been running, Signore."

He leaned forward and smiled. "His time is nearing an end, your majesty. There are many among us who would welcome the change."

"I thank you, again, and hope you are right."

Kissing my hand once more, he then rose and took a step back. "By your leave, I will go to make ready the boat that will take you to your destination."

"Of course," I said, and he bowed and exited the room. I remained alone for only a few minutes before Sybill and Wolfie returned with our bags.

"Everything all right?" Sybill said.

I reached out and took her hand, smiling. "For the first time in ages, I think it might be."

Wolfie went to retrieve his belongings, and when he came back, Casanova had a gondola ready for us. I kissed him on both cheeks as we said goodbye. Then he and Wolfie exchanged bows before two servants came to collect our things and lead us down to the back entrance again where the boat waited. This time, Sybill got on board without complaint, and as we pulled away from the steps, Casanova came out to wave goodbye from the landing. I hoped I would have the chance to see him again under better circumstances.

Again, we wended our way through narrow waterways before suddenly entering into the main canal. From there, we left the island of Venezia, the lights of the city twinkling on the waves as we headed across the mouth of the gulf. I felt grateful the winds were low and the water calm that night. Only a sliver of moon still hung overhead, and a few scudding clouds passed over its face. Our progress seemed to take ages, my anticipation dragging out the time, though less than three-quarters of an hour actually passed.

At last, the gondola turned and aimed toward one of the islands. A stone wall encircled the small chunk of land, behind which stood a brick building like a fortress. Over the top, I could just see the outline of a tower with a cross shining in the pale moonlight. The gondolier pulled up to a pier where a man swathed in black monk's robes stood at the bottom of a set of marble steps, waiting. Wolfie and I exchanged looks as the gondolier tied up and began handing the monk our luggage hurriedly.

"I think perhaps there has been a mistake," said Wolfie.

"No mistake. Is San Lazzaro," the man said, not pausing for an instant.

"Wait, is this a monastery?" Sybill said warily.

"Yes. Is holy place." He grunted with effort, still removing our things onto the shore.

"Hmph," Sybill snorted. "We're vampires. Won't we burst into flames or something?"

Wolfgang laughed, shaking his head. "Wives' tales. Do you feel demonically possessed?"

"Well, no. I just..."

"No offense, my dear, but you have seen too many horror movies."

She scowled, and I saw from her expression she bit back what she wanted to say to him. Without a word, she stood and stepped off onto the pier.

Once she walked out of earshot, Wolfgang leaned in close to whisper, "Do you think this is the right place?"

I shrugged. "Where else can we go?"

He nodded and took my hand, giving it a little squeeze of encouragement. With a resolute sigh, I disembarked with Wolfie, and as soon as we were safely on land, the man untied the gondola and immediately slipped away as though he could not get away from us fast enough. I did not have time to feel insulted, however. The monk bowed his head, gathered our bags, and turned to climb the marble steps without a word.

"Wait!" I started after him in surprise. "Where are you taking us?"

The monk simply shook his head and kept walking, turning to cross an open courtyard ringed by trees. Our footsteps echoed against the high walls in front of us as Wolfie asked again in Italian. The man gave no reply. I tried German and French, to no result. Instead, he walked purposefully toward a steel gate where he stopped and rang a bell. When the door opened, we had no choice but to follow. All three of us trailed after him, and another monk shut the gate behind us with a resounding clank, securing the exit with a steel bar. The sound, so reminiscent of a prison door, made me flinch inwardly, though I kept my expression in check and gave no visible reaction. As I had done so many times throughout my life, I forced my feet to continue moving forward at an even pace in spite of the trepidation in my heart.

Our silent guide led us inside and through the halls of what we realized was a cloistered monastery, passing through a colonnaded courtyard before walking into another enclosed corridor opening out onto a reception hall. There, he set down our bags and gestured us to follow him on into another area.

Wolfie and I both exchanged glances of uncertainty, but this time Sybill had a flash of insight. "Vow of silence," she said.

The monk nodded, clearly having understood her, and something in me relaxed then, allowing him to lead us on.

We passed through a darkened library with glass cases and shelf after shelf of ancient tomes lining the walls. In one room stood a mummy, and I saw Sybill's mouth open and shut with surprise as we continued past without stopping. At last, we rounded a corner, and our guide slowed his pace. In a corner of this room stood a large wooden desk lit by a single kerosene lamp. A man sat, his back to us, and we could see him writing furiously in a leather-bound notebook. A silver handled cane stood leaning against the bookcase beyond, just within his reach.

Hearing our approach, he turned. I saw the familiar dark curling shock of hair against his pale forehead. Even in the gloom, his eyes were still clear and blue, sparkling with mischief. "What took you so long?" he said.

"It is you!" I said, stopping still and staring with wide eyes, my hands trembling.

He gave a crooked smile, gazing back at me with eyes twinkling mischievously. "I knew you'd find me out eventually, Marie. Honestly, I am disappointed. I thought you'd figure it out much sooner than this. You're losing your touch, old girl."

Standing up, he stepped forward and put his arms around me, drawing me into a close embrace. In my ear, he whispered softly, "I have missed you terribly."

I kissed his cheek, then pulled back, cupping his face in my hands, looking deep into his brilliant eyes. My voice choked. "I have missed you every day."

At my side, Sybill looked him up and down and then turned back to face me. I knew her brain was bursting with a million questions. However, the answers would not be possible just yet. There were too many of my own to ask first.

Clasping his hands behind his back, Wolfie cleared his throat and bowed. "Wolfgang Amadeus Mozart, at your service, sir."

"Oh, bother that service thing. We're vampires. We serve no one. Well, except her majesty, here, of course." And with that, he laughed and stuck out his hand to shake. "George Gordon, Lord Byron. Poet of some renown. Before I met our mutual acquaintance, that is. It's Noel Baron in this incarnation. It's truly an honor to meet you."

"Wolf Weber is what they call me these days. Your reputation precedes you, sir. It's a pleasure."

They shook hands, but though their words had been friendly and both of them were smiling, I could see them silently sizing one another up. Hoping to put a stop to that, I took Sybill's hand and pulled her forward. "Albé, darling, this is Sybill, your sister in blood."

Byron turned to face her, still grinning, and Sybill seemed visibly shaken with his good looks. Her jaw dropped, and I saw how his blue eyes captured hers. "Sister, eh? Pity. Thwarted yet again." He took her hand in his and lifted it gently to his lips, brushing her fingers with a kiss. "Not that such things ever stopped me in the past."

He lifted his head and winked at her then, and I saw her gulp, still gaping.

"She is not for you, Albé," I said, stepping in to pull his hand from hers.

Waggling his eyebrows, he gave a naughty curl of his lip, chuckling. "Ah, but am I for her? That's yet to be seen. What are you calling yourself now, my dear?"

Sybill licked her lips and said, "Eva Mars."

"The first lady of war?" he said, raising one eyebrow. "Let us hope your name brings you strength over strife, dear sister."

"Short for Evangeline, Albé." I said. "Stop scaring the poor girl."

"Ah. 'Evangeline, the bearer of good news.' Yes, I like that better." He let go of her hand then, and his eyes softened. "Never mind me, dear girl. I may have been the inspiration for the first vampire in English literature, but I'm still a poet at heart."

"How is Doctor Polidori these days?" I said.

Byron shook his head and shrugged. "Still dead, thanks. He persists in looking for a cure, but I don't think he will ever find one, poor fellow. Nuisance, really. I wish he could find a way to be mortal once more. At least then he'd stop whining, and I'd finally be able to kill him and be rid of him once and for all."

"A cure?" I said, furrowing my brow. "Why would anyone want a cure?"

Rolling his eyes, Byron laughed with a hint of bitterness. "Isn't that just my luck? I give someone the ultimate gift, and he spends the rest of eternity trying to get rid of it." His lip curled in a rueful sneer, and then he pulled a flask from his jacket pocket and drank deeply, sitting back down on his stool. "But you didn't come here to ask about my sorry excuse for a love life, surely? You certainly didn't come to ask about me. If you were really so concerned, you'd have been here a bit sooner. So what is it you want, Marie?"

His words stung, and I scowled as I replied, "I have been looking for you for years."

"Oh really? Well, that's odd. You must not have been looking very hard. I have been here for donkey's years. Yet you never called, you never wrote...you never even sent a Christmas card. Now that hurt, Marie." He drank deeply once more, then waggled his finger at me. "I just knew my queen mother would worry for her own dear boy's safety. But then, we both know you better, don't we?"

Wolfie stepped forward, scowling, his hands curling into fists. "Leave her alone."

"No, Wolfie," I said. "He has a right to be angry with me."

"Thank you for the permission," Byron's voice dripped with irony. "I can't tell you what a relief it is to finally be allowed to feel something. Better late than never, eh, Marie?"

I had to put a hand on Wolfie's chest to hold him back this time. Keeping my voice even, I said, "I deserve that too, I suppose."

"Marie, darling, god forbid any of us gets what we deserve." His sardonic laugh cut me deeply. "I have to say I'm disappointed in you, Herr Mozart. I never thought you'd have been anyone's lapdog, but I suppose you've been made a slave to her thighs, just like all the rest."

This time, I could not stop him, and Wolfie knocked the flask out of his hand. Blood sprayed across the room, splattering the desk along with the pages of the book in which Byron had been writing. "Oh, bloody hell. Now look what you've done. I'll have to rewrite that whole page."

"I ought to kill you where you stand for speaking to her that way," said Wolfie, his nostrils flaring.

"The wolf has some bite," Byron said, taking his cane in his hand and standing to face Wolfie. His voice sounded calm, but the warning hidden beneath the words I recognized all too well. "Trust me, dear boy, I haven't said a word that isn't true. You know she doesn't give a damn about you or me. She is here because she needs me. That is all. Isn't that right, Marie?"

"Why must you be this way?" I said, touching his hand that held the cane.

"What way is that? Honest?" He laughed, shrugging me off. "I'm afraid my days of lying to myself are over. Don't worry, though, my dear. I might just let you use me anyway for old time's sake, provided you keep your dog on a chain when he's around me. I don't mind insults or fisticuffs, but I cannot abide a man with no respect for my work. That's just rude."

Flinging my hands up, I said, "Oh, you are impossible!"

"Not impossible. Just shockingly unlikely." He winked again, turning to look at Sybill and proffering his arm to her. "Dear me. Where are my manners? Dearest sister, you must be famished and exhausted after your long journey. Allow me to play the host, won't you? These monks understand my needs. They will tend to yours as well, so long as we are peaceful in their house."

She raised an eyebrow, gazing back dubiously.

"I'll be a good boy. Cross my heart." He flashed her a winsome smile no one could resist, and cautiously she took his arm. "There now. Isn't that better? I feel like we're family already. Here, I'll show you to your quarters, let you get settled in, and then we can get down to serious business afterward. Fair enough?"

Annoyed and hurt, still I had to see the sense in that. I let him lead us toward the door, brushing aside Wolfie's annoyance with a warning glance in his direction. "We do need to talk, Albé. It's important."

Sullenly, Wolfie walked behind, not taking his eyes off Byron for a second, and I could feel him seething as he followed in my wake.

"Yes, yes," Byron nodded, still walking back toward where our bags had been left. "After you've rested and we have all fortified ourselves. I have a feeling this is going to be a long conversation and one for which we'll need all of our strength and mental acumen. Am I right?"

We reached the reception hall once more, and I took a deep breath before saying, "Yes. Maddening, but you are correct."

"Mad? Me?" His lip curled once more, and without prelude or warning he scooped up the heaviest of our suitcases and tossed it across the room to Mozart who caught it with a grunt of protest. "Just a rumor."

Continuing as though he had not spoken, Byron then picked up Sybill's small rolling bag and handed it to her with a wink, leading her away. I scowled at my own luggage. Wolfie picked it up, looking like an extremely annoyed porter. We had no choice but to hurry behind, trying to catch up.

"The discussion will keep," I said, my voice rising to echo in the corridor. "But not for long. It is a matter of life and death."

"It always is with you. Some things never change." His voice sounded soft as silk, but a hint of warning lurked behind it, and I knew as he led the way toward our rooms, I had my work cut out for me if I wanted to persuade him to help. I only hoped I still held a place in his heart and the ravages of the years standing between us had not eroded away the love that once bound us together.

Open Doors

Raul

I awoke to the echoes of footsteps reverberating against the hard stone, but I had been alone for so long, uncertain how long I'd been left alone in that dank hole. When the door of my cell opened, a man entered carrying a kerosene lamp. Though the light was dim, it hurt my eyes. Clinging to the stone with claw-like fingers, I retreated into the shadows of the corner, and I heard a strange, wild hissing. It took a few moments before I realized the sound came from my own cracked lips.

The man set the lamp down in the center of the cell, peering at me with curious glittering eyes. "Ah, my guest. Bonsoir. I apologize for not having greeted you sooner. Unavoidable circumstances detained me."

His words washed over me, and I had difficulty focusing on the meaning of them, my hunger taking over all rational thought and leaving me struggling as though in a fog. I knew my fangs were bared, and I though I could smell he was a vampire, I also knew he was well fed, in my eyes swollen like a tick. I wanted to rip him apart to taste the blood, have it dripping down my chin and from my fingertips.

Clearly, he saw the predatory gleam in my eye. He smiled, taking it in stride, and then snapped his fingers. A young woman walked robot-like into the room, obviously glamoured, though her expression was full of terror. He had taken her will from her, but not her fear or awareness. It was monstrous. And I was starving.

"Bon appétit," he said, taking a step back, gesturing toward the woman as an offering.

The creature took control of my body and, with an inhuman roar, I lunged toward the woman, fangs out, fingers like claws. I gorged on her, breaking her open, slaking my thirst with her death, sucking every delicious drop as I tore her body into pieces. Inside, a captive to my urges, I felt shocked and horrified, forced to look on while the monster I had become groaned in ecstasy with the kill, swallowing the blood in gurgling gulps and even sucking the marrow from her bones. I could feel my veins expanding as the woman's blood spread through my system and out to my extremities. Every cell came to life, and I closed my eyes, reveling in the sensation profoundly both orgasmic and terrifying. Tormented by the dichotomy of my mind, I was powerless to stop my actions.

When nothing remained of the woman but shattered bones and ribbons of flesh, I lifted my head to look at the vampire who had watched on with an expression of benevolent curiosity. "Do you need another, my friend? Or have you had enough?"

Though I felt the raging beast inside me thrill to the idea of having more, I took control and suppressed that murderous urge. "Enough," I said warily, licking my lips, unsure of his motivations.

"Good," he said. "I expect you have questions, do you not?"

Confused, I stared at him without reply.

This too, however, he seemed to understand and take in stride. "Come now. Let us be friends."

"Friends?" I said at last, blinking. "You've kept me a prisoner here, and you want to be friends?"

"Oh my dear boy, 'prisoner' is such an ugly word. I never intended that. I simply gave you time to consider your loyalties." Despite his calm tone, I saw his fangs show as he spoke. "I am perfectly willing to allow you to leave this place, provided you give me what I want."

"What you want?" I said, spitting the words out. "I don't even know what the hell that is."

Covering his mouth with his fingers, he laughed, then. "I want you to tell me about your maker, the whore, Marie Antoinette, of course, Raul."

He said my name so matter-of-factly, I was shocked into silence and stared at him wide-eyed.

My face must have betrayed my disbelief, because he smiled a little more at my reaction. "Come now. You knew exactly what I wanted. All this refusal of yours was for naught. We knew precisely who you were from the first. Your desire to keep her identity secret, while honorable, is foolish and misplaced."

"If you know everything, then what do you need me for?" I glared in challenge, fangs showing, rising from my hunched position on the floor to look him in the eye. My hair, still dripping with gore, fell across my face, and I knew I must look as horrific as I felt.

He laughed again, shaking his head at me as though I were a child. "Save the theatrics, my boy. I do not need you at all. 'Want' is the word I would use."

"Why?" Holding onto my anger, I had folded many meanings into the question. I wanted him to tell me why I'd been kidnapped, tortured, and driven nearly to madness purely to satisfy what seemed like a whim. I wanted to know why he'd chosen me. I wanted to know why he hated Marie so much.

"Because it pleases me," he said. "I would have you know the truth about your situation. But most of all, I hate to see a young vampire so completely full of self-loathing and wasted potential. It pains me to know how much you must hate your own nature, when you should glory in it. You are immortal, yet you live as though you have no right to be so. What a sorry state of affairs. She has done more damage to you than I ever could."

While his words made me angry, they also stung. He had seen into my soul and recognized the secret I'd buried all this time. I hated being a vampire and all its ramifications, even though I knew Marie thought she gave me something precious. The thirst for blood disgusted and ate away at my sense of self. She didn't understand my feelings and felt hurt by them, so I'd learned to keep them to myself, letting them kill me slowly, all the while wanting nothing more than to have the torment end. I'd been in such denial, not only had I hidden my thoughts from her, I had suppressed them from myself as well. Doing so gave me a perpetual sense of anger and frustration with my own weakness. The entire time I had lived with Marie, I had withdrawn into books and music, hiding from the truth about myself. Only when I had met Sybill had I been forced to acknowledge being a vampire made me hate myself and separated me from the only chance I'd ever had for happiness. His words ripped through me like a knife, slicing into my heart so deeply I gasped.

"Let me release you from your pain, my boy. This life should be joyous. You only need reach for it." He held out his hand to me, unfazed by my blood-drenched appearance. "Come. Let us talk. That is all I ask. You will decide for yourself. Simply take the first step, and you will see this prison is of your own making. I can help you free yourself from your own suffering."

Something inside me broke, and, tearfully, I took his hand with a grateful heart, letting him lead me away.

Question and Answer

Sybill

"Sister?"

I heard a knock at the door followed by a soft whisper. I blinked awake and lifted my head off the pillow to glance across the room. "Mmpf?"

With a creak, the door opened, and as I rubbed my eyes, Byron crept inside, a mischievous grin curling his lip. "You still asleep?"

Groaning, I flopped back on the bed. "I was. Not now. What's up? If you tell me I've got to pack and leave all over again, I will cut you. This is my fourth bed in a week, and I'm sick to death of moving around."

"So surly." His eyes crinkled good-naturedly as he laughed, walking over toward me. He had a slight limp I hadn't noticed before, and clearly he held that silver-handled cane for more than just an affectation. "Wonder why I stayed lost for so long?"

"Ha." I sat up, running my fingers through my hair and yawning. "Okay, fine. I'm awake. What do you want?"

"Why, to get to know you, of course. You are my sister, after all," he said, taking a seat on the side of my bed, his face full of amusement as he tilted his head in appraisal. "Good lord, your hair is like a wild thing. Sorry, but I don't understand these modern styles. Is it supposed to do that?"

"Why? Will it scare you out of ever waking me up again? If so, yes. I did it totally on purpose." I struggled to sound annoyed, but I couldn't help the smile that crept across my face as I spoke. "You can call me by my real name. It's Sybill."

"Lovely name. You can call me Albé," he said with a little bow of his head.

"Where's that nickname from?" I said, wrinkling my forehead as I tried to puzzle it out.

"It's a play on my name, my dear. Lord Byron. L.B. Albé." He grinned and then reached out to ruffle my hair. "Now get up. I've got lots to talk to you about before the old lady interrupts our fun."

"Hey!" I said, squirming away and sliding out of the other side of the bed. "Fun? This is fun to you?"

He looked me up and down in my sleep shorts and tank top, and then he winked wickedly. "Definitely. Nice tattoos."

"Don't be creepy." I crossed my arms over my chest self-consciously. "Get out so I can get dressed."

With a chuckle and a smirk, he stood and covered his eyes with one hand, still peeking through his fingers. "Come now, Sybill. We're family."

"Out!" I threw a pillow at him.

He scurried to the door, laughing loudly. "I'm going. But hurry. I'll be outside waiting. I've got breakfast for you too, so chop, chop."

I sighed and rolled my eyes. "Fine. I'll be there as quickly as I can."

When I emerged from the room, he stood twirling his cane in one hand, leaning against the wall and whistling. Smiling, he stopped once he saw me and held out a steel travel cup toward me. "Here. You'll need this."

Taking it from him, I lifted the lid to peek at the contents. Blood. Still warm. "Thanks," I said and took a sip. "Mmm. Where did this come from?"

"The monks. They take turns making a donation."

"Well, that's thoughtful."

He shrugged. "Not really. I think it's part safety precaution so I won't go on a biting rampage and part payment for the work I'm doing."

"Which is?" I said, taking another drink.

"Well, I did translations for them years back. They're all Armenian, you see, and almost all of their books are unknown in the Western world because no one really speaks Armenian. They've all but been wiped out. This is one of their few safe havens. Anyway, when I returned to this place a few years back, I offered to translate some of their oldest books in exchange for my room and board. It's a good arrangement all around."

I nodded. "I wondered. You don't seem the religious type."

He smirked. "Even the devil believes in God, my dear."

Taking a last sip, I then put the lid back on the cup and looked at him. "What should I do with this?" I said, waggling the cup with uncertainty.

"Oh, we'll be walking past the kitchens. We can drop it off on our way. Shall we?" He proffered his arm to me, and I let him lead me down the hall.

We went through several doors. I didn't recognize any of the passages from the night before. True to his word, we came to an open arch through which we could hear the sounds of dishes clanking. Byron took the cup from me, leaving me there in the corridor while he carried it in and handed it to one of the monks. Then he returned, and we walked on. "I can't tell you how good it is to have someone to talk to. These monks aren't much for conversation."

"I noticed," I said.

He opened a door, and we went down a short flight of steps into a square room, clearly used as a large pantry. Bags of rice, flour, and potatoes sat alongside cans of food on wooden shelves, and there were also a large number of jars filled with some sort of red jelly. "Rose petal jam," he said, sweeping his hand toward the jars. "It's their specialty. Do try not to knock any of them over. I don't want to have to explain to the Abbot what happened."

"I'm insulted," I said, letting go of his arm and turning to face him. "Do I look like a klutz?"

He laughed and shook his head. "I'm just getting to know you."

"So what did you bring me here for?" I looked around the room, realizing the only door was the one through which we'd entered, and there were no windows at all. "Should I be worried you've separated me off in here?"

I meant the question as a joke, but the look on his face told me I'd struck a nerve. "I may be many things, Sybill, but I would never hurt a woman, especially not when she is family to me. You are in no danger, I can assure you."

"I didn't mean it like that," I said. "You have to admit, though, this is a strange place to bring me."

"I had to be sure we wouldn't be interrupted or overheard. You never know where spies might be lurking."

Quirking an eyebrow, I said, "Spies? You mean the monks? I don't think they're talking to anyone."

"Trust no one, my dear. Except family, of course." He smiled when he gave this exception to his rule, and he clearly included himself in that statement.

"I thought you didn't trust Marie," I said, crossing my arms over my chest.

"Trust her?" His lip curled as he replied. "I do. Implicitly. That doesn't mean I don't find her infuriating and self-centered, however. Speaking of the old girl, how much has she told you about your new un-life? Knowing Marie as I do, I'm betting you've been mostly on your own. Am I right?"

Frowning, I nodded. "Pretty much. She did teach me how to hunt when I needed to, but that's about all I know."

"Tsk. That won't do at all." He took a seat on a sack of potatoes, propping his foot up on a nearby step stool, and looked up at me. "Right then. Ask away. I'll answer any questions you have."

I blinked for a second to think, then put one hand on my hip and said, "Okay, how does it work?"

"How does what work?" He raised an eyebrow at me, nonplussed.

"The turning thing. How did I become this?"

"I assume by 'this' you mean 'a vampire'?" Teasing me, the corners of his mouth struggled against a smile.

"Well, duh," I said. "It's just, I don't feel much like most of the stuff in the movies fits."

"Ah. That's the work of our international vampire disinformation team. They're good, aren't they?"

"Seriously?" My eyes widened, and my jaw dropped.

"No!" He laughed at me outright. "You really are a newborn, aren't you? Sorry. I kid. Honestly, the truth is rather boring. Well, I think it is, anyway. Polidori, my doctor, has been studying it for years and thinks it's fascinating. Each to his own, I suppose."

He sniffed before he continued. "At any rate," he said, "the 'turning thing,' as you put it, is a virus. You, my dear, have been infected."

I scowled. "You've got to be joking."

"I'm afraid not. Vampirism is a terminal illness, as you have well surmised, though not quite fatal. Funny old world, eh? Polidori could explain it better, but apparently this virus is some sort of super-bug, I suppose you'd say. It causes cellular mutations. He's doing testing now, but it seems to be something like rabies, only much more fast-acting and with several other accompanying symptoms."

"You're telling me I have rabies?" I gaped in horror.

"Not exactly, but sort of. Yes. There's no cure." He shrugged. "Polidori's working on one. He's been at it for over a century. God knows why."

It took a moment for this information to sink in. "Wait. Why the blood thirst?"

"Oh, that's simple enough. Your body needs the extra infusion of human blood in order to slow down the mutations. So long as you give it what it wants, you can keep yourself from going insane. When you're a new vampire, you have lower tolerance to the thirst. That's why it is so important we give you what your body needs as soon as you wake each evening. By the time you've lived as long as Marie and I have, you learn to adapt. She and I could go a week before we experience serious adverse effects."

"Are those effects permanent?" I could feel myself starting to panic, my throat closing up.

He thought about that, looking up toward the ceiling. "Some of them are, yes. You see, once the mutations spread to your brain, it slowly eats away at the tissue, and if it goes on long enough, you end up being ruled by your animal instincts. A bit like a zombie, really. It's not pretty."

Speechless, I sank down onto an enormous bag of rice and stared into the distance, my eyes glazing over.

Seeing the shock in my expression, he leapt from his seat and hurried over to touch my shoulder. "Oh now, Sybill. Don't worry. We won't let that happen to you. We'll take care of you. You can see many of us never get to that point."

Trying not to cry, I looked up. "I guess I just thought, you know, being a vampire meant you had superpowers. I know I must sound stupid, but how could I know? I mean, you called it a gift. What kind of gift is it if you just turn into a biting machine?"

"Come now. It's not as dire as all that. There are a lot of benefits, starting with not dying. I'm rather partial to that one, myself." He sat down next to me again, reaching out to take my hand. "Why don't you tell me what you expected, and I'll tell you whether those ideas are accurate or not? Fair enough?"

I took a moment to think about his offer and then nodded. "Okay. Here goes. Crosses?"

"Myth. We're not demons."

"Silver?"

He showed me a watch he wore on his wrist. "Like this, you mean? It's pretty, but it doesn't affect us."

"Holy water?"

He shook his head. "No effect at all."

"Stake through the heart?"

Frowning, he nodded. "Well, that one is true, but only because it's the major organ that pushes blood throughout your body. I know it seems as though your heart doesn't beat, but when you drink blood, the muscles do contract slightly, just enough to send the infusion through your veins and out to your extremities. That's why when you feed, your senses are heightened, though the effect quickly fades once your heart slows to a stop once more. There's nothing special about a stake, really. Anything that stops your heart from working will do. A small caliber bullet would likely just be a painful nuisance and slow you down for a while, but it wouldn't kill you. Anything larger, however, if it damages the heart, it could kill you, yes."

"Quick healing?" I raised my eyebrows hopefully.

"Absolutely true. There are exceptions, of course. If you lose a limb, you won't grow a new one back, but you will heal over and stop bleeding extremely quickly. There's no risk of an infection in the wound." He smiled. "Quite handy, really."

"What about your limp?" I said, looking down at his foot. "Why hasn't that healed?"

A pained look came over him. "I've had it since childhood. It's a club foot. I'm rather sensitive about discussing it. It will never heal."

"I'm sorry." I bit my lip and squeezed his hand. "I didn't know."

"It's fine. Just please, don't treat me differently because of it. I don't like pity." He squeezed my hand back, letting me know he forgave me. "Go on. Ask something else."

I nodded, thinking before I went on. "What about garlic?"

"Wives' tales." He sneered. "No merit to that at all."

"Sunlight? I've been told we can't tolerate it, but I don't know why."

With a sigh, he said, "That's the most inconvenient symptom. Our skin becomes overly sensitive to ultraviolet radiation. We will blister in a matter of minutes. It won't kill you, and you won't burst into flames, but it is extremely painful and takes a long time to heal. Polidori is working on a liquid sunscreen, but thus far, nothing has worked."

"I've seen I'm faster and stronger than normal humans," I said. "How about flying? Or turning into a bat or whatever?"

He laughed. "Sorry to disappoint you, but you're not a magician or a shape shifter."

"Hmm." I felt a little bit silly for asking, but also a little disappointed to be wrong. "Well, I've seen that glamour thing in action. How does it work?"

Raising his eyebrows, he smiled. "You know, I'm not really sure. I know some predators are able to hypnotize their prey. I think it's something like that. I'm sure Polly would have some detailed scientific answer, but that's all I really know. It's handy, at any rate. I'm happy to teach you if you like. It takes practice, but once you get the hang of it, it's an extremely useful skill."

"Would you?" I said, excited by his offer. "That would be so great. I feel like..."

"Like she hasn't taught you anything? Yes, I'm familiar with the feeling." He smiled at me kindly. "Don't worry. You're my sister. I take my role seriously."

Full of gratitude, I put my arms around him and hugged him. "Thank you so much. I've felt so alone and overwhelmed. Honestly, I need someone to keep me from being so lost."

"We all need that, don't we?" He held me close, and when at last I pulled back, he smiled again and said, "Speaking of teaching you things, how much do you know about protecting yourself? I don't want to frighten you, but the time may come when you have to fight to keep yourself from being killed. I can help you there too, if you need it. Have you ever fired a gun?"

I nodded immediately. "Oh, yes. My father made sure I knew how to use both a pistol and a rifle. Just target practice, but I'm not afraid to defend myself if I have to and am a decent shot."

He smiled with approval. "Good. How about hand-to-hand fighting?"

"You mean I don't magically get ninja skills along with my superpowers?" I winked, teasing.

"Sadly, no." He laughed. "But don't despair. I used to be a boxing champion. I'll be happy to teach you what I know."

"My father gave me basic self-defense lessons, but that would be helpful, thank you," I said.

"How are you with a sword?"

I felt taken aback by this question. "You're kidding. Like, a real one, you mean?"

"Yes. Why? Were you hoping for Jedi lightsabers, because those don't actually exist."

"I've never even seen a sword that wasn't a toy except in a museum or at the Renaissance festival."

"At the what? No. Never mind." He shrugged, lifting up his cane in both hands, and with a twist, he pulled out the handle, revealing a hidden sword he then brandished in front of me. "I'm skilled in fencing, and I can teach you, but it will take time to master. You'll have to be patient.

For most people, handling a sword isn't something that comes naturally. It takes work and discipline. The good thing is, however, now you're a vampire, you have all the time you need to become an expert at just about anything you set your mind to. In the meantime, we'll just have to try to keep you out of any situations requiring swordplay."

"Do you seriously think that situation is very likely?" I raised an eyebrow dubiously at the sword he held in his hand.

"Let's just hope not." That answer didn't comfort me. He returned the sword to its hiding place, twisting the handle to lock it within the cane once more. "Any other weapons you're skilled with? Bow and arrow? Axe? Crossbow?"

"Uh, no. I'm a city girl. There's usually not a reason for axe-wielding where I'm from."

He shrugged again. "We'll add them to your training along with the sword."

I blinked. "You're not joking, are you?"

"No, I'm definitely not. Decapitation is the only foolproof vampire-killing method, and you might need it someday. But don't worry. I'll make sure you learn everything you need to know." He looked at his watch. "The old lady will be getting up by now. We had better head back before she thinks we're having a secret affair."

My jaw dropped. "But you're my brother."

"We aren't actually siblings, you know. That is only a way of explaining our strange situation. We do have a connection, though, don't you agree?" He leaned in close, and his eyes were suddenly sultry and deep. Licking his lips, he gazed down at me. "I'm not the only one who thinks so. Marie seemed a little concerned about it yesterday. Maybe she had reason. What do you think?"

He reached out to caress my cheek with the palm of his hand. I shivered in spite of myself. His change in behavior startled me, and I felt uncertain how to react. "You...you should stop that."

"Do you really want me to?" He touched my lower lip with his thumb, and though I pressed myself back against the wall, he moved in closer still until our noses brushed one another.

I swallowed hard, gazing back into his deep blue eyes, then put both hands on his chest. "Yes," I said, and pushed him back.

With a wink, he roared with laughter then. "I just wanted to see what you'd do." He stood, reaching out a hand to me to shake. "Come, Sybill. I'll be a good boy, I swear."

If I could have blushed, I would have. Abashed, I put my hand in his, one eyebrow raised. "That wasn't funny."

"Oh yes. It was hilarious." He chuckled for a moment, before he gave me a wicked grin. "But I won't do it again. Not unless you want me to, anyway."

"I thought you were in a relationship with this doctor of yours," I said.

"In my view, the two are not mutually exclusive. Besides, the thing with Polly and me didn't last long and happened years ago. Well, for me, anyway. I'm not sure the poor boy has let go of his sentimental attachment." He shrugged at the last as though he didn't feel any real concern.

"I love Raul," I said, as though that was the last word on the subject.

He nodded, his eyes still fixed on mine. "Ah, yes. This mysterious brother of mine. He is a lucky man."

"Well, not right now," I said. "Someone kidnapped him."

"If he won your heart, he is the luckiest man in the world. Even in captivity, you would give any man a reason to live." He bowed, lifting my fingers to his lips.

Pulling my hand back, I shifted nervously on my feet. "You really shouldn't talk to me like that."

Straightening till he looked me in the eye, he leaned on his cane and laughed again. "You will have to forgive me, Sybill. In life, they called me 'mad, bad, and dangerous to know.' But I am fiercely loyal to those I love. Family is more important to me than anything in the world."

"We only just met," I said. "You keep saying we're family, but how do I know you mean it?"

"I would never joke about such a thing." His expression looked deadly serious.

"Oh really? Well, then answer me this." I planted my feet, crossing my arms over my chest. "If family is so important to you, why did you leave Marie?"

"Who said I did the leaving?" The pain in his voice as he spoke sounded palpable and raw.

Confused, I tilted my head and searched his eyes. "She said she lost you."

"Is that how she put it? I see." He curled his lip as he spoke. "Well, let's just say we have a difference of opinion then."

"Why don't you tell me your side of it?" I said. "I'm listening."

He shook his head and cleared his throat, looking away. "Someday I will tell it all to you, and you can judge for yourself who is in the right. For now, we have to go."

I could tell I had hurt him deeply, and I felt a twinge of remorse. Reaching out, I caught his arm to stop him from walking away. "Wait. Albé, I'm sorry. I didn't mean..."

"No need to apologize," he said, but his voice rang thick with emotion. "Come. She's waiting."

That ended our private conversation, and I became distracted in thought afterward, though I didn't say anything more to him as we walked back the way we had come. What had caused the long estrangement between him and Marie? I felt grateful for his honest answers to my questions and for his offers to help me with self-defense, but at the same time, his personality had a wildness, an unpredictability, that left me feeling unsure of my footing around him. Had he been seriously flirting with me, or had that been truly a joke as he had claimed? I couldn't tell. Most of all, though I felt a close rapport with him developing, I didn't know if my own reactions to him were purely sisterly. It made me feel guilty to even acknowledge I found him attractive, though I certainly did.

I loved Raul deeply, but a part of me wondered if I had simply fallen in love with the idea of being with him rather than the reality. After all, Raul and I had only had one night together. That didn't seem enough to base a commitment upon. I had held onto the dream of being in a relationship with him to give my thoughts focus as we had traveled from one place to the next, but I didn't know if holding onto that dream was realistic. Once we found him, would he would want to be with me at all? Perhaps I wished for a fairy tale that could never come true, envisioning Raul in the role of Prince Charming, when in fact I barely knew him. Until I'd met Byron, Raul had been my emotional anchor, but now I felt adrift, and the uncertainty frightened me.

From the Ashes

Vincent

Two days after the Palmer House Hotel explosion, I rose from the rubble as night fell, my body covered in cuts from broken glass and wet from fire-hoses that had been used to quench the blaze. My situation could have been much worse. I suppose I should have been grateful I happened to be in my penthouse suite. The floors pancaking down on top of one another in the building collapse obliterated anyone below. As for me, the only thing that kept me from being killed was being in exactly the right spot at the moment the hotel imploded.

I sat in a chair in the corner when I first felt a shudder and heard the deep percussive booms of the explosion. Then I was tossed into the air and felt myself hurtling downward with an agonizing lurch, the free fall seeming to last for ages. Somehow, while everyone and everything around me became crushed to oblivion, I was thrown into a corner with steel reinforced concrete on all sides. Parts of the floor, wall, and ceiling wrapped around me in a triangular, tent-shaped space, keeping the majority of the debris from falling my way. It also prevented the wall of fire that blasted the bomb site like the wrath of God. No mortal could have withstood the heat I endured.

No, I was a lucky bastard, that's for sure. A human would certainly have died from the impact. I alone survived.

Getting out of there wasn't easy. Without vampire strength, I'd have been trapped until a clean up crew came with heavy equipment to clean up the site. That would have made for quite an uncomfortable situation since explaining how I survived might not make much sense given the circumstances.

Everything happened for a reason, they say. Fact was, though, even if there was a reason, it might not be one most people liked. I knew the reason for what happened to me and my place. It was all about the dame. Goldie. Marie.

She didn't set the bomb. Of course not. But she might as well have. I lost everything and everyone because I did her a favor. Eventually, I knew I would find the person who blew up my hotel, but that wasn't my real problem. It was Goldie. I was a chump to help her. I didn't let anyone make a fool out of me. She brought all that trouble to my door. Goldie knew just what she was doing. Oh, she was beautiful all right, and she played dumb when it suited her, but that dame didn't make it this long without being smart. And she'd left a trail of bodies behind too. Fellows who were too dumb to see they were being played. She'd thought I'd be one of them. While I was out scrounging in the dark for some blood and a clean set of clothes, she was already over there with her Prince Charming, living it up on my dime.

That was where she went wrong. Vincent DeLuca wasn't not just some bonehead she could use and toss away.

Some might say I should have let bygones be bygones. Not me. I would find her, and when I did, she would answer for what she cost me.

Family Meetings

Sybill

When we got back to the guest quarters, we found Marie pacing in irritation. Mozart had an odd expression on his face, as though we had interrupted something he was about to say. Marie, on the other hand, clearly was impatient to see us, perhaps because we had halted an argument with our entrance.

"Where have you been all this time?" she said, stopping in her tracks to turn and glare at us.

"Just showing my dear sister around a bit," Byron said, putting on the charming smile I was starting to recognize, trying to gloss over the tension in the room. "She expressed a curiosity about the place, and you know how I like a stroll."

Knowing I don't have a talent for tact or lying, I nodded my head and hoped that would do for a reply.

Her eyes narrowed. "Stroll. Ha. You just wanted to keep me waiting."

"Now, mother dear, why would I do that?" He moved in close and kissed her cheek. "Come. Let's not fight. I'm sorry for my tone of yesterday.

You know how I get sometimes. I was surprised to see you, that's all. I'm better now I've got used to the idea."

Though I knew she itched to say something more, she held back, and I was grateful not to see their argument perpetuate. "I missed you," she said softly, and the genuine feeling in her voice made him smile.

"I missed you too," he said, pulling her into his arms for a moment. Mozart scowled looking on, but I hoped his jealousy would fade.

Clearing my throat, I stood up straight. "So are we going to have this important talk or just stand around hugging one another? You said we have a lot to discuss. Shouldn't we get started?"

They separated, and I could see Mozart relax a little as he tried to hide the emotion so visible a moment ago.

Marie nodded, her eyes still fixed on Albé's. "Yes, but I think your doctor should be here too, don't you?"

"No, I don't think so," he said with a frown. "He'll only whine because no one is paying attention to him. And Polidori is not my doctor. I fired him."

She smiled as though this were a familiar conversation. "He's actually quite clever, darling. Perhaps he will have some ideas we hadn't thought of."

Shrugging, he rolled his eyes. "I doubt it. You'll only go giving him a big head asking what he thinks. If you insist upon it, I will play nice. Just don't tell him you think he's clever. He'll only behave like an insufferable git."

"What's a git?" I said, raising my eyebrows with amusement.

Byron opened his mouth to answer, but Marie cut him off. "No, you don't. Enough, Albé. He's part of this family, whether you are happy about it or not. You turned him, and therefore you have a responsibility to include him in family affairs."

"I've been paying for that mistake for almost two hundred years." He sighed. "Ugh. Fine. You win. But we'll have to go to him. He will never leave that laboratory. Lord knows why he hasn't given up by now."

Wheeling around, he pointed at me, eyes narrowing. "And you. No questions. I refuse to listen to him go on and on about his experiments."

Blinking, I smirked. "Me? Never. You have me confused with someone else."

"I mean it. If he starts explaining about peptides and nucleotides and I don't know what else, I will stab myself in the throat with a scalpel." Coming over to my side, he offered me his arm.

"So dramatic." I couldn't help but laugh.

Tartly, he said, "Oh, ha ha! Fine. Don't listen to me. You'll see what I mean."

Mozart walked over to Marie to lead her the same way, and I saw her hesitate. However, she put on a regal smile and wrapped her arm around his. A shadow passed over his face, and I knew though she was putting a good face on things, sooner or later, they would return to their fight. Judging from their body language, I doubted the outcome would please him.

We walked in yet another section of the grounds I hadn't seen before, passing an open courtyard with a formal garden at the center. Frost covered the ground, and the stone fountain stood dry and cold. A colonnade encircled the space, and we walked along it, our footfalls reverberating on the flagstones. Walking through a set of large wooden double doors, we entered another wing of the building, and I got a strange sense of the monastery being much larger than it had appeared upon our first arrival.

This new area smelled like it had been unoccupied for quite some time. The air was musty, stale, and still. Dust motes rose from every surface as we passed. All the rooms were dark, and the doors were closed. Moreover, silence was noticeably deeper than in the rest of the monastery. The further we went, the more I felt as though we were trespassing. Even Mozart stopped humming. Throughout the earlier part of our journey, he was actively composing his new piece, and the music that filled his thoughts was a constant companion to us, regardless of time or place. Yet here, his muse fell mute. Was it another sign of a rift between him and Marie, or did he sense just as I did that we were invading the place?

I didn't have time to ask or ponder this thought further, however, because Byron suddenly turned to the left. We went through a darkened archway and descended a staircase. A light shone at the bottom, and I could hear a strange buzzing. A strong stench of formaldehyde made me wrinkle my nose, and beneath it I detected the dry scent of vampire. When we reached the bottom of the steps, we turned to the right, suddenly finding ourselves in a stone, windowless room. Steel shelves filled with jars and strange instruments lined the walls. Fluorescent lights hung from the ceiling, giving everything a greenish pallor. In the center of the room stood a man wearing medical scrubs, a blue surgical gown covering him to his knees, a surgical cap, face mask, and goggles. He leaned over a metal examining table, sawing through the top of a naked male cadaver's head with a hacksaw. The blade stopped just as the crown of the skull dropped onto the table with a clank, revealing the brain.

Marie made a little noise, and the man looked up with surprise. He set down the hacksaw and glared at us. "Dammit, milord, I am working. This is not an amusement park. You're contaminating my specimen. Now I'll have to go find another dead vampire to dissect. Do you know how hard I worked to find this one?"

"Charming. Sybill, meet Doctor John Polidori. Polly, this is my sister, Sybill. I believe you've met my mother. Oh yes, and her companion, Herr Mozart. I'm sure you two will have loads to talk about." Byron turned to look at Marie who covered her eyes, trying not to gag, then looked back at the body on the slab. "Cover that up, won't you, old chap? We have guests. At least pretend to be a decent fellow, if you don't mind."

I kept my eyes on Polidori and gave him a weak smile and a small wave. "Hey there. Sorry."

He rolled his eyes, pulling off his latex gloves and throwing them into the trashcan before removing his face mask and goggles. "Don't mention it."

Pulling a sheet off one of the nearby shelves, he threw it over the body, hiding it from view. Then he took off the surgical gown, splattered with blood and brain matter, tossing it into a bin in the corner, before walking over to the sink to scrub his hands and arms.

"You aren't going to catch a disease from this poor dead bastard, Polly. I don't know why you are so fastidious." Byron chuckled and led us over to the corner to wait.

Drying his hands on a towel, he threw it into the bin along with his surgical cap. His hair was dark and curly, and his face was almost delicately handsome. "I don't expect you to understand surgical technique."

"That's not surgery. That's an autopsy."

"Did you come here to interrupt me and quibble, or is there a purpose for this visit?" I could tell this must be an ongoing argument, and Byron seemed amused by the banter, while Polidori clearly was not.

"Tsk tsk. Temper, Polly. You'll make our guests feel unwelcome." Byron smiled, his voice dripping with sarcasm, and I saw his fangs revealed with the grin.

Though he obviously wanted to say something further to Byron, Polidori struggled against the urge, gathering his face into a more friendly aspect. "I apologize. Where are my manners? Sybill, it is a pleasure to meet you. I did not know I had acquired an aunt. Marie, it is lovely to see you again. You're looking well. Herr Mozart, it is an honor, sir."

He bowed stiffly, and Byron snickered. "That'll do, Polly."

"I wish you would stop calling me that," said Polidori, grating his teeth.

"Yes, so you have told me for the last two hundred years." Byron smiled, making it clear he had no intention of changing his behavior in the slightest.

Drawing a deep breath to calm himself, Polidori stood a little straighter, clasping his hands behind his back. "To what do I owe the pleasure of this visit, may I ask?"

"By all means. Ask away," said Byron, smirking at him, letting the silence build for a few seconds until it became uncomfortable. He didn't intend to make this easy.

Polidori sighed, pinching his nose with annoyance. "Why are you here?"

"Family," said Byron, the humor leaving his voice and his lip curling into a snarl. "To which you belong. You would do well to remember."

The two of them glared at one another for a long moment before Marie, who had finally recovered herself, stepped forward. "Gentlemen, we do not have time for this sort of tit-for-tat. We have a mission of great urgency, and I need you to put aside your differences and talk like civilized men. Another man's life hangs in the balance, and indeed so do the fates of all of us in this room, so stop this absurd bickering."

I wanted to cheer, but I looked away and rocked back on my heels, pressing my lips together to stay quiet. Mozart's face looked grim, and I sensed again in him a growing agitation as though he felt like an outsider in the situation.

"Of course, your majesty," said Polidori with a deep bow. "Right this way."

Not making eye contact with Byron, he led us directly from the lab into a sitting room beyond. Though the walls were stone, there were wool carpets arranged artfully on the floor and strikingly modern leather and steel sofas and chairs. Sleek lights hung from the ceiling, giving the room a tasteful, comfortable, Italian flair. If the door behind us had been closed, I could have forgotten entirely about the dissection in the next room. However, no matter where I sat, the slab lay unavoidably in the corner of my vision, making my eyes and my mind wander back with distraction.

"Please," he said as we all sat down, "how may I be of service?"

"Thank you, Doctor," she said. "I assume you have been made aware of certain enemies of mine. No doubt Albé has warned you regarding their relentless pursuit and of the danger we all face should their plan succeed."

"Indeed, madam. I am well acquainted with the name and nature of our adversary," he said.

"Well, I'm not," I said, the words bursting forth before I could stop them. Everyone turned to stare at me, and I felt a defensive anger well up inside. "You're all acting like there's some sort of boogieman after us. Just who are we running from, and what are you all so afraid of?"

"You haven't told her?" Byron gave Marie a sharp look.

Marie frowned, holding her hands palm up as she gestured toward me. "We had no time. I had to get us to a place where we could talk about these things in safety. What would you have me do? Since the day I met her, there hasn't been a moment we weren't being pursued until just now."

"Excuses," he said, his lip curling in anger. "This poor girl has been through so much for you. She deserves to know the truth."

"Thank you," I said, taking his hand and giving it a squeeze. Mozart reached out to Marie to offer his support, but she brushed away his touch, and he pulled back as though he were stung. She took no notice, however, looking at me with a steady gaze. "I don't know who captured Raul, but the person they work for is my long time enemy, the Marquis de Sade."

"De Sade?" I said. "As in, the guy who wrote all that porn?"

Byron snorted a laugh, but quickly stifled it, covering his mouth with his hand and feigning a cough.

"The same." Marie nodded, and her eyes were suddenly world weary and sad. "The word sadist comes from his name, and with good reason. The Marquis has pursued me for over two centuries."

"But why? I mean, he's just some crazy writer guy, isn't he? What's he got against you?"

"I would not call him just anything. The Marquis is a devious, charismatic, and manipulative psychopath who fixated on me as the root of all of the problems he experienced throughout his life. He believes I am responsible for his incarceration as a violent and dangerous sex offender, though he never denied the truth of the charges brought against him. He merely deemed the punishment objectionable. Somehow he felt because of his social status, there should have been no consequences for his actions. He also blamed me for his loss of reputation and wealth, though he clearly squandered what little money remained in his inheritance and he'd ruined his reputation without any help from me whatsoever. When he realized the vampires among those of us at court disagreed with his blatant displays of violence, ones we could not hide or ignore, he blamed me for turning them against him. He hated our policy of restraint, saying vampires had a natural place at the top of the food chain and we should dominate human beings in any way we saw fit without restraint or remorse."

"Top of the food chain?" I wrinkled my nose. "Gross."

Byron snorted again, and this time he did not bother disguising it.

Ignoring Byron's reaction, Marie nodded and went on. "Yes, quite. His writings and behavior threatened all of us. If the human population of France realized what we were, we knew it would mean our downfall. The Marquis, however, did not care what humans thought. He was convinced our kind should control the entire world. My advisors and I agreed he must be kept a prisoner for all our sakes. However, his words spoke to the Revolutionaries, and he glamoured them into believing overthrow of the government was not only possible but necessary and we all deserved death. Once they'd put me in prison, he dropped his title, calling himself 'Citizen Sade,' and he convinced those in power he was a man of the people with sympathies aligned with them. Ignorant of his true nature, they released him and made him a judge. He had a penchant for blood, and under his rulings, many of my friends from court were executed. I realized then his supreme hatred of me. He wrote a series of treatises, wrongly accusing me of all sorts of crimes, the product of his madman's imaginings, including the idea I had committed incest with my own son."

"Revolting nonsense," Polidori said, curling his lip with distaste.

Marie smiled at him in agreement. "The Marquis had a flair for the dramatic, and he loved the attention he received. He wanted to see the public baying for my blood. Under his urging, they condemned me to death."

"He's still chasing you?" I leaned forward to hear more, eyes wide.

She nodded, smoothing out her skirt over her knees. "When he heard a rumor I had escaped, he began his relentless hunt. I traveled first to the small town of Ravenna, not far from here, in order to remove myself from his reach. That is where I met Albé. When I discovered the Marquis had found my location, we removed to Rome, where our dear Doctor lived. Byron turned him, and we were then going to travel as a group to Greece, but Polidori and Byron had a…disagreement, shall we say?"

Both men nodded, shifting in their seats uncomfortably.

Marie looked at them both before continuing her story. "Polidori left for England while Albé and I went to Greece. When we arrived, however, Greece was in the throes of a war with Turkey. I had seen enough fighting to last several lifetimes, but Albé believed their cause was just. He wanted to stay, believing himself honor bound to aid the Greek people in their fight for independence. I insisted our only option to ensure the Marquis couldn't find us would be leaving for the New World. We agreed I would leave and he would remain behind to help the troops, then join me later once he completed his work there. I sailed for New Orleans, and that is where we lost one another. He never found me again."

She looked over at Byron for confirmation, and though his face appeared solemn, he nodded. "That is not quite how I remember the discussion, but I do not wish to quibble. Let us leave the argument in the past and forge a new relationship now we are reunited."

"So let me get this straight," I said, trying to wrap my head around what I'd been told. "For the last two centuries years, the original sadist has been looking for you, and that's who you think has kidnapped Raul? We need a plan, because if that's true, I don't want to think about what they've done to him. This wackjob has to be stopped."

"I like your fire," Byron said, giving me a nod of encouragement. "It is time to put an end to the threat."

"Agreed," said Polidori. "How can I assist?"

"We need to find him and eliminate him," Marie said. "Over the years, the Marquis has only increased in strength and abilities. I have always advocated for restraint, working to mask the symptoms of my condition to the extent that it is possible. The Marquis, on the other hand, gave himself over to his more monstrous instincts, letting the disease proceed. We are, therefore, at a distinct disadvantage since the results of this decision are unknown. Doctor, I hoped your research might give us some insights and help us find a weakness."

Polidori rubbed his forehead thoughtfully. "I have studied vampires with advanced states of the disease, but I am afraid I cannot give you precise data pertaining to the Marquis' unique case. Clearly, he has not allowed himself to succumb completely to the symptoms, for those who have done so experience a rapid transformation from human into, what I call, revenants. They are mindless and monstrous, driven purely by baser needs, the hunger taking over and eclipsing all rational thought. This state is brought on by long periods of blood deprivation, and can be complete in a matter of a few months, given the right circumstances. Some people also seem more genetically predisposed to rapid onset, including those whose immune systems are weakened. This series of stages of the disease accounts for variance in anecdotal accounts written by humans across various periods of history."

Out of the corner of my eye, I saw Byron roll his eyes with annoyance as Polidori gave just the sort of medical detail he found so annoying.

For the rest of us seated in that room, however, the information was new and necessary, and I found myself leaning forward to hear more.

Warming to his audience, Polidori continued his explanation. "A human who contracted the disease without sufficient blood prey in his or her geographical location may exhibit far more advanced symptoms than one who is in a dense population with a large pool of blood prey to draw upon. Most of those infected with the disease express a desire to keep their illness hidden for as long as may be possible, and therefore they strive to find ways of obtaining the blood they need while still retaining their own personality and memories and way of life. There are also variations due to blood type and there is an indication that ingesting the blood of younger hosts might stave off the advancement of the disease."

"Yes, yes. This is all fascinating, I'm sure, but get to the point." Byron waved his hands to interrupt. "What does this have to do with the Marquis?"

I saw Polidori close his eyes for a second to compose himself, then he went on in a clear and clinical way, turning to look at Marie as he spoke. "Given his personality and pathology before being infected, I am unable to draw any certain conclusions about the state of his illness. I have never seen a vampire of his age who did not have the disposition displayed by yourself, your majesty. You have worked diligently to mask and hinder the advancement of the symptoms, but with the Marquis, he may have sought to bring on symptoms he felt were advantageous or useful to him. That makes him an unpredictable subject for diagnosis. Without capturing and examining him here in the lab under controlled conditions, I am afraid I can only speak in generalities."

Marie nodded at this explanation. "I understand. What we need, then, is some way to weaken him. Tell me of your vaccine trials. Is it possible to reverse the disease and make the Marquis mortal again so we might eliminate him?"

"The results of my clinical trials, madam, have been inconclusive." Polidori shook his head and frowned as he went on. "Some subjects seem to respond to the treatment, but generally I find those results are consistent only among the recently infected. Those who have experienced the disease for longer periods of time demonstrate widely erratic results from the vaccine. Believe me, if the vaccine were predictably effective, I would have used it on myself by now. I cannot predict the outcome should the Marquis undergo treatment."

"But would it weaken him, man? That is the pertinent question," said Byron, tapping his cane on the floor for emphasis.

Polidori shrugged. "Weaken him? Yes, most likely. But the correct dosage is difficult to calculate without testing his blood in my laboratory. I would not recommend the attempt given the unknown variables in these unique circumstances."

"What if he were to receive the maximum dose?" I said, narrowing my eyes and leaning closer to the doctor.

His forehead furrowed. "Again, I cannot predict. The dose might kill him, or it might simply weaken him. It might even cause mutations I have not seen before. As I said, his is an unusual case, and I cannot know..."

Lifting my hand to stop him from talking, I waved away his concerns. "But it's more likely we could defeat him either way, right?"

"More likely, yes," he said with a reluctant nod. "Still, without sufficient testing..."

"Right then." I turned away to face the others. "That's settled. Vaccine it is. Now we just have to figure out how to find him and deliver it."

"Now wait just a minute!" Polidori stood up, glaring at me. "You can't just barge into my laboratory and demand I give you the serum that has been my long life's research. My vaccine is a cure, not a weapon. I won't participate in this scheme of yours. I have seen the ravages of the vaccine on those for whom the treatment failed, and I would not wish that on anyone, even this madman you seek."

Jumping to my feet, I got up close to him, hitting my finger on his chest for emphasis. "A man's life is at stake. A man I care about. I'm not going to let you tell me no when you can help me save him."

"Sybill, please," Marie said, leaning forward in her seat.

Polidori's eyes flashed in anger. "Get her out of here, Albé. I'm warning you. I won't be a party to this plan. The vaccine isn't ready, and I will not allow my work to be used in ways that go against my Hippocratic oath."

"Hypocritical oath, you mean," I said, hopping up and down in fury.

Byron stood behind me, wrapping one arm firmly around my shoulders and pulling my body back against him to keep me from hitting the doctor in the face. "Come, Sybill. He may be a fool, but he will listen to reason."

"We don't have time for that!" I shook violently and struggled to get free. "Raul is captive there right now, and god knows what this wacko is doing to him. I'll be damned if I'm going to sit around talking anymore!"

Polidori stormed over to the doorway and pointed through his lab toward the archway leading to the stairs. "Get out! All of you!"

Marie stood up, and Mozart rose to stand behind her with a grave expression. "Take her back to her room, please, Albé. We will find another way."

Blood tears streamed down my face, and I sobbed as Byron marched me out of there. I fought him all the way back, but he remained resolute and unyielding, and at last I realized I couldn't break free. When we got back to the place I had slept the night before, he walked me in much more gently, shut the door behind us, and laid me on the bed. I curled up into a ball, and he sat beside me, stroking my hair. "We will think of something, Sybill. I swear to you. We will think of something."

Seething

Polidori

A soft knock came at my door just as I was updating my journal on the day's research Though I hate interruptions, when I looked up from my desk to see not Byron, as I had anticipated, but the beautiful, headstrong young woman I had only met on the one occasion and who, I had been instructed, was my aunt by vampire reckoning, I heaved a sigh of resignation and set the book aside.

Rising from my seat, I gave her what I hoped would appear to be a friendly smile, bowing slightly at the waist. "Good evening, miss. To what do I owe the pleasure of your company?"

Covering her mouth with her hand, she laughed, stepping into the room, and I looked up with one eyebrow raised in curiosity and irritation. "Have I said something funny? Pray, do tell me how I have amused you so I may make a note of it for future reference."

"Oh god, you're serious, aren't you?" A frown crossed her features, and she moved closer, looking me in the eye. "Look, we got off on the wrong foot. I said things the other day I shouldn't. I was angry and frustrated.

I don't know you, and it wasn't fair of me. I'm sorry. Honestly, I didn't mean to sound rude just now. It's just I'm not sure how to act when people are so formal, you know? Where I come from, nobody talks like that. I thought that was just in old books and movies. I'm not making fun, honest. Can we, like, start over or something? Only, please don't talk to me like I'm some Jane Austen character, all right? It makes me nervous. I feel like I should be offering you tea and crumpets, and I don't even know what the heck a crumpet is."

I gaped at her open mouthed at these pronouncements, and even more so when she stepped right up in front of me, smiling, and held out her hand. "Hi. I'm Sybill. Pleased to meet you. What should I call you? Doctor Polidori seems so formal. After all, we're family, right?"

Awkwardly, I took her hand, and she shook it as firmly as any man, a fact which was completely startling to say the least. And yet, despite her brashness, there was a warmth in her demeanor that was strangely disarming. My cold greeting to her made me suddenly ashamed, and in that moment I decided I liked her, in spite of her odd manners and our argument the day before.

Smiling back in return, I nodded, her hand still clasped in mine. "I was the one who was rude. I apologize. Forgive me. As you say, we are family. Please, call me John."

"John. All right then. Thanks." Releasing my hand, she glanced over at the journal I had left on my desk, then back at me with a worried brow. "I'm not bugging you, am I?"

For a moment, I stood still, puzzling over the meaning of those words, and then following her gaze, I shook my head and smiled. "It's nothing urgent. Please, come in and have a seat. I would like for us to become better acquainted."

"Really? You would?" She raised an eyebrow dubiously, though she followed me on into the parlor beyond and took a seat on the sofa. "You don't have to say that, you know. I mean, I get it if you're working. I hate being interrupted when I'm working in my studio. Messes up the flow, know what I mean? You know, you should get yourself a sign for your door so people know when you're busy. I could pick one up for you next time I go into the city if you want."

I couldn't help laughing, though her rapid speech and topic shifts were a bit overwhelming. "That won't be necessary, though I thank you for the kind offer. Until now, it's only been milord and myself. The monks don't come down here. They aren't sure what to make of me, I'm afraid. They understand that I am a healer, and they respect that. After all, they once cared for lepers. But they don't understand modern medicine, and I think they don't quite trust that God would approve of my methods. They may be right."

"How do you guys know one another, anyway? You and Byron, I mean. Were you friends before, you know, you were..."

"Turned?" I finished, though I knew she had implied another kind of relationship, one I wasn't ready to discuss with her. "We were not friends, no. We were close for a time, however. As close as any servant can be to his master, I suppose."

She raised an eyebrow, crossing one leg over the other as she settled into the cushions. "Servant? Okay, I feel like I need to hear this story. There are so many questions in my mind, but I'd rather hear your version of what happened first. If you don't mind, that is."

"Of course. I'm happy to tell you. I don't know if you'll find my story interesting or not, but I will do my best." Giving her a smile, I sat back in my seat and began my tale. "I can still remember the day I received a letter informing me of my interview with His Lordship. Fresh from my medical training, still baby-faced and full of self-confidence, the youngest graduate of the University of Edinburgh's medical program, I was used to being the star pupil, the know-it-all, the focus of attention and envy of others. All my life, people called me a prodigy, and I believed every word of their praise. My interview with his lordship was only one more opportunity for validation. Someone famous would say my name, agree that I was worthy, and give me a place at his side so all the world could see I was the top of my profession."

She nodded, her eyes fixed on me, and it gave me courage to continue.

"Looking back now, I realize that day was a tipping point for me," I said. "For one shining moment, when Milord informed me I had won my position, I thought I might burst with happiness. I was sure I would prove worthy of attention and praise and find my way into the limelight. But how can a candle shine its light while standing next to the sun? And how does it keep from being burnt away? I didn't know the difference between education and genius, intelligence verses overwhelming creativity. In his eyes, I would always be a tradesman. No one prepared me for that reality or told me my recitations of facts, so lauded when I was a child, made me seem an insufferable prat. I was never teased or bullied. My studies isolated me from other children and their cruelty. Thus, when Milord first made a joke at my expense, rather than laugh it off as others more worldly than myself might have done, I became incensed. I remember how my cheeks burned with the shame of it, and I thought I might leave him then and there."

Sybill's forehead wrinkled with concern. "How do you know how he felt about you? Maybe he didn't mean to hurt your feelings."

"Mean to. Hmm." Looking down at my hands clasped in my lap, I laughed softly, more at myself than at anything she'd said. She wanted to believe the best in him. Of course she did. Everyone always did. "Perhaps. I suppose the boys he grew up with were not so tender-hearted or so ill-acquainted with the world. When he saw my over-reaction, he found it humorous. He laughed at the way my face reddened with indignation at a slight, and my humiliation only increased when he encouraged others to follow his lead. I couldn't bear their laughter. The angrier I grew, the more he seemed to want to 'put me in my place,' as he put it. My place. Yes, he made it very clear that I would never be his equal."

I shifted slightly in my seat, then looked up at her directly, deciding to address the question she had implied but not spoken aloud. "Worst of all, he broke my heart. I had never known the touch of a lover, woman or man, until I met him. Maybe he thought it was a kindness, what he did, stealing to my room in the night, asking for forgiveness for the day's hurts and rousing feelings in me I had never experienced. Of course I forgave him. Night after night, he bound me to him. If I am being charitable, I can admit his understanding of love was bound up with pain and suffering. His mother's mercurial moods prepared him for that expectation, and certainly I got to know his highs and lows intimately. In the morning, he was all prickles, jovial in the afternoon, insulting over the dinner table, but ah, the nights made me feel for a while that nothing else mattered. Imagine my devastation when I discovered he had another lover. A woman. And then I learned there was another man. Indeed, he shared his bed with innumerable paramours. I was not even special to him in that regard. Yes, he broke my heart in every way another person can."

With a sympathetic sigh, she reached out and touched my hand, and I took it in my own giving it a gentle squeeze before going on. "By the end of the summer, he had ruined me for anyone else. My soul was crushed. I thought I was broken forever, but I didn't know the meaning of the word."

From the other room, a familiar voice rang out, startling us both.

"Honestly, don't you grow tired of playing the martyr?" It was Byron, and I turned to see him holding my journal in his hand, flipping through the pages with a smirk on his face.

Leaping to my feet, I ran to snatch the book from his grasp. "That is private!"

With a laugh, he curled his lip and raised an eyebrow. "Not when you leave it out for anyone to read. You haven't told her the juicy bits yet. I like the juicy bits. But you knew that."

Sybill still sat in her seat, looking on with wide eyes, while I stood, shaking with embarrassment and anger. "Is everything a game to you?"

Stepping in close, he ran his fingers across the curve of my cheek, licking his lips to provoke me. "I do love to play."

"I hate you," I said with a shiver, forcing myself to turn away.

"No more than usual, I'm sure." He laughed bitterly, carding his hand through his hair, then glanced over at Sybill before turning back to look at me. "Please, don't let me interrupt your story...doctor. She hasn't heard some of the most scandalous parts." Just like that, he winked, leaned forward, and kissed my cheek with a loud smack, then gave me a quick spank on the backside before whispering in my ear, "I do hope you add in some descriptive details. These winter nights are so long, and you know how I hate being bored."

Pulling away, I glared at him fiercely. "One day, I swear I will kill you."

"Yes, yes. So you've said, many times." Swaggering toward the door, he called over his shoulder, "Boring!" and then walked out, slamming the door behind him.

Enraged, I shouted at the closed door, "We need to talk about boundaries!"

As his footsteps retreated back up the stairs, I heard his cold laughter echoing against the stones.

I turned back to face Sybill, still trembling with frustration. "I am sorry you had to see that."

"Don't apologize." She rose to her feet, walking over toward me, a sad little smile on her face. "Why do you let him tease you like that?"

Shrugging, I heaved a sigh, pressing my lips into a line for a moment before answering. "He thinks he's humorous and finds my reactions amusing. I shouldn't let my emotions get the better of me. He tells me I take myself too seriously, and I suppose he is right. Perhaps I am too thin-skinned."

"I can talk to him if you want," she said. "Ask him to back off. He'll listen to me."

"No, no," I said, shaking my head. "That is very kind, but I would hate to cause a rift between you. I will speak with him later in private. He and I have a long history, and sometimes I think he only speaks so because he feels defensive. He may have overheard our conversation and thought I wanted to turn you against him. I assure you, I would not do such a thing."

Though her brow furrowed, she nodded her agreement, reaching to take my hand and give it a squeeze. "I believe you."

Her display of affection was touching, but it also made me a little uncomfortable, unused as I was to sharing my feelings with others. "I fear I have given you the impression I am the hero of the some story. That is far from the case. I am no victim, nor is he a villain. I cannot tell you all of my story now, but someday I will, and you will see there is enough guilt and recrimination for us both. Neither of us is innocent nor entirely evil. He did many good things on my behalf, and he never stopped trying to save me, though I cannot think why he should bother."

She shook her head. "You're a good person. Anyone can see that."

I couldn't help my bitter laugh at her assessment. "Good? No. I most assuredly am not. You don't know me very well yet, so you will have to take my word for it. I have blood on my hands, and my soul is drenched in darkness."

"I think you are too hard on yourself."

"No. If I had any true conscience, the best thing I could do for everyone is kill myself and have done."

"John, no," she said, flinging her arms around my neck. "Please, don't even joke about that."

I staggered back, pushing her away forcefully. "Sybill, I am quite serious. I am a dangerous person. Perhaps for you most of all. You don't know what you're talking about with me. If you knew the truth about me, you wouldn't so quick to be kind."

The dismay and pity in her eyes was so palpable, I had to look away. She didn't understand. How could she? She was still new to this monstrous life, and she couldn't conceive of the darkness to which I had fallen. Part of me wanted to reach out and sever her head from her body right there and then to spare her the inescapable and never-ending guilt and shame which stretched out ahead of her, compounding year upon year into the distant future.

With that thought, suddenly the gory scene came to life in my mind. I felt my fingers grip her hair, my arms tighten around her throat to hold her tight. I heard her screams and felt the scrabble of her nails against my skin. In my vision, I felt the strain as every muscle and sinew was torn with audible snaps and then a rush of her blood, pumping like a fountain, drenching me, spurting from her body as it jerked a few moments longer, not yet recognizing the arrival of a swift and remorseless death. In this vivid waking dream, as I dropped her corpse to the basement floor, I felt the creature in me roar in triumph, licking the blood from my hands in hideous delight.

I stepped back from her, agitated by my rising blood-lust, and strode over to my desk stiffly, not looking up as I spoke. "Do forgive me, but I'd like you to go now. I have work to do."

I could hear the sadness in her voice as she took a deep breath and began to move toward the door. "Sure. Okay, John. Just remember you can talk to me if you need a friend. Anytime."

As the door shut behind her, I closed my eyes and covered my face with my hands. "Friend," she had said, without comprehending to whom she was speaking. A friend was the last thing I could be to her, and all her good intentions only made that fact more abundantly clear. I opened my journal and returned to my notes, steeling myself to keep my gentler, weaker feelings from taking over.

Respite

Byron

She found me in my usual haunt, sitting at my small writing desk, poring over a passage I've been struggling to translate properly.

"Am I bothering you?" she said, standing hesitantly several paces away, biting her lip.

With a soft chuffing laugh, I set down my pen, then looked up and smiled. "You are never a bother, lass. Come, give us a wee break from the monotony of this blasted rhyme for a bit. It's enough to drive a man mad, this translation business."

Returning my smile, she came to stand behind me, peering down at the page as she placed both hands on my shoulders. "You're tense. Want me to help?"

She was already rubbing, but when I nodded, she began kneading firmly, making me groan as the knotted muscles began to loosen.

"Ah, lass. You've got witchcraft in your fingertips and no mistake."

Laughing, she dug in with her thumbs and I groaned again. "You have an accent. I hadn't noticed it before. I mean, well, I knew you were British, obviously, the first time you spoke, but just now I heard a hint of something else. Scottish, huh?"

"You've a good ear. My elocution tutor from Cambridge would be most displeased to know it." Eyes closed, I gave in to the sensual pleasure of her touch, sighing softly as my aches and pains eased.

"Cambridge?" she said. "Well, la-dee-dah. Look at you, Mister Fancy-pants."

"That's *Lord* Fancy-pants, thank you very much. I didn't stay long. A year. Long enough to learn what I needed in order to become a Member of Parliament."

"You were in politics?"

"Well, don't sound so surprised."

"Sorry. It's just you don't seem the type."

"Oh? And what type might that be? Old? Fat? Pompous? I can be pompous if you like."

"Pssh. No, thanks. I can do without. I meant you just don't seem pushy. I can't imagine you making speeches and kissing babies. That sort of thing."

"I'll have you know, I'm quite a favorite with babies."

"Is that so?"

"Yes. That's so. Even had a few of my own at one time."

"You? A dad? Huh. I can't picture that either."

"I was a wonderful father. You can ask anyone. Well, no. You can't. They're all long gone now, but believe me if you could ask them, they'd tell you I was a wonderful father."

"Okay. Okay. I believe you. How do you and John know one another?" she said.

"John? Is that what he asked you to call him? Who am I kidding? Of course he did." I laughed sardonically, then shook my head dismissively before going on. "He's told you the story, I'm sure."

She shrugged. "I heard his side. I want to hear yours."

With a weary sigh, I closed my eyes for a moment. "Very well. John Polidori was my physician back two hundred years ago now. Damn me, time really does fly, doesn't it? He was nineteen. The youngest graduate of Edinburgh's medical school. Came highly recommended. He was easy on the eyes too, as you can no doubt see. A bit naive, of course, but I figured he wouldn't always be telling me not to do the things I loved. I took him with me to Europe."

"That was a big responsibility for a teenager."

"In retrospect, yes. It was. Too much, as it turned out. He made himself a nuisance. He was jealous of me. Even more jealous of my friends or anyone I gave more attention to than him."

As she looked at me, she tilted her head curiously, knitting her brows. "Jealous? Why?"

"Good lord, who knows. Pride, I suppose. He challenged one of my friends to a duel over it, and I had no end of trouble keeping him out of constant squabbles. I even had to bail him out of jail once for assaulting someone. He was more dramatic than any character on the London stage. And he didn't comprehend that though I was friendly, I was his employer, not his friend. There are certain things you don't do or say when you work for someone, and he didn't understand that distinction."

She laughed at that, then shook her head. "Why didn't you send him home then?"

"I tried. I fired him. Gave him enough money to return to England and even wrote a letter of recommendation for him so he could start fresh on his return without embarrassment. He was stubborn, though, and instead of going to England as I expected, he walked south to Italy with my money in hand and tried to ingratiate himself with relatives there. He made a mess of things with them too, I'm afraid. Ran up debts.

Living with me had grown him accustomed to fine things, you see, but he could not afford that lifestyle. He was young and foolish. No one had taught him to be frugal or sensible. Long afterward, he tried to confront me again at the opera in Milan. It was a nightmare."

Her gaze was direct, and she bit her lip for a moment as if deliberating before she finally said what was on her mind. "He said you were lovers and you cheated on him."

It was my turn to be surprised. "Is that how he put it?"

She shook her head again, frowning. "Well, not exactly, but he did say he didn't realize he wasn't aware there were others at first."

"Ah." I laughed, then shook my head. "If so, he was a bigger fool than I realized. I'd just been through a messy divorce, and the testimony was widely circulated in the papers. There were all sorts of rumors. It was well known I had both male and female lovers. I was sexually involved with other servants. Why would I think he would become attached to me? He was possessive. Obsessively so. And he didn't understand why I wouldn't give up all other company in favor of spending time with him exclusively. Of course, that expectation was absurd. I could hardly throw over societal rules for a servant. What he wanted was impossible."

"Did you love him?" Her question was quiet and cautious, and the kindness behind it was touching.

For a moment, I hesitated. I knew the answer, but I had not voiced it aloud in so long, I was almost ashamed to admit the truth, even to myself, and when I replied, my voice dropped to a near whisper. "Love him? Of course. I still do, though not in the romantic way he wanted. I couldn't give him that. Not ever."

I heaved a heavy sigh, then turned my head to look back over my shoulder at her. "Poor boy. That's why I felt responsible. Still do. It's my fault, you see, what happened to him. All of it. When he confronted me in Milan, I felt guilty for how he'd turned out. By then, I'd been turned, so I thought I could make up for the innocence I'd stolen by giving him eternal life. He still hasn't forgiven me."

"You could tell him, you know. Say you're sorry, I mean. It's not too late."

"Oh, dear girl, I'm afraid it is far too late for us to truly understand one another, though in his case it is a willful misunderstanding."

This time, it was her turn to sigh. She squeezed my shoulders gently, gazing back at me with a sad look in her eye. "You've given up, then. Why? Are you angry with him?"

"Angry?" I paused for a moment to ponder the question. "No. And yes. I sometimes think he enjoys being miserable. Why can he not simply accept his state of being, embrace it, and get on with his life? Oh no. Not he. Instead, he wastes his time on these ridiculous schemes of his, letting his resentment fester. And for what? I gave him a goddamned gift, and he treats it like a curse. Insufferable man. Yet in spite of everything, I made him what he is, for good or ill, and I cannot let him go until I have made it right with him, however long it takes. As for why he stays with me, I assume it is out of spite."

She nudged me, rolling her eyes and smirking. "Come on. It's not that bad."

Laughing bitterly, I curled my lip in a sardonic smile. "It's exactly that bad. Truly, we must be the most stubborn men ever born. This uneasy connection between us has lasted for nearly two hundred years, and still we cannot let it go."

"You love each other," she said, and it wasn't a question, nor was there any judgment in her tone. She was simply stating the facts as she believed them to be.

"A strange kind of love."

"Still. I'm not wrong. He loves you too, though he doesn't know how to show it, I think."

"I think this is quite enough introspection for me today." Chuckling, I shifted in my chair so I could face her more directly. "What about you?

Have you come to terms with eternal life, do you think? Or are you angry with your maker too?"

She suddenly looked uncomfortable and uncertain, reaching up to touch her hair and looking away at the pattern on the floor.

"Ah. So it's like that, is it? Don't worry, lass. I'm not going to tell your secrets."

"What was it like for you?" she said, her voice uncharacteristically timid and soft, and I knew she was shifting the subject to my own experience so she could gauge what my reaction might be to her response.

"To be honest," I said, "I haven't really spent time thinking about it. I'm much the same man I always was, but I became much stronger and resilient in an often senselessly brutal world."

"But were you angry with Marie for turning you?"

"Oh lord, no. Why should I be? It's a gift, isn't it?" However light my words sounded, though, I couldn't hide the irony. "Look, I know you've undergone a massive change. I remember how conflicted I was at the time. Part of you is horrified, thinking what a monster you've become, and another part of you finds the whole thing exhilarating. All that strength, your heightened senses, it's intoxicating. Have you had time to explore your new powers? To find out what you're really capable of?"

She shook her head, her dark eyes gazing back at me with a myriad of unasked questions.

With a slap of my palms against my thighs, I nodded and stood, determination in my eyes. "Right then. You and I are going into the city."

Startled, she stared at me and blinked, stepping back half a step. "What? Now? Isn't it dangerous?"

"Pish posh. You'll be with me." Reaching for my jacket, I pulled it on with a laugh.

At last, I saw a smile light up that beautiful face. "Did you seriously just say 'pish posh'? I think that's the first time I've ever heard someone say that outside of a classic novel or some British television show."

"Yes, well, there's a first time for everything, isn't there? Come on. Night is wasting." Clasping my cane in one hand, her hand in the other, I began tugging her away, heading for the docks.

Her eyes wide and glancing around furtively, she stumbled a little as I led her out the door. "Wait! Won't Marie be mad about it? Us just sneaking off?"

"You don't strike me as a shrinking violet. We can handle whatever or whoever we come across. Besides, she wanted us to bond. Look at us, bonding."

"I don't think she had us leaving the island in mind." She looked around once more, as though she thought we were naughty children skipping school.

I winked at her, grinning broadly. "What she doesn't know won't hurt her."

Laughing, she followed me down the steps of the jetty to where the boats were tied up, and I helped her aboard one of the motor boats there. "You really are mad, bad, and dangerous to know. You know how to drive this thing?"

At that, it was my turn to laugh, my hands making quick work of the ropes before I clambered onto the deck and took a seat behind the wheel. Grinning, I turned the key, and the motor roared into life. "Guess you'll find out, huh?"

Thrown back in her seat as I sped away, she held on tight and practically squeaked with excitement. Seeing the exhilaration and happiness on her face was worth any tongue lashing I might have to endure from Marie after the fact. For this beautiful woman beside me, becoming a vampire meant nothing but fear and heartbreak. She needed to see her experience wouldn't always be that way. Sybill needed to know there could be joy in what she'd become. If Marie wasn't going to show her, it was up to me to give back her hope in what the future might hold.

Raising my voice over the noise of the motor, I glanced over at her, watching as the spray flew up in our wake through the waves. "What have you seen of the city so far? I don't want to bore you with the same things you've already done. Not when Venice has so much to offer."

"The only thing I saw was the view going in and out of that place where we met with the coven. You know, Casanova's place. And even that, we didn't see more than a couple of rooms." Her eyes were still on the way ahead, the moonlight shining on her face.

"What? No sightseeing at all?" I raised my eyebrows, then looked away, not wanting her to see the pity I felt for her written in my expression. "Unconscionable. That won't do at all."

The lights of the city twinkled across the water, adding an ethereal glow to all of the ancient buildings, adding an air of magic and mystery upon our approach. I found safe mooring near the Basilica of San Marco. Tying us off, I was exhilarated as I hopped ashore, I turned with a smile and held out a hand to her. "Milady, the city awaits. What do you want to see first?"

Eyes sparkling, she placed her hand in mine, and with a laugh, she alighted beside me. "Everything!"

The excitement in her voice was electrifying, and I watched her expression as I led her forward toward the main square. "A tall order. I am afraid, my dear, it would take years to see everything Venice has to offer. For this first night exploring her many wonders, perhaps you can tell me what you wish to see above all. A musical performance, perhaps? Architecture? Beautiful views? Great works of art?"

"Art? Oh yes, please! Titian was from here, wasn't he?"

At this, I raised an eyebrow, walking up a set of steps to cross a small bridge over one of the narrower canals that fed the center of the island city. "You sound like a student of his work."

"Well, I am...was an art major. I planned to become a painter." I heard a sadness in her tone, and I realized she was only now coming to understand that all her previous life plans would need to be adjusted in light of her change in circumstance.

"Is that so? Someday you shall have to show me your work, then."

Just as I spoke, we rounded the corner of a large building, and suddenly the square lay out before us. Because of the wintry season, there were fewer tourists milling about, so she saw the place much as the natives do. I heard her gasp, and her grip on my hand tightened, her fingers lacing with mine.

"Oh," was all she said, but her look said everything her lips could not.

I told myself then, no matter how angry Marie might be at our having escaped to roam the city on our own, the punishment would be worth enduring.

"Indeed. That was exactly my reaction upon my first arrival here. Shall we go see the basilica?" The enormous statues that adorned the top of the building stared down at us, and I followed her gaze upward before making a half turn and pointing at the building opposite. "Or perhaps the tower? Bird's eye view of the city?"

Wordlessly, she nodded, an enormous smile spreading across her features.

"Tower it is, then, I said, leading her to the door that led to the tower steps.

A man was just locking the metal gate at the entrance. Clearly, he had no intention of allowing any other visitors to climb the staircase, but I placed a hand on his shoulder and caught his eye. In flawless Venetian, long practiced through my years here, I asked him to allow us access, exerting my influence on his mind. Nodding slowly, he unlocked the gate and pushed it back for us.

"Attendere per noi, per favor, signore," I said, eyes still fixed on his.

"Si, signore," he replied, closing the gate behind us and then leaning against the wall.

"What did you say to him?" she said as we began our ascent.

"I only asked him to wait for us. Someone has to let us out again, don't they? And anyway, we don't want to be disturbed while we take in the view. He will ensure we have the place to ourselves."

"How do you know he won't turn us over to the authorities?"

"Because I saw his mind. He thinks you and I are meeting for a romantic tryst, and he is quite a sentimental fool. Most Italians are, come to think of it."

"Hey, my family is Italian," she said.

"Well, that explains a few things," I laughed, helping her on the uneven stone steps.

She arched an eyebrow and smirked. "Are you stereotyping me?"

"Never," I replied, "though some stereotypes exist for reason. Don't tell me you haven't made assumptions about me from the moment we met. British lord. Poet. Come on. Admit it. You had preconceptions about who I was from day one."

"All right. Fine. I admit it. Happy?"

Grinning, I leaned in and whispered conspiratorially. "Just tell me one thing. How do I measure up in comparison?"

Laughing, she gave me a sidelong glance. "I can honestly say you have been a non-stop surprise."

"Well, I do try. I'd hate to bore you."

"Trust me," she said, "boredom is the last thing anyone could feel around you."

With that last word, we topped the last step and walked out onto the observation area. She went silent, letting go of my hand and rushing to the rail in wonder. Her eyes scanned in all directions, gazing down at the city laid out beneath us, street lamps casting a glow on all the ancient facades. Moonlight highlighted the edges of rooftops, and in the maze waterways and out in the harbor, the city showed its lively heart as boats went to and fro.

"This is amazing," she said in a breathy whisper.

Following her as she circled counterclockwise to take in the view from all directions, I covered my lips with my fingertips, a crooked smile tugging at the corner of my mouth. "I'm glad you approve."

"I should have brought my phone so I could take pictures," she whispered as if to herself, and for a moment, I saw a cloud pass over her features.

"What's wrong?"

She looked down at the crisscross lines of the decorative pattern of patterned stone paving the square below. "Nothing. Doesn't matter."

"Nonsense. Of course it matters. What's bothering you? You can tell me anything."

"It's just...Raul hasn't seen any of this, I bet. I can't help worrying, you know? What if they've hurt him? Maybe even killed him? What if he's scared and alone? It just...I feel guilty having fun when I know he may never get out of wherever they've got him." She turned, then, and looked at me with a furrowed brow. "Sorry. I appreciate you bringing me. I do."

Reaching out, I touched her shoulder gently. "No apology necessary, lass. May I ask you something, though? If it's not too painful to think of him, that is."

"Of course. Anything."

"How long were the two of you intimate? I'm sorry if it seems an indelicate way to ask. Clearly, the two of you were lovers."

She laughed self consciously, looking down for a moment and shaking her head. "You'll think I'm ridiculous."

"I most certainly will not."

Her eyes met mine with a hint of self-conscious embarrassment. "We slept together one night. It just...it happened really fast. Raul was intense. He came to see me at work maybe a few times. I gave him my number. God, it sounds stupid now. Like some kind of sordid fairytale. He was charming, though. I know you haven't met him, so you don't know what he was like. He had such charisma. I couldn't resist. He tried to stay away. Jesus, he was so worried about protecting me. He couldn't resist me either, I guess. He didn't want to lie to me about himself, he said, so he told me the truth about who and what he was. We ended up having sex. Then he disappeared. Next thing I knew, Marie showed up at my apartment, pissed off, trying to kill me and then...bam. She turned me. Just like that. We've been running ever since. At least until we found you, anyway."

I kept quiet as she struggled to explain, and when she wound down, I stepped in a little closer, brushing her cheek with an outstretched hand. "Ah lass, forgive me, but you hardly even know him, do you?"

She shook her head and looked up at me sadly.

"My god. What was Marie thinking, dragging you all the way here because of a man you had only just met? She's been treating you as though you are his destiny. How do you feel?"

She shrugged, heaving a soft sigh, her voice lowering to a whisper. "I don't know, honestly. Everything happened so quickly, I haven't had a chance to think."

My hand slipped into her hair, my thumb still brushing her cheekbone. "Of course you haven't. Please forgive my forwardness."

"No, please don't apologize. You're the first person to ask me anything about my feelings at all. I appreciate you caring enough to ask. I needed to talk about things. About him. Not just running and being dragged into Marie's schemes. I mean, I want to find him too. I do. I care about him. It's just, he and I don't really know anything about one another. I don't think he even knows my last name. Awfully hard to talk about forever with a man who barely knows the most basic thing about me."

To this, I didn't reply, just nodded and gave her a grim smile of understanding.

She looked down in embarrassment. "God, you must think I'm some kind of whore or something, sleeping with someone I hardly know."

"Ha!" I covered my mouth to quiet my outburst, then shook my head, giving her a tender smile as I reached to lift her chin and bring her gaze to meet mine once more. "Believe me, Sybill, I am the very last person who would ever judge you in that way. If you knew half of the stories about me, you would know better. You strike me as sensible, capable, and rational. We haven't known one another long, but in that time you have impressed me as a woman of strong character and moral fibre."

"Moral fibre. Sounds like a breakfast cereal." Though her words were sardonic, her smile showed me she was pleased by what I said, and she moved close, wrapping her arms around my waist impulsively, pulling me into a hug as she whispered into my ear, "Thank you."

Enfolding her in my embrace, I held her quietly for a moment, breathing in the scent of her hair. Her body was not as soft as it looked, and I guessed Marie must have had a hand in her choice of wardrobe. These clothes were meant to accentuate her feminine curves, but beneath was a toughness and resilience I prayed she would never need.

Just then, the clock tower bells began to toll the hour, breaking the spell of our embrace. The sound was overpowering, and though she couldn't hear me, I laughed and the two of us turned and headed back down the stairs once more. Just as I had instructed, the man was waiting for us, and I thanked him with a wink before turning away with Sybill toward the open main square. Warm light spilled from the cafes that encircled the periphery, and waiters bustled about with their trays, carrying glasses of wine, delicate desserts, and coffee drinks to the customers seated in their outdoor areas. Kerosene heaters were spaced around the tables to keep them warm despite the winter chill.

"Where to now?" Sybill asked, linking her arm in mine.

Grinning, I led her away down one of the narrow alleyways where the bright lights faded, giving way to mysterious shadows and intrigue. "There is still time to walk to the Accademia to see some of those great works of art. We can't see everything before they close, but this won't be our only excursion, I hope."

"Oh yes, please," she said, leaning her head on my shoulder and hugging my arm against her. "You know, this is the first time I haven't felt frightened or anxious since all this began. I haven't had time to relax from the moment I was turned. This night out is just what I needed. Thank you. Really."

"You don't need to thank me. You aren't the only one who needed to get out, you know. I hate to tell you this, but I am not entirely selfless. Shocking, I know, but it had to be said. Thank you for reminding me how important it is to enjoy life once in a while. I needed this as much as you did, and I enjoy your company."

"Sweet-talker."

"Mmm. Is it working?"

Snickering, she looked up at me with a cheeky grin. "Well, I like you. How's that?"

"I'll take it."

Tourist season was long past, and Carnival was still ahead, so the thronging crowds the medieval city was known for were absent, leaving us to experience the wonder of Venice in relative quiet. A hush had fallen over the stones, and in the cool of the evening, fog rose on the waterways, creeping around the corners from the canals. The city built on the water suddenly seemed to be floating in the clouds, and though I had lived here for over half a century, the awe of the moment was not lost on me.

Leaning in close, she whispered, as though the fog might be listening. "This place is like something in a dream. It almost doesn't seem real. Know what I mean?"

We stepped out to find the bridge to the Accademia laid out before us, and again, she gasped. I pulled her closer, pausing a moment to allow her to appreciate the view before tugging her onwards. "This way," I said, though my eyes were fixed on her expression rather than the path ahead.

Her surprise and sheer delight were enough to feed my soul for decades into the future, and I fixed the image of her smile firmly in my memory so I could remember it when times got darker and I needed a reason to go on. As we crossed the bridge, a gondolier below, masked in fog, began to sing a piece from an Italian opera, and his voice filled the air around us. I felt her shiver, a reaction I knew had nothing to do with cold since we were immune to its effects. In that moment, I decided one day, when our immediate danger had died down and there was time, I would take her to the opera.

We stepped down from the bridge onto the opposite side of the canal, and the imposing facade of the Accademia rose before us.

A few people were still milling about, stragglers hoping for more time with the masterpieces. We only had half an hour until the building closed. Just long enough for a taste of what the city had in store.

We walked through the main doors, and though the guard was inclined to turn us away, I convinced him otherwise, and he let us pass without requiring an entry ticket.

"I make regular donations," I whispered to Sybill as we passed the little gift shop. "Don't worry I might be short changing them. I assure you, I am not."

She laughed softly, her fingers tightening on my forearm, and as we stepped into the first room, she goggled open mouthed at the enormous wall-sized canvases on all sides. "Ho-ly...."

"Well, there is a lot of religious iconography, yes," I quipped with a smirk. "I'm afraid I'm a rather secular guide, however."

Staring up at the restored ceilings and brightly colored frescoes, she shook her head and shushed me. She turned slowly in wonder, bringing me with her as she made a circuit of the room, and then in a reverent whisper, she said, "Take me directly to whichever work you think is best before I get overwhelmed. Otherwise, we may never make it out of here."

"Very well," I said, chuckling. "Though perhaps you should close your eyes and let me guide you there. Otherwise, I'm afraid you might just collapse from shock."

Though I'd intended my words as a joke, she took them as a serious suggestion, closing her eyes and tightening her grip on my arm. "Surprise me."

Chuckling, I placed my free hand over hers which rested on my forearm. I patted her hand gently, leaning in to whisper. "No peeking, lass."

She gave a little smile, and her grip on my arm tightened slightly as I began leading her away with confidence toward the rooms I thought would impress her the most. I had viewed the collection many times through the years as the displays were renovated to suit the evolving taste of its patrons. Restoration of the masterworks was an ongoing process, and I always delighted as the soot-stained paint was cleaned and restored to its original vibrant state of splendor.

Though there were several enormous wall-sized paintings by Titian in the gallery, the one which affected me most was his most atypical. All of his other works showed a mastery of brilliant color, and his figures were rendered with extraordinary detail and understanding of the human form, unrivaled by his contemporaries. To me, he was every bit as talented as Michaelangelo. Yet the painting I led her to was not like any of his others, and it was quite likely Sybill had never seen it before in any textbook during her studies. I wanted to surprise her, show her something she would not expect.

The museum was laid out in chronological order, so the mural I led her to was the last of the works by Titian in the collection. I walked through these ancient rooms, filled with masters from the height of Venice's power and influence. True to her word, Sybill kept her eyes closed, trusting me to guide her from room to room.

At last, we reached the room I intended and I slowed my pace, bringing us to stand near the center of the room at enough distance to allow her to take in the entire scope of the painting.

This was Titian's last work, unfinished at the time of his death. Where his other works were bright and polished, this was dark and filled with a sense of urgency and distress, Titian's Pieta. It appeared that Titian had still been working on the underpainting, the shadows swallowing everything. Only the central figure of the Virgin Mary had features that were in focus. Even Jesus was half-finished, missing the normal details one would expect of the artist, his hands only roughly drawn. At their feet, the artist himself appeared on his knees, beseeching a Mary who could see nothing beyond her loss, her son cradled in her arms while the rest of her was lost in shadow. At her other side, Mary Magdalene seemed still in motion, gesturing with an outstretched hand as if to call out in distress, but she is looking off the canvas into the void, and the edges of the painting were framed in an ominous darkness. Even the cherubs looking on seemed demonic and menacing, and the statues of Moses and the female prophetess, the Sybill, depicted to the right and left of the central figures seem almost monstrous and foreboding.

I had seen the painting hundreds of times, and it never failed to halt me in my tracks. Titian had intended the work as a plea for the Virgin Mary to save him and his son from the plague, a plea that fell on deaf ears since both of them died of plague before the oil paint was dry.

"Open your eyes, lass," I said, leaning in to whisper the words against the shell of her ear.

I don't know what I expected from her reaction – wide-eyed wonder, perhaps, or even a gasp of surprise. Instead, as she gazed up, her expression was one of horror and dismay. She stared with a tremulous unease, her hand tightening on my arm like a vice.

"Get me out of here," she murmured. "I think I'm going to be sick."

She shut her eyes again, then turned her head to bury her face against my shoulder. "Get me out of here. Please."

Not knowing what to say, I simply did as she asked, placing an arm over her shoulders protectively as I led her to the exit.

Only when we were outside did she stop shivering, and we paused by the canal while she wrapped her arms around me. I stroked her hair and held her, but it took several long moments before she finally let out a deep breath and finally relaxed with a shudder.

"I'm sorry," she said, her head still resting against my chest.

"Shh," I said. "Nothing to apologize for, lass. Are you all right?"

She gave a small shake of her head, and her voice came muffled against the fabric of my coat. "It's stupid."

"What is?" I reached down to lift her chin so I could gaze into her eyes.

Her face half in shadow, the look in her eyes held a desperate sadness I didn't understand and which made my heart clench in pain.

"I just...I had this horrible feeling. Dread. Panic. Claustrophobia. I don't know why. I can't explain it. I only knew I had to get away or I might drown in it."

"Because of the painting?"

She nodded, chewing her lip. "It's stupid. I'm sorry. I couldn't help it. I've ruined our evening."

"Nonsense," I said, flashing her a reassuring smile as I cupped her cheek in my palm, my broad thumb playing at the corner of her mouth. "You're just hungry, maybe. We can get you a bite, and you'll be right as rain."

"But the museum..." she whined softly.

"...Will be here another time," I said, completing her sentence. "Immortals, remember? We will come back to see the rest, I promise. Being what we are gives us the advantage of time. You have time enough to enjoy it all. We have forever."

I kissed her brow and gave her a gentle squeeze. "Come," I said. "The night is young. Let's get you a bit of fresh blood, and everything will be better again. You'll see."

With a sigh, she frowned, then shook her head. "No, I think I need to go back. I'm sorry. Can we do this another time?"

Though I was disappointed, I didn't let it show. Instead, I smiled a little more and nodded. "Of course."

She said nothing, but her expression shifted to one of grateful relief. My arm still around her shoulders, I walked back in silence with her to where our boat waited.

Only once we had put some distance between us and the city did she seem to truly relax, easing into conversation with me about the constellations overhead and about the various islands we passed. I answered her questions as though there had been no awkwardness before, and that seemed to put her on steadier ground. I wanted to apologize for having shown her the wrong thing, but I had been around her long enough to know she would only take that as a reason to feel even worse, berating herself internally for making me feel uncomfortable. And so I kept the apology to myself, planning instead to make it up to her in some other way.

The further we got from the city, thinner the traffic, and by the time San Lazzaro came into view, our little boat was the only one on the dark waters of the lagoon. I slowed down, cutting the motor so we could enter like ghosts, unheard. As I did so, I caught sight of another small boat pulling away from a secret side entrance that led to an underground entrance to the monastery. That passage was used only by the monks themselves and one other, and I had no doubts who was at the helm, though his face was hidden in shadow. Polidori. If Sybill hadn't been with me, I'd have trailed him in order to discover what he was up to. I didn't want to involve her in any further drama between me and Polly, however, and so I simply filed my observation away and drew her attention away toward the pier, asking her to hop ashore and help tie us off.

Sybill clearly had very little experience around boats, and we were in the midst of a good laugh about her knot work when I heard a rustling behind us.

"Do I even want to know where you've been?" Marie's voice was full of tension and fury.

Sybill stood and looked up and stared in shock. Nonplussed, I finished tying off the lines properly, then rose and turned to face Marie. "She's not your teenage daughter. She doesn't have a curfew. I took her out to see the city. In case you hadn't noticed, she's had nothing but panic since she met you. I thought it was high time she enjoyed at least one evening."

"And the fact we have enemies searching for us everywhere? I suppose that detail is inconsequential." Even in the dark of night, I could see her glaring at me, her expression hardening.

Sighing, I rolled my eyes, taking Sybill's hand in mine. "Do you really think I care less about her safety than you do? And tell me, mother dear," I said, my words dripping with sarcasm, "do you honestly think she's safer with you than with me? You came to me for protection, if you remember."

"I came to you because we needed help, and because I thought you would know how to keep us safe. I didn't come here for you go gallivanting off with her the first time I turned my back."

"Gallivanting?" Sybill scoffed. "I'm a big girl. I don't need a babysitter, and I can take care of myself. Not that it's any of your business, but we were just looking at art. He's been a perfect gentleman, and we were totally safe."

"Totally safe. I see. And you know this how? In your expert big girl opinion, how exactly are you certain you were not seen? There are spies everywhere, and you have no idea who to trust." Marie turned her baleful gaze back toward me, and her next words came out with a flash of fang. "Fine. Since you seem to think you have everything under control, you do as you please. After all, what do I know? I've only managed to evade these people for the last two hundred and fifty years. Why should you listen to anything I have to say?"

I sighed. "Marie..."

Cutting me off with a wave of her hand, she shook her head. "No. If you are so clever, by all means, do whatever you like. That is what you do best, after all."

Before I could say another word, she turned and walked away, leaving us behind with only the sound of the waves lapping the pier.

"Shit," said Sybill, letting go of my hand.

"Mmm," I said, still watching as Marie disappeared from view.

"She's gonna hate me now," Sybill said, looking down.

"She's just jealous and feeling threatened," I said, placing an arm around her and leading her toward the monastery gates. "Just give her time. She's the queen, and she's used to having the final word. Let her have it for now."

"Jealous? Of what? I thought she wanted us to get to know one another."

As the gate closed behind us, I chuckled. "She's afraid I'll love you more than I love her. She can't admit that, of course. That would make her seem needy. But it's there in the back of her mind. Fear of being left behind or forgotten."

"That's ridiculous. She's your maker. And anyway, she's the one who stopped looking for you all this time."

For the first time, Sybill was taking my side against Marie, and I couldn't help feeling conflicted about that. On the one hand, I didn't want to drive a wedge between them. The bond between maker and progeny was sacred, and even if Marie and I hadn't had a perfect relationship, I didn't want to ruin that for them both. However, there was a selfish part of me that swelled with pride and gratification that, given a choice, Sybill chose me first.

"I didn't exactly look for her either," I admitted in spite of myself.

Sybill gave me a nudge, wrapping an arm around my waist as she looked up at me with bright eyes. "What were you doing all that time, anyway?"

Though the question was innocent, the answer was complex, and I wasn't sure she was ready to hear all of what I might say with a sympathetic ear. Some of it wasn't just mine to tell, after all, and I didn't think she was ready to handle the truth about my past with Polidori. Not yet. She didn't know us well enough yet to keep an open mind.

"Oh, that's a long story," I said, smiling as if alluding to secret delights, though the truth was far darker and more frightening than she had any way of knowing. "Maybe someday I'll tell it."

"That's a polite way of saying 'I don't want to talk about it,'" she said, one eyebrow raised, though her tone was teasing.

"Not tonight," I said gently. "But I promise to tell you the truth soon."

This seemed to satisfy her, and she leaned in against me and whispered, "Deal."

High and Dry

Mozart

Marie walked into my room and let out a stifled scream of frustration, shutting the door with a loud clamor and then kicking it with her toe for good measure before leaning her forehead against it.

"Ugh! That insufferable man! I swear, he does nothing but vex me." She sighed, then pushed back from the door, standing with eyes closed, clearly struggling to maintain her composure.

"Darling," I said, rising to my feet and crossing swiftly to her, "you mustn't let such trifles upset you. He will come around. You'll see."

Moving in behind her, I reached out my hands, placing them on her shoulders, intending to soothe her, but she hunched her shoulders and shrugged me off, turning away and raising a hand to fend me off.

"Don't. Don't 'darling' me. Don't you dare. Honestly, you men with your 'darling' this and 'darling' that. I am not your darling. I am not a darling at all, understand me? I'll not have you or anyone else patronize me in such a fashion."

I pulled away, eyes open wide and staring at her in complete shock. "Marie...patronize? I would never dream of such a thing. I only meant..."

She cut me off before I could finish that thought, whirling toward me, glaring, her hand upraised as if to silence me. "No. Don't do that either."

"Do what? I haven't..."

"You know exactly what. Don't try to explain to me what you intended. I don't want excuses or explanations of how I misunderstood. I understood very well. You mean to shackle me. Make me behave. Keep quiet and do as I'm told. Smile and make things pleasant for you. Well, I won't. I won't go back into a gilded cage. Not for you. Not for anyone. I'm not here for your amusement. I'm not made to please you. I am the queen. More than that, I am a woman. A human being. I have just as much right to anger and frustration as any man, I and refuse to be quiet simply because you find it unladylike. Who do you think I am? Some doll to dress up and make you look good? Feed your ego? Is that it? Men. You're all alike. Get out. Just get out and leave me alone."

"But...this is my room," I blurted like a petulant child.

"Out! Get out!" She raised her hand as if to strike me, eyes blazing, and in that moment, I saw her fangs bared for the first time, like a wild vicious thing.

I felt myself go cold and defensive, and I'm certain my face went even more pale than ever. Nostrils flared with steely rage, I clenched my jaw. No jokes or attempts to calm her would avail me this time.

"Very well," I said, backing toward the door, hands upraised defensively. "As you wish."

With that, I made to bow my head politely, still trying to hang onto a shred of gentlemanly demeanor and dignity. As I did so, I heard a low growl from her, and then she bent down, removed her shoe, and threw it at me, striking my arm.

Before she could hurl the other shoe, I slipped out of the room.

As I closed the door behind me, I heard a resounding thud at eye level against it that echoed through the long corridor.

I stood there awkwardly in the hallway, listening to the sound of rattling and clattering inside as though she were throwing things in a hysterical tantrum. My mouth went dry as I remained there, motionless and stunned.

A soft sound at the end of the hall made me turn to look. Dressed in a cloak, Polidori stood with an amused smirk on his face. A large bundle sat at his feet as if he'd only just set it down.

"Trouble in paradise?" He was practically smirking at me, and that expression of amusement was unbearable.

"You would know, I suppose," I said, unable to hide my tone of derision and blame. "I understand I have his lordship to thank for her state of pique."

This time he laughed outright. "While ordinarily I would be quite willing to lay blame at Lord Byron's feet, I overheard enough of your conversation to know you earned that chiding without any help from anyone else."

I moved toward him, fists clenched, and he chuckled outright.

"Now now. Don't be angry with me. You should know better than to try to control a woman like that."

"I will thank you, sir," I growled, "to keep your opinions to yourself, and in future, pray refrain from lingering outside my chamber door to listen and spy at keyholes."

"Oh you are angry aren't you? Tsk." He shook his head, still laughing softly as his dark curls fell across his forehead. "Do you really suppose I want to listen in on your little melodrama for entertainment? Pardon me for saying so, but you flatter yourself, Maestro. I happened to have been walking this way. It was mere coincidence. Next time, if you are going to argue, do it outside if you want privacy. Monasteries are not exactly havens for secrets. From the outside world, maybe, but not from the other occupants."

"Is that so?" I stammered, knowing how absurd and childish I sounded even as I spoke the words aloud.

"There there." He stepped close and patted my shoulder. "Don't take it to heart. It'll pass I'm sure, this little spat of yours, and this time next week, you'll both have forgotten all about it."

It was all I could do not to strike the man, and I'm sure the look on my face told him exactly what I was thinking, but he laughed again, stepping away and shaking his head.

"Now you know why she was upset. No one likes being patronized, Herr Mozart. Especially not a queen. You'd best remember that if you intend to remain in her company."

For a long moment, I stood there stammering, my tongue seemingly stuck in my mouth and incapable of speech. Slowly, I realized he was right. She had been right. I was trying to bend her to fit an image I still held in my head of the soft-spoken, lovely girl I used to know long ago when we had been children and she had been an indulgent playmate.

Of course she wasn't that same girl any longer. Life had brought too much pain and heartache and forced her to become a woman of power and influence, only to have that power stripped away. I knew the echo of her, but this person, all these long years later, having lived under a shroud of loss and spending so long hiding and running, I realized with sudden chilling clarity I didn't know her at all.

My cheeks puffed out, and then I exhaled heavily, struggling to maintain my pride.

Polidori nodded once, gave me a tight-lipped smile, and then picked up his bundle and turned away without another word, stalking off toward his laboratory, leaving me standing there, cast off like an afterthought.

Slipping a hand into my pocket, I pulled out my phone and stared down at the screen. No new messages. It seemed no one thought of me in Chicago, nor anywhere else for that matter. Not one person missed me in all the world.

Yet this extraordinary woman beyond the door had welcomed me, brought me with her across the globe. The selfishness of my desires made me embarrassed. I needed her, but she did not need me in return, and there was not a soul I could rely on other than myself.

I frowned, dropping my head, and with a sigh, I placed the phone back in my pocket.

From our arrival in this place, I could feel the weight of the past hanging over Marie like a pall, and no amount of cajoling on my part could lift it.

Though she never said so, I was the outsider. The others were family to her, and she took their connection very seriously. She saw them as her children, and being around Byron after such a long separation shifted her focus to building trust between the two of them. She felt emotionally overwhelmed with the renewed closeness, and I was marginalized in her attention.

Intellectually, I understood the reasons, but knowing why didn't reduce the sting.

Sensing the tension in her, I did my best to alleviate it, but where earlier my attempts to distract and amuse her met with approval and even appreciation, now it seemed to serve only to irritate and annoy her. Her patience with the others was endless, but with me in private, she was irritable and snappish.

My problem was suddenly clear to me. Where she had many people to distract her and talk to about her frustrations, I had only her. I had let myself become an extension of her and had allowed that role to be the sole reason I spent any time with the others at all. I presumed that my relationship with her would give me a legitimate reason for my existence within their ranks, assuming a permanence that was by no means assured. As I stood there contemplating the closed door that separated me from her, I became suddenly aware of just how alone I had become. I had no other confidante or friend here, not one person to whom I could turn for companionship, and the responsibility for that situation fell entirely on myself.

In addition, my life up to this point had revolved around my ability to entertain, but here I had no outlet for those impulses except for her. I needed to find some measure of creative outlet, some way to express myself, or I feared not only would I lose her, but I would lose my place here along with my mind. I had to find a way to connect with the others and to feed my soul.

Music. The dearth of it in my daily life was driving me mad. From the moment we left Chicago, I hadn't had access to an instrument of any kind, and I felt as though my true self was in shackles.

Squaring my shoulders, I stepped away from the door, turning and walking away in search of the library. I didn't know if any of the others would be there, but it was the only alternative I could think of which might yield an improvement in my predicament.

The contrast between the opulence of the busy hotel where I had been living and the austere and contemplative beauty of this quiet place was startling. Even in the dead of winter, the courtyard at the heart of the monastery was green, but the monks fluttered about the place in their black robes like a murder of crows, and aside from their comings and goings, the place felt empty and cold as a tomb, my footfalls echoing on the stones.

San Lazzaro was the name given to the monastery. Saint Lazarus. Brought back from the dead. I found it ironic given that the monks were harboring five vampires in their midst, giving us blood in exchange for...what exactly? Byron's translation work might have made their tolerance sensible when it was payment for only Byron and Polidori, but with three more of us included in the mix, how long would such acceptance last? Perhaps, I thought, I could make myself useful in this regard.

I entered the library through the main doors generally used by tourists during the day. This area was brightly lit and modern, overwhelmingly decorated in stark white with clear glass gleaming all around. Blinking at the harsh contrast from the gloom I had just come from, I squinted and shielded my eyes, making quickly for the exit into the older section of the facility. As soon as I walked through the doorway, I found myself in much darker surroundings, floor to ceiling shelves surrounding me on all sides, and I breathed a sigh of sweet relief. This area was much more to my liking with its dark wooden shelves, patterned terrazzo floors, and decorative frescoes on the ceiling. I could almost forget the modern world entirely. The decor had not been updated except for the introduction of electricity, and the sweet vanilla scent of old paper made the space feel inviting and warmer than the rest of the building.

I walked slowly from one room to the next, allowing myself time to really look at the sheer volume of books in their collection. When we first arrived in this place, I had been so concerned with our safety and with Marie's well-being, I didn't take time to notice details that surrounded us. I was never much of a reader, too caught up in my work to have time for such pursuits, but I could appreciate the quantity of the books here. These Armenian monks had a fair number of books in their own language as part of an effort to save their cultural heritage, so the library was full of books that were extremely rare as a result.

When I entered the room that housed several mummies kept in glass cases, I paused, walking over to the one that lay prone on display in the center of the room and peering down at it in fascination. I had never seen a mummy up close, and as I looked at the figure, the skull dark with age and exposed to view, I couldn't help the shudder that ran through me. Had I not become a vampire, my own body would have long since moldered to dust and bone. The prospect was both sobering and horrifying. My entire family, all my companions were long dead. When had I last allowed myself to think about my wife and children? It was less painful to forget, but in the moments when thoughts of them came flooding in on me, it was hard not to let guilt overwhelm me.

"Alas, poor Yorick, eh?" The voice behind me made me jump in surprise, coming as it did from much closer than I would have anticipated. It was Byron, of course. He must have been watching me for several moments while I was lost in thought.

Turning to face him, I looked up in a little confusion. "I beg your pardon?"

"Hamlet," he said, pointing to the mummy as though this explained it all. "Never mind. What brings you to my domain, my dear fellow?"

The way he asked was like a little barb, though the smile stayed on his face, so I wasn't sure if he was intending his words sarcastically or not.

"I was curious if the monks here have a pipe organ or piano I might use. I was in the midst of a new composition, you see, and I should very much like to continue where I left off. If I could get access to use such a thing, of course."

My question seemed to take him aback, judging by his expression. He quirked an eyebrow, reaching up to stroke his chin thoughtfully. "There is a pipe organ, yes. Sometimes there are concert performances here which feature it. We would have to get the monks' permission for you to have access, but I think given who you are, they might be willing to make allowances."

Grinning broadly for the first time since our arrival here, I clapped Byron on the shoulder. "Excellent news! Would you make introductions for me? I am rubbish at that sort of thing. Ask anyone."

"You don't say," he said, this time his sarcasm plain, though I chose not to take offense. Laughing at his own joke at my expense, he then took a more conciliatory tone, nodding his agreement. "Yes, I could do that. They trust me here. Outsiders make them wary. I think they might be more agreeable if the request comes from my lips. I have had ample time to study their language and culture, and as a result have earned their trust."

I bowed low with an antiquated flourish. "Thank you, my lord. That is very kind of you."

"Oh please, don't bother with that 'my lord' nonsense. Albé. I insist."

"Very well. If you will agree to call me Wolf." Smiling, I pronounced it carefully for him with my own native German "V" rather than the English "W," a subtle but important difference to me.

Repeating after me, he smiled a little crookedly, reaching out to place his hand on my shoulder. "Friends, then, yes?"

"Friends," I agreed, feeling much warmer toward him than I had ever expected. "You know, when we first arrived, I will admit to a degree of jealousy. I hope you will forgive me. I can see it was misplaced."

"Yes, well, I get that a lot."

One look at his smirk showed me that he was joking, and he winked at me. Yes, this was a man I could befriend after all, I thought. I laughed, patting his shoulder in return. "I should get back."

"Ah yes. She should have wound down by now, I expect. It was about time for her to lose her temper. Don't worry. The storm passes quickly."

We began walking together back the way I'd come, and I chuckled a little sheepishly. "How long were you and she …"

One eyebrow raised, he laughed again. "Do you really want an answer to that question?"

We paused by the door together, making it clear this was where he would leave me. I pondered his question for a moment, then shook my head, looking down self-consciously. "I suppose not."

"Good man. Let the past stay there." He placed his hands in his pockets and took a half-step away. "I promised Sybill I would sit for a portrait tonight. I had better go."

"Are you and she, you know…" I let the obvious question hang there in the air, unspoken.

"Sybill and I? Lord no."

He answered so quickly, however, I knew he was trying to deny his own feelings, perhaps even to himself. Still, it wouldn't do to say so to him. He was obviously not ready to discuss it yet.

"My mistake," I said, but the look I gave him left no doubt of my suspicions. "Enjoy the rest of your evening, Albé."

With that, I nodded, then turned and walked away, leaving him alone to contemplate things on his own. As I walked back to my room, I hummed my new composition under my breath, my thought already turning with excitement at having access to an instrument once more.

I didn't know what I would find on my return or if Marie would be there, still angry with me. The door stood open upon my arrival. She was gone, and I could see at a glance she had cleaned up any evidence of her outburst. The broken pieces of a glass lay at the bottom of the trash can alongside a picture frame which had housed an image of the Virgin Mary. Breathing a sigh of relief, I stepped into the room, closing the door behind myself, and crossed to the bed. I sat heavily on the edge of the mattress, leaning forward, my elbows resting on my knees.

Part of me wanted to go seek her out to discuss what had happened, but a larger part of me balked at the prospect. If she had gone in search of solace, perhaps that was for the best. It might give her a better perspective on things and allow her the peace of mind needed in order to have a meaningful dialogue.

No, I decided, it was better to let her come to me when she was ready and use the time in between to focus on other things. Trying to make her behavior fit my expectations and wishes would only drive a wedge between us. With this thought foremost in my mind, I went over to the little table in the corner of the austerely decorated room and sat in the straight-backed chair, fished a pen and piece of paper from the drawer, and began writing the new piece, humming softly to myself as I worked on through the night.

REVELATION

Raul

Once they removed me from that dank hole, my enigmatic rescuer and host gave me over to his servants. They did not speak to me, simply gesturing to express what they wanted me to do. I bathed, dressed in black trousers and a turtleneck sweater with matching black boots they gave me. They slicked my hair back from my face as though preparing me for a fashion shoot, and then they brought me from the bowels of that place into an upper room lit only by candles. Blackened streaks covered the bare stone walls as though they had been scarred by a fiery catastrophe at some point in the past. This cold, austere, and imposing backdrop stood in contrast to the elegant antique furnishings decorating the space. In the midst of this seeming war between violence and comfort sat my host in a simple but well-tailored three-piece black suit, white shirt, and gray silk tie. He smiled and sat up as I entered, and the servants closed the door behind us, leaving just the two of us alone.

"Ah, much better," he said, looking me up and down with an appraising eye. "Marie always did have impeccable taste. Please, sit. Let us get to know one another, shall we?"

The situation seemed such a great contrast to where I had been only a little while before, and my consternation must have been visible as I sat opposite him on one end of a large red velvet sofa.

"You must have questions. Go on. Fire away. I am ready to answer." The grin on his face appeared both predatory and restrained, but I got the feeling he intended this expression to put me at ease.

"Where am I?" I said, leaning forward with my elbows on my knees. "Who are you?"

He laughed, and suddenly his ferocity stripped away. In that moment, he seemed genuine and kindly. I wondered if I had been projecting my fears onto him earlier, seeing only what I expected to see. "Direct approach. I like that. The first question is simple. The second will take time to answer. This place," he said, moving his arm in a sweeping gesture, "is where I spent a good deal of my childhood. You are in Le Château de Lacoste in the south of France. I apologize you are not able to see it in its rightful state. The mobs ransacked and burnt the place years ago."

"As for who I am, that is a complex story." He relaxed back in his seat, putting his arm along the back of the sofa. "I am, as you are well aware, a vampire, and you must have guessed I am an old and powerful one. I don't know what Marie has told you, but I have been seeking her out for a long time. She has done terrible things throughout her long life. It is my job to punish her. I have the burden and the privilege to carry out punishments of all kinds. Usually, my services are requested by individuals or organizations who seek creative and thorough solutions to problems of justice."

"So, you're basically a hired assassin?" I raised an eyebrow, puzzling out the meaning in his words.

Again, he laughed. "Oh dear boy, killing someone isn't punishment. Surely you can see that. While death may be the final result of my work should my clients demand it in the name of justice, that is certainly not the primary goal, nor is it necessary to achieve my purpose. No, I would much rather keep someone a prisoner than kill that person."

His mouth twitched at this last statement, and he licked his lips.

"Marie? Are you planning to kill her?" I gazed back at him steadily, trying not to let my voice betray my anxiety.

"Oh dear boy, if you knew what she had done, you would not be so concerned." Shaking his head, he looked back into my eyes. "I can assure you, I would much rather not see her killed."

"But the guillotine," I said. "She told me she thought that's what her fate would be. Are you telling me she lied? I thought that's what you were going to do to her. Cut off her head."

"Let me tell you about the guillotine, young man. The guillotine is certain, sudden, and foolproof as a method of execution. I saw hoards of people baying for blood, as the blade came down. They stood there for hours to watch. And do you know who the people initially intended to kill with the use of that device?"

"The aristocracy, right?" I had a vague grasp of history and really only remembered what I had seen on television or in movies.

He shook his head. "That is how it appeared, yes. That is how the history books recorded the use. But the guillotine's primary purpose was to exterminate our kind. Vampires."

"Wait a minute." I shifted in my seat, clasping my hands and leaning a little further forward. "You're telling me that the French Revolution began as a vampire hunt?"

"Well, there were political and economic reasons as well, but yes, the primary objective was a vampire genocide. Did Marie not share this little piece of information with you?" He smiled, but his smile did not reach his eyes.

I sat back in surprise, shaking my head. "No, though she did say she thought it ironic her husband signed the decree making the guillotine the primary form of execution only to have it used on himself soon after."

"Ah Louis." He chuckled low and then sighed. "He did not know what his wife had become. Poor fool. He kept himself separated from her except for official duties, and so one can understand his ignorance, I suppose. But yes, I agree. Ironic, indeed."

"You mean, he didn't know about her? That means he wasn't a vampire." I thought for a second. "I always wondered how she could have children if both she and her husband were vampires. So did someone turn her after they were born? It would have to be, right?"

Nodding, he crossed one leg over the other. "Once she had produced an heir and a spare, as they say, yes. Her elder son died before the Revolution began. She had a baby girl who died less than a year after being born. Or didn't she tell you that either?"

"No," I said with a frown. "She didn't. How did they die?"

"The doctor listed hemorrhaging as the official cause, and historians called it tuberculosis, though I rather think some member of her court lost control. Children's blood is so deliciously fresh, you see." He flashed his fangs as he spoke. "Once you bite in, it's nearly impossible to stop."

Running my hands through my hair, I thought for a moment, then looked back at him, studying his face. "How do you know all of this, but you weren't killed right along with all the rest?"

"Why, our dear Marie has kept yet another secret from you? Tsk. So many lies. I can't believe she didn't trust you enough to share the truth with you." He smirked. "Well, no matter. You are here, and I have no such fear of honesty. She had me incarcerated in the Bastille, and when I entreated for release, she ignored my plea. In fact, when word began to spread the mobs might storm the prison and release us all, they quickly moved me to another, more remote location so I would not be among those who were liberated. That woman's vindictive decision to ensure my captivity is the reason why, all these years later, my pursuit of her is relentless. Marie has many crimes to answer for. My imprisonment is only one such case. There are scores of others that cry out for justice. I intend to deliver."

Narrowing my eyes, I shook my head. "How do I know any of this is true? I don't even know your name."

"Have you not guessed it yet?" He laughed. "Why, dear boy, I am the Marquis de Sade."

I blinked, mouth agape, staring at him. "The Marquis de Sade. I thought you died of old age in an insane asylum or something."

"Insane? Oh no. The records may have branded me insane, but I assure you, I had perfect control of all my senses. The vampires who, like Marie, favored hiding what we were simply found me inconvenient. I challenged their notion vampirism is something to fear and to disguise. For that, they branded me a heretic, a criminal, and a madman. I most certainly did not die, as you can see. I had a loyal servant who found it most agreeable to impersonate me, taking on the role of infamous letch. My reputation had already made me a favorite among certain types of women, and men for that matter. He died happily in bed with one of them, and they were never the wiser. As for me, I disappeared for a while. The climate in France had grown dangerous, and so I sought a more remote location for myself and my daughter."

"Daughter?" I sat up. The idea of this man having access to a child frightening me. The term sadist came from his name. He was the S in S&M. Knowing his identity, I couldn't imagine him as a parental figure in any sense of the word that didn't fill me with horror.

A grin spread across his face. "Yes. You have met her already, though clearly she did not introduce herself to you. I gather your meeting was less than cordial."

"She killed people I cared about." My hands shook with effort as I struggled to keep from saying Sybill's name, but I couldn't hide the feral growl in my voice. "She left me locked in a dungeon to starve. 'Less than cordial' doesn't even begin to describe how I feel about her."

"Allow me to apologize for any offense she might have caused you. My condolences for your loss. Her actions, however, she took for the sake of justice. She is dedicated to her task, you see. She does not take kindly to those who stand in her way. Surely you can understand this. If your father gave you such a responsibility, is there nothing you wouldn't do for him?"

His question struck a chord, but not the one he expected. I wanted to strangle the man. Unable to sit still any longer, I looked away and stood up, shoving my hands in my pockets as I walked across the room to stare out the window. "You don't know my father. You don't know me."

For a moment, he looked me up and down predatorially. Then his voice came soft and seductive. "Oh, I think I do."

"Shut up!" I whirled to face him, pointing my finger. "You don't know the first thing about me."

Biting his lip, his mouth curled into a smile. "That anger of yours is delightful. What brought it on, I wonder? Something unpleasant between father and son? Life in your childhood not as rosy as you wished?"

"Fuck you, man!" In a rage, I picked up a chair by the window and hurled it at him with a roar.

Faster than I had ever seen anyone move, human or vampire, he ducked and then suddenly stood beside me as the chair crashed harmlessly to the floor. He pushed me against the wall with his forearm, baring his fangs. "I admire your fire, my son. I know where it comes from. We have more in common than you know."

"Why are you telling me all this?" I kept my eyes fixed on his in challenge, refusing to break.

Pushing against my chest again, he brought his face closer to mine, staring right back. "Because you need to understand. I want you to know the whole truth about yourself, about the world and your place in it. You need to stop repressing your anger, and start using that fury to fuel your actions. Properly harnessed, that rage in you could accomplish astounding things. But until you accept yourself completely, in all your imperfection, and embrace your true nature, you will never reach your potential."

"I never wanted any of this," I said, my voice cracking with emotion. "She turned me without even telling me what would happen."

"That makes you hate her, doesn't it? That you didn't have any power to choose." His arm crushed into my breastbone painfully. "You feel weak and helpless because she did this to you without your permission. Just like your father."

My lip quivered as I fought back tears. "Yes."

He let me go, and I slumped against the wall. "Good. Admitting the truth is the first step to freedom. Shall I tell you how I came to realize I had been given a gift with my turning? Perhaps if you see it from my perspective, it will help you to understand how her control of you has tainted what ought to be a beautiful gift."

Rubbing my chest, I nodded slowly, fighting back tears.

"Come. Let us step out onto the balcony, and I will explain further." He walked across the room, gesturing me to follow as he opened a door leading to the outside. Together we found ourselves on a large open rooftop area with a view of the valley far beyond. We were high on the tower of a ruined castle, and from the parapet I could see the entire landscape below bathed in darkness. Stars in their millions shone down from above. I could see this place had once been immense, but little remained in a habitable state. Yet even in ruins, the place held a real beauty. I could understand why he would be drawn to such a place.

He stopped to lean on the wall, gazing out at the landscape with a wistful smile. "My childhood was full of abuse of all kinds, psychological, verbal, physical, sexual, and it came at the hands of those who should have cared for me most. My parents did not wish to bother to be parents at all. I merely stood in their way. They sent me to live with my uncle, a clergyman, who first molested me at a young age indeed. I hated the man, and I saw despite widespread knowledge of his behavior toward both me and others, there were never any consequences for the things he did. He called me a liar who betrayed the family's trust when I tried to tell what had been done to me, and as punishment, my family sent me to a boarding school where the clergymen abused me as well. I had no one to trust or look to for justice — not family, church, educators, or the law. By the time I became a teenager, I had vowed when I became a man, I would be the one doling out the punishment. No one would ever abuse me again. To me, sex was a means of power, and used in conjunction with violence, I recognized it as the surest way to achieve control over others. I learned to find my gratification in domination.

"Having heard I had grown into a handsome young man, my uncle sent for me, and I felt helpless to disobey. Though having to return to him made me angry, I went all the same. Little did I know what he had planned for me, however. He had not called me there to make me his victim once more. No, he wanted to offer me a place at his side and a gift beyond price that would change my entire existence forever. The gift of the blood."

"Words cannot do justice to the hatred I felt for that man. He had violated me in all ways, night after night throughout my early years, and I nearly became physically ill when I saw his face again. However, what he said to me next would shock me to the foundations of my soul. He offered to make me his heir and to mentor me. When I began to laugh, he chose to reveal his true face at last. That of the monster. He explained to me what he was and what he was capable of doing. He showed me his abilities, killing one of his own servants right before my eyes. His power inspired absolute awe within me. Then he did the unimaginable. He offered to give me the same gift, and I knew, hate him or not, I had to have that same power, whatever the cost. Despite my loathing of him, I gave myself over to his bite in order to begin the change."

"As soon as he gave me his blood, I could feel the change begin, and once complete, I felt filled with elation, giddy with hunger, and overflowing with delight at each sensation. For the first time in my life, I felt as though I truly belonged in the world and unafraid at last. I could do anything. Go anywhere. I was free. That which you might call monster, I found to be the expression of my true self unchained at last. I have never looked back. Not once in all my long years. I embrace my whole self, unreservedly and completely. One day, I hope you will do the same. That is my dream for you. To feel the completeness that only comes when you stop pretending to be anything other than perfect and powerful. When that day comes, you will understand your own true purpose."

He paused in his telling, and I looked at him sharply. "Your uncle? What happened to him?"

"Justice," he said, fangs gleaming in the starlight.

A look passed between us, and in that moment, I had clear understanding of what justice might mean to a man like this. I nodded, pondering the depth of all Marie had left out of her stories to me, and I wondered what else she had neglected to explain. Did I really even know her at all?

He seemed to catch my train of thought, though I had not spoken. "I am telling you all of this because I can see Marie has taught you to skulk in the shadows and hide what you have become, even from yourself. You must understand you are not simply a human being who has vampirism. That sort of thinking diminishes the glory of the truth. Vampirism is not a punishment. It is magical and transformative. You were a human, but you have become a vampire. You are forever changed."

Gently, he put his arm around my shoulders, his voice softening as he went on. "It is a way of being, a permanent alteration each cell in your body has undergone. Your human life is over, but accepting that fact leaves you open to the wonders of your true self. In order to be happy, you must let go of who you used to be and fully embrace what you are now. Rejoice in the totality of what you have become, for every aspect is sacred. You are powerful, strong, and immortal. Death and fear have no dominion over you. You, dear boy, are a miracle made manifest."

I felt a shiver run through me as he spoke, and I found myself enraptured by the idea I might finally find peace at last. The stars twinkled down from above, lending a mystical quality to his words.

Seeing my reaction, he smiled and leaned in conspiratorially, and continued talking in fatherly tones. "Vampires and humans can never be together in any context that is not predatory. It is an abomination to believe otherwise. Vampires like Marie are foolish to think it is admirable or even possible to attempt to restrain the killer instinct within each of us, to try to hide ourselves in human populations and live a lie. Why should we? It goes against our natural urges. We were made to kill. Denial of that fact means self-loathing. Any human we become attached to is a pet, and that relationship can only result in two endings — turning or death."

Just then, he paused, looking out over the horizon. "Dawn is coming. We should retire and continue tomorrow."

As he finished speaking and led me back inside, I couldn't help but think of Sybill. Did she still live? Fearful asking might result in catastrophe, I could not dare to ask or even speak her name. I desperately wanted to keep her safe and insulate her from danger. But perhaps the Marquis told the truth. Maybe my being with her was impossible. Much as I hated to admit it, I began to wonder if the only contact between vampires and human truly should be that of predator and prey.

A good deal of what he had told me made sense. His story resonated with me. He had been so honest, revealing even the most painful things in his past without remorse or hesitation. What would it be like to have such acceptance of the entire truth of myself? I knew there were things from my life that hurt me so badly, I had repressed even the faintest thought of them. He showed such courage in relating his past, hiding nothing, however vulnerable he might have been at the time, and the contrast between that childhood weakness and his current strength seemed a powerful and even admirable trait.

He left me in a guest room near his own. I sank down into the bed with a sigh. It had been so long since I'd slept in anything other than a cell. Though I had a million questions swirling in my mind, I fell asleep almost immediately, and for the first time in what seemed like ages, I did not dream at all.

PART II

Furious Dancing

Marie

There was a soft knock on my bedroom door. I opened it to find a monk there, holding out a small piece of paper. He stared down at the floor as if he feared I might glamour him.

"Thank you," I said, taking the note from his outstretched hand.

Without speaking, he bowed, then turned away silently, crossing himself as he retreated down the hall. Superstitious nonsense. Still, I could hardly blame him for his ignorance and fear. Truly, the fact they allowed us to remain in that holy place astounded me. Byron must have done a good deal of explanation and pleading to convince them.

I shut my door and opened the note. Despite the typewritten format, I could tell at a glance from the phrasing the identity of the sender without needing to read the signature at the bottom.

Dear Madame,

If I may be so bold, I believe that before our next formal meeting, you and I should discuss ways of proceeding.

I beg you to be my guest this evening at my place of business. I assure you my intentions are honorable. I have sent my assistant to escort you. Her name is Jenny. She is waiting at the vaporetto dock in a private boat. I give you my solemn vow you will be safe in her care. You may trust her in all things, as I do.

Yours faithfully,

Casanova

His message was an immense relief to me. Clearly, he was as concerned by the coven council's behavior as I was, and meeting apart from them was exactly what the situation required. I needed someone to confide in and ask advice from, and his civility and straightforward manner was impressive. We had a common goal, and working closely together was the only logical way to achieve it.

I changed quickly into one of the smart suits I purchased back in Chicago, stepping into a pair of Italian spiked heel boots. Though I didn't feel the cold, I put on my fur coat. Leaving St. Louis with Sybill felt like a lifetime ago, though it was only a few weeks. Touching up my lipstick, I approved of my look in the mirror. I was not used to the red hair yet, but the color was better than I had anticipated. With a smile to myself, I took my purse in hand and walked out, heading for the quay beyond the monastery walls.

As he had said, a small wooden motorboat waited for me. A long-legged woman sat examining the screen of her cell phone as I approached. She looked up when I drew near, clicking the button to turn off the screen.

"Hey there. I was about ready to send in the troops to get ya." She rose to her feet to help me aboard, taking in my outfit with a raised brow. "Great shoes. Not exactly safe on a boat, but as long as you stay sitting down, you should be okay. I'm Jenny, by the way. Nice to meet ya."

Her abrupt manner was startling, but I simply thanked her as I took my seat.

"No problem." Smiling, she loosed the lines, took her seat at the wheel, and started the engine. "Hang on."

With that, she sped out with a great curving splash of water. I just had time to grip the rail to avoid being thrown overboard.

"Where is it we're going?" I shouted over the noise of the motor and the rush of the waves.

We bounced along, and she kept her eyes ahead, hand on the throttle. "Oh, it's his nightclub. Didn't he tell ya?"

I shook my head, trying to take things in stride. "He just said business. What kind of nightclub is it?"

She laughed. "Disco bar, would you believe it? I laughed when he hired me a few years ago. I was like, 'Disco? Seriously dude?' But I guess the word means something different to these Italian folks. It's not like all John Travolta the way I pictured. It's a dance club. Best one in town. You'll see."

Though she was clearly a vampire, her way of speaking was so much like Sybill's, I knew she had to be fairly recently turned. "Where are you from?" I asked, struggling to be heard over the roar of the boat.

"Iowa, born and raised. Town so small there wasn't even a public library." She laughed, shaking her head. "Had enough of it, finally. I won a trip to Europe in a radio contest. Got turned on the third night. Haven't been home since."

"Do you miss it?"

"Hell no! Would you?"

"I've never been there." I hung on for dear life as she zigzagged through the slower boat traffic of the lagoon.

"Well, I love it here, and I'm not going back. Gio, he's a good boss, you know? And he lets me do my own thing." We were swiftly approaching the Grand Canal, and she slowed the engine at last.

"Gio?" I turned to face her, puzzled.

"Giacomo. You know. Casanova. He goes by Gio when he's out in public."

I nodded, though I may never get used to the informality of this century. "I see."

She slowed a little more and pulled into an open boat slip, then cut the engine. "Hang on. Let me tie us off." Running forward, she looped the line around a cleat on the shore. "There. Now, what should I call you out there in front of, you know, humans?"

"Goldie O'Shay," I said, watching her put the gangplank out for us.

"All righty, then. After you." She gestured toward the shore, standing to the side to let me pass.

I stepped down onto the ancient stone flagstones, and she followed close behind before crossing in front of me. "It's this way. C'mon."

With long strides and head held high, Jenny led me through a maze of dimly lit narrow passageways between buildings. After a few minutes, we turned a corner and stepped out into a wider walkway. We passed a couple of closed shops, then stopped abruptly. There was a long line of people waiting behind a velvet rope in front of a building. I could hear a pulsing beat from deep inside an ancient facade.

"Subtle," I said, pointing up over the open doorway at the glowing sign emblazoned with the words "Casanova Disco."

Jenny laughed. "Right? Come on. I'll take you to him."

A bald man covered in tattoos stood at the door, checking identifications with a flashlight, giving out wristbands, and collecting cover charges. He looked at Jenny and nodded for us to go through. Jenny grabbed a couple of wristbands and handed one to me. As I put mine on, I heard someone who was waiting in the line start to complain, but we were quickly past and walking through an inner door.

The building had obviously once been a theatre. Just to our left as we walked in was the bar, lit by blue neon, and the busy bartenders handed out mixed drinks of all kinds. Tall tables and stools encircled a sunken dance floor. Bodies moved frenetically, pressed up close to one another, lit with swirling multicolored lights. On a stage at the far end of the club, a DJ stood at a mixing board, and three girls gyrated on stage at the front. The music pulsed through the room so forcefully, I felt my ribs vibrate.

Jenny wove her way through the crowd toward an archway at the right side of the dance club. A velvet rope stretched across the base of a set of steps that led upward. We approached a man in an Armani suit who nodded at Jenny, then opened the rope to let us through before closing it off again. We climbed up and came to a set of closed curtains where another man in a suit stood guard. He pulled the curtain aside for us, and Jenny led us through.

Casanova was sitting on a circular leather couch in what had once been a box seat for the theatre. When we approached, he grinned and rose to his feet to greet us.

"At last." He reached for my hand and brought it to his lips. "Dear lady, you honor me."

Jenny smiled at him. "Need me to stay?"

He shook his head. "Thank you, no, my dear. I will call for you when our conference has concluded."

"Okie dokes, boss. See ya later, then." She turned to me and nodded. "Nice meeting you."

I smiled, nodding in return. "Thank you. It was very nice meeting you as well, Jenny."

She walked back out, and Casanova led me over to the couch where we sat side by side. "I hope you will forgive me for meeting you here. In this place, we can speak openly with one another and not be concerned about being overheard."

The music was loud enough to drown out most conversation, but with our vampire hearing, we could sit close together and speak in complete confidence. "This is perfect."

He leaned forward to pour dark liquid into two wine glasses from the table in front of the couch, and he handed one to me. Blood. It was still warm.

"Thank you," I said, taking a sip. Delicious.

Casanova drank from his glass and then set it on the table before looking back at me. "Let us be honest with one another. The coven is impatient. I fear that they will not wait for you to demonstrate that you won't bring the wrath of the Marquis down upon them."

"Well, they will have to." This last came out more harshly than I had intended, and I lifted my glass again to hide my irritation. "I am going to get Raul out of there. End of story."

He gave me a sympathetic smile, reaching out to touch my knee. "Madame, I understand your concerns. It is only natural that you would wish to protect the boy. Believe me, I am only trying to prevent the council from acting rashly."

I took a deep breath to calm myself before I spoke. "I trust you, sir. You have been good to me and mine, and for that I am in your debt."

"Nonsense," he said, but a smile spread across his face, and I could see that my gratitude was something he found deeply pleasing. For a moment, I wondered if sooner or later he would decide that I did owe him after all. Would the price be too high once the time came to repay him?

I took a sip of my blood to gather my thoughts. Casanova was taking a great risk in helping me and an even greater one by meeting me here in the open. What would the coven do if they found us here together? They already thought he was taking my side against their interests. I tried to figure out what was in it for him. Why would he risk so much on my behalf? What did he hope to gain? It was as though we were playing a game of chess, but I could not see the whole board.

Something in my expression made his brow furrow. "Dear lady, what is it that troubles you?"

Setting down my empty glass, I shook my head and smiled, waving my hand dismissively. "I worry for my family. That is all."

Leaning forward, he took my hand and brought it to his lips. "Family is everything, is it not? I hate to see you in such distress."

The multicolored lights reflected in his eyes, and I watched them for a long moment, trying to find the truth behind his gaze.

"Signore, you are too kind. Please, do not trouble yourself over me. I am a survivor and have been through worse times before."

Casanova moved closer yet, leaning toward me until his lips brushed my ear. He reached up with one hand to cup my cheek, his other arm around my shoulders in an embrace. I froze, but didn't move away, his unexpected touch sending a shiver down my spine. Rather than kiss me, however, he began to whisper, his fingers caressing my skin all the while. "I believe that there is a spy amongst us, hidden in the coven. Someone is looking to do you harm and is poisoning the coven toward you. I will find and root the person out, but in the meantime, we must be discreet in our meetings with one another, yes? It would not do to give anyone reason to doubt us both."

Taking a cue from him, I reached up and ran my fingers through his hair, then traced feathery kisses up his neck till I reached his ear. "Why risk seeing me at all? Why bring me here?"

He laughed softly in my hair, then pulled back to look me in the eye, his thumb brushing my cheek. "If I said I was a gentleman, you would laugh. But old habits die hard, dear lady. And I am not dead yet."

I smiled. "You may regret this one day, you know."

"Ah, dear lady. My life is filled with them. What is one more?"

Turning my face, I kissed his palm, then pulled back from him to stand. "I will try to be patient."

"That is all I ask." He stood and took my arm in his, leading me back toward the curtain at the rear of the box. "Notice that I did not say we should not meet at all. I couldn't bear that. One day soon, I hope we can meet to talk of more pleasant things."

"As do I." On tip-toe, I kissed his cheek and then gave him a smile. "Goodnight, Signore."

"Goodnight, my queen." He let me go then, pulling back the curtain. "Jenny will meet you at the door to escort you home."

We bowed to one another, and I turned to walk away, heading back down the steps to the main dance floor of the bar alone.

The dancers were still moving as though in a trance, and the beat of the music thrummed through their bodies like the blood in their veins. I could smell their sweat, their sex, their urges and desires, and for a moment I was tempted to step among them and be lost in the frenzy of the dance. But a queen cannot lose sight of her mission, and I had no time to waste in physical pleasures, however fleeting. With a sigh, I straightened and strode back out through the bar and onto the street.

I could not see Jenny, so I turned this way and that, peering over the heads of the drunken revelers who were wandering out into the night. Then, far down the wending alleyway, I saw a dark figure beneath a hanging street light. I narrowed my eyes, trying to get a better look when I felt a tug on my arm. I turned to see who was touching my arm, and there was Jenny, smiling at me.

"Sorry it took me a second to find you. I hope you weren't waiting too long."

I glanced back down the alleyway, but the figure was gone. Forcing a smile, I shook my head and looked back at her. "No. I was only here a minute."

"You ready to go then?"

I nodded, and she led me back to the boat at a quick pace.

"Are we in danger here?" I was stepping aboard, and before I got to my seat, she was already letting the dock lines loose.

"Oh honey, we are always in danger." She chuckled softly, then started the engine. "That's just the name of the game around here. Trick is to keep moving. If they can't catch you, they can't kill you."

We zoomed away into the night, and this time I sat silently gazing out over the water, lost in thought.

Fathers and Daughters

Ernestine

The night drive from Avignon was a slow one through the meandering country roads of Provence, and with the waning moon, little of the view was visible. I knew the way well, however, and perhaps could have navigated it blindfolded.

Long ago, a gentleman's carriage pulled by four horses brought me here from Paris. I didn't know who to thank or what to expect from my new home, nor did I comprehend the immense and permanent impact my benefactor would have upon my life.

As for the man himself, he became father and mother and mentor all in one to me. He saved me from the bloody streets of Paris, and here at the Château, the horrors of the guillotine and The Terror were forgotten. He gave me fresh clothes, a new name, and a beautiful room overlooking the valley below. He provided me with the best tutors who taught me mathematics, literature, and the understanding of many languages. Natural philosophy, which today is called science, became the greatest of my studies. I had an aptitude and a fascination for understanding the ways in which the world worked, and he gave me every opportunity to expand my knowledge in this regard. I owed everything I became to him, and in turn I was eternally grateful.

When at last I grew to adulthood, he told me how pleased he felt with the woman I had become. He said I was proof to all the world a woman could be equal to a man in learning and still be worthy as a companion for all his days. I did not understand his meaning, and he told me my innocence did me credit. He said he agreed with Rousseau's assertion society caused all human failings, and therefore he kept me in the Château to protect me from the corrupting influence of others. I assured him I felt content to live there with him forever, and he laughed, telling me I little understood what I said. When I insisted nothing would make me happier than to remain with him, continuing my studies and living a quiet life at his side, he paused to look at me with an appraising eye. Then with a smile I will never forget, he said, "So be it."

That night, he turned me. He gave me the gift of the blood, and for that reason, I will always be in his debt. I asked him at my turning what I should call him. He said he meant to teach me everything he knew, all his wisdom, and therefore he would always be the Master to me.

All these years later, as the car rounded the bend in the road and the hilltop ruins of Le Château de Lacoste came into view, the sight still filled me with a sense of nostalgia. This place felt like home to me, more than anywhere I ever lived either in the years before The Terror or since. I never saw what the castle looked like before the mobs tore it apart and burnt the rest. In my memory, the place always had been a ruin.

Scaffolding covered the southernmost façade, and the winter moonlight glinted on the cold stones, giving it a mystical glow. Only a small portion of the place was habitable, but he was slowly rebuilding according to his childhood memory of the place. He planned one day to see it restored to its former glory, and at last he had amassed the power and wealth necessary to see that dream to fruition. Being a part of his plans was an honor and proof I'd earned his love.

The driver stopped the car at the main entrance. I instructed him to take my bags to my room while I went to see the Master. With much to tell him, I hurried two steps at a time up to the parapet, knowing his habits and love of the view.

"Father?" I said, opening the door out onto the rooftop. "I'm home. I have wonderful..."

My voice broke off as he turned to face me. He had been leaning on the parapet as I had anticipated, looking out over the city below, and as he heard me approach, he set aside his musings to look upon me and smile.

"Dear child," he said, hands outstretched to me benevolently.

Walking to where he stood, I dropped to my knees before him, bowing reverently. "Master."

Remaining in that humble position, I waited patiently under his gaze until at last his hands touched my head in benediction. Raising my head to look at him, I gazed up at my Master like a dutiful child.

"Give your full accounting," he said. "I wish to hear of all your work on my behalf."

"Yes, Master," I said.

Unfolding the entirety of my efforts and discoveries, I told him all, leaving nothing out for fear of displeasing him. As I explained about capturing Marie's progeny, he pressed his fingers into a peak, touching them to his lips. He said nothing, only listened.

Next, I told him of my encounter with Marie's servant, my failure to obtain any useful information from her, and my killing her in front of the progeny as a warning to comply with my wishes.

He made a slight sound at that, not of judgment but of listening, then nodded. "Go on."

I told of my pursuit of the deposed queen to Chicago, of Vincent DeLuca's refusal to see me, and my subsequent destruction of his headquarters. When I got to the description of DeLuca's basement blood production facilities, his eyebrows shot up. I knew that look. I wouldn't be let off lightly for having made such a spectacle. However, he didn't stop me there. Instead, he gestured for me to continue.

Warming to my subject, I went on to tell him of my dealings with our spy, and while it had not yet borne fruit in capturing her, my master smiled, clearly pleased with the fact that Marie remained, as yet, still unaware of our efforts.

When at last I finished my accounting, I bowed my head again to await his judgment.

"This tale of yours bears us both good and bad, my child. I fear in many ways, your actions may bring about negative consequences for our plans. Killing Monsieur DeLuca, was unwise, my dear. Very rash. I cannot yet foresee all of the potential outcomes from such an act, but those I do see are not to our favor and may perhaps prove quite dangerous for you and for me."

He paused then, and I felt a chill down my spine that had nothing to do with the weather.

"I am sorry, Master," I said, keeping my head downcast and penitent. "I betrayed the trust you placed in me. I willingly accept whatever punishment you feel I deserve."

His laughter cut like a dagger. "Oh, child, it is not so dire as all that. Not yet, anyway. You may yet salvage the potential good that is to be gained from your endeavor."

Looking up, I met his gaze with gratitude. "Thank you, Master. Yes. I wish only to be your humble servant. What would you have me do? Anything you ask of me, I will complete."

His hand stroked my hair fondly, though his eyes remained hard. "There now. My lovely girl. Such a dutiful daughter. The man child you captured, the one who belonged to our enemy, I wish you to bring him to our cause. I believe we may find some use for him. You will go to him and turn him to our advantage. You will show him the error of his ways. I wish him to become like a brother to you. I see in him a man who might be very useful indeed. Do this, and all is forgiven."

Aghast, I gaped up at him and stammered. "M-Master, the man hates me."

"Then you must convince him otherwise."

"But Master, he is useless. He cannot provide us any actionable intelligence. Would we not be better to rid ourselves of him and concentrate on other avenues of pursuit?"

He raised a brow at my questions. "Are you challenging my orders, child?"

There was a harshness in his tone and a warning. I knew what he had done to others who displeased him, and though I was his favorite, I suddenly realized how tenuous that position might be.

Shaking my head, I dropped my gaze in shame. "No, Master. I will do as you command. I am your instrument. I wish only to please you."

"I am very glad to hear it. Still, I want to ensure that you understand fully the gravity of the position you put me in. Tonight, you will return to your room. Twenty lashes will suffice, I think, to prove that you have learned your lesson. Once you are through, leave your whip outside the door for inspection. I expect to see it well bloodied."

"Yes, Master. Thank you."

Bending down on all fours, I kissed his feet to demonstrate my submission, and I heard him laugh softly as I did so. "There's my good girl. Always so obedient. Now go. Tomorrow you begin your new task."

Without another word, he turned and walked away from me to overlook the valley once more. Chastened, I was dismissed. Keeping my head bowed, I slowly rose to my feet, turning to walk toward the door that led inside.

Over his shoulder, not turning to look at me, he called, "On your knees, cherie. You will crawl back down to show your remorse."

Stopping in my tracks, I did just as he commanded, dropping to my knees and crawling across the rough stones toward the door. Knees bloodied, I whispered as I made my way back to my room, "She will pay for what she's done one day. I swear it. The queen will pay."

THE MARTYRDOM OF FAME

Byron

The moment Polidori stepped out of his basement laboratory, I hounded him for information. "Is it working yet?"

"These things take time. The serum isn't ready."

"Dammit, Polly. We can't keep dawdling. We need this to work."

He glared at me, setting down a carrying case of test tubes full of blood. "What would you have me do? My first concern is for public safety, not to mention the safety of those of us who might be directly infected if I'm not careful."

"Infected? What the devil are you talking about? We want to give the serum to the Marquis, not to the general public." I rolled my eyes, a long suffering sigh escaping my lips. "Gods, how did a nervous Nelly like you manage to persuade anyone to give you a medical degree?"

"Charm and good looks," he deadpanned.

"Polly, I am serious." I placed a hand on his arm, brows knitted with concern.

"Well, it's about time," he said. "Look, the serum is untested. It contains a mutated form of the virus. Vampirism is blood-borne, yes, but I cannot predict the vector the mutation might take. For all I know, it could become airborne, or it might pass through exchanged fluids. Even a small amount might be enough."

"There isn't time to worry about every contingency, Polly. Be reasonable."

He crossed his arms over his chest. "Who is the trained medical professional here, you or me?"

"That's not..."

"If you think you're so smart, you do these tests yourself." He bent down and picked up the carrying case, shoving into my hands, and inside I heard glass vials clink against one another.

"Polidori." My voice was a hissing whisper that echoed on the stones.

He snatched the case back. "You know the risks. You have seen what can happen. Let me do my job, and get out of my way. If you ever accuse me of being a bad doctor again, you're on your own. You'll have to find someone else to put up with your bullying and shenanigans."

Before I could reply, he pushed past me and marched down the hall toward his rooms, head held high.

Annoyed with myself for letting Polidori get to me, I decided the best remedy was to bury myself in my research. After all, my willingness to complete the translation of the ancient texts was what allowed us this place of refuge.

I made my way back to the library, wandering past row upon row of ancient tomes. In spite of my irritation with Polidori, I couldn't help but smile at how much the books made me feel at home. Though I am certainly no monk, it was a relief to have a place where I no longer had to worry about discovery. The monks asked no questions and required very little in return for their hospitality. We had a roof over our heads and blood when we needed it. What the abbey lacked in excitement, the place more than made up for in safety.

At last, I reached my private corner. Several books still stood waiting for me on the desk, and my notebook lay at the ready. I eased myself down onto the stool and began my work for the night. In order to get my mind in the right frame of mind to write, I often reread something I had written in the past, just to switch on that creative portion of my brain. I kept several volumes of my poetry near at hand, and at that time, I was making my way through Don Juan.

Somewhere behind me, I heard soft footsteps, and I knew it was Sybill. Her scent wafted toward me, and it was all I could do to sit still without reacting to her presence.

As she came closer I read aloud from the book in my hand. "There are four questions of value in life, Don Octavio. What is sacred? Of what is the spirit made? What is worth living for and what is worth dying for? The answer to each is the same. Only love."

"Isn't that a quote from that Johnny Depp movie...you know...Don Juan de Marco?" She stopped next to me, peering into my face with a smile.

I snapped the book shut and looked up. "If so, then it was stolen from me."

"Huh? You wrote that?" Sybill's eyes opened wide.

My eyes rolled involuntarily as I tossed the book aside on a nearby table. "One does not like to brag, lass. Do not make me feel I am a preening peacock, I beg of you."

"I'm sorry. I just don't know much about poetry. As an art major, I never took more than the required English lit classes." She reached out to pick the book up. "I really liked what you just read, though. Could I borrow the book?"

"You don't have to read it to flatter me." Embarrassed I had brought it up, I turned back to my translation, got out my pen, and began work where I had left off the day before, trying not to look at her.

She opened the book and flipped through the pages, leaning over them closely in the darkened room. "This poem is crazy long. Is this all one thing?

Jesus, that's a lot of work." Suddenly, she looked up in alarm. "Wait, you've got to be like famous and stuff, aren't you?"

I shrugged noncommittally and kept writing.

"Oh my god. You are. I feel so dumb. I'm sorry. My English teachers were more into American lit instead of British. You must think I'm really rude."

Looking back over my shoulder, I saw her biting her lip. "It was a long time ago. People forget. It's fine. I wasn't Shakespeare or anything, lass."

"No, but I bet you weren't far off from being that well known, were you?" Her furrowed brow showed me she feared offending me, and I was ashamed because in spite of what I'd said, I had been showing off.

"You can borrow the book," I said softly. "Maybe you'll like it, or maybe not. Judge for yourself."

With a smile, she leaned in and kissed my cheek. "Thanks, Albé. I'll take good care of it."

"You'd better. It's a first edition." I winked at her, then turned back to my work again.

"So, what is it that you're writing, exactly?" She was hugging the book to her chest, and she tilted her head to one side as she watched me.

"I'm writing an English translation of a book of Armenian poetry that still keeps the poetic flavor of the original. If I did a word-by-word literal translation, you might get the meaning but not the feeling or soul of the work. I am letting the rhyme and meter lead me to keep the essence of the poem alive."

"What's the poem about?"

I chuckled. "Shepherds. The Abbot chose it. I'm afraid you might find it a little dry."

She stood looking over my shoulder with a puzzled expression. "You're handwriting all this? Why not use a computer? It's so much faster."

"I never got used to writing on a computer. My fingers are awkward on a keyboard. Pen and paper feels more permanent, and taking my time as I write allows me an interval of thought before each word is inscribed. Old habits, I suppose."

"I could help you, if you want. We could use a voice dictation software so you could read it out loud and have the computer type it up for you."

Pushing back from the table, I turned to face her. "I don't own a computer."

She shrugged. "We could get one easily enough. I'm sure someplace in Venice sells laptops. I'll be happy to set it up for you. You don't have to have internet or anything since all you're going to be doing is putting it all into a file. You could just plug it in here right by the desk, read it out loud, proofread, and boom. Done."

I threw my head back and laughed. "Boom, huh?"

"Mmm hmm. Just like that." She beamed at me, and I could see this was her way of making amends to me for not recognizing who I was. "If you wanted, that is. I mean, if you don't, that's fine. I'm not trying to tell you what to do or anything. I just thought..."

"It's a good idea. Thank you."

"I can even teach you about computers, if you want. I'm pretty good with them."

Chuckling, I shook my head. "One thing at a time, lass."

She nodded. "Gotcha. Well, I guess I'll leave you alone so you can get back to work. Thanks for the book."

"Anytime. If you want to come sit with me sometime, I'll be happy for the company, as long as you're quiet."

A huge grin spread over her face, lighting up her eyes. "I'll bring my art stuff next time. Maybe tomorrow, if that's okay."

"I'll have a desk set it beside mine for you." I couldn't take my eyes off her.

"Cool." She stood grinning back at me for a few seconds, and I thought for a second she might lean in for a kiss. Instead, she shrugged, straightened her spine, and made a half turn toward the door. "Okay, well, see ya!"

With that, she walked away. I stared after her until she disappeared around the corner, then I gave an involuntary shiver and turned back toward the desk. "She's just a girl," I muttered. "You have work to do."

Focusing on the page, I knew already I would be there all night, and the predictability of the action gave me comfort. I relaxed into my seat, and buried myself in the translation, shutting out all thoughts of Sybill for the time being. I lost track of time until I heard the chime of the grandfather clock announce the hour. It was nearly dawn. Time to take my rest. My pages would wait. There was much still to do, but the life of a vampire is long.

Tryst of Fate

Marie

A soft knock came at my door in the early evening. Anticipating Mozart had come to try and woo me again, I sighed and got out of bed, pulling on my dressing gown. "One moment," I said, taking a moment to brush my hair and put on a pair of slippers.

I didn't want a confrontation with him, though I knew it was inescapable. Eventually, he and I needed to talk about what was and wasn't between us, but I dreaded the inevitability. Once we had the discussion, it would be over, and there would be no changing my mind or undoing it.

He latched on too quickly and tightly, and I felt trapped every time we were together. I couldn't help the reaction. We simply were not right for one another. I could never be what he needed, and he was not at all right for me. As a friend, yes. A long term lover, no. He was the only one who didn't recognize what was obvious to everyone else, and I worried removing his illusions would break his heart in the process. Still, I couldn't perpetuate a doomed relationship either.

With a heavy heart, I paused one more moment before the mirror, gathering myself for the conversation I dreaded, then crossed the room, bracing myself as I opened the door. "Sorry to keep you waiting. I..."

As the door swung open wide, I stopped abruptly, startled. Rather than Mozart, it was Casanova standing there, eyes full of mischief, taking in my attire. My robe clung to every curve of my body, and I could see from the way he looked at me, he appreciated the view.

Lifting a hand, I held the top of my robe closed more firmly to my neck. "Oh, Signore Casanova. Forgive me. I was expecting someone else."

"It is I who begs your pardon, your majesty," he said, bowing low and taking my free hand in his to kiss. "I should have sent a messenger first, but the matter is urgent. I hope you will forgive my intrusion."

"Nonsense," I said, laughing softly at his quaint decorousness. "You are not intruding at all. Please, won't you come in?"

He rose to his full height once more, his lips curling into a crooked smile, and he stepped inside, letting me close the door behind him.

Standing with him in my bedroom, I was immediately keenly aware of the intimacy of the space. This man had been the greatest lover the world had ever known. His romantic conquests were legendary. The room felt suddenly small, the bed absurdly prominent like the proverbial elephant in the room. Like all things I wasn't yet prepared to discuss, I ignored it completely, taking a seat in the side chair by the fire and gesturing toward the other for him, as if this were the most ordinary thing in the world.

"Won't you be seated?" I said, still holding the robe closed at my neck while the other hand did the same at my knee.

With a low chuckle, as if having sensed my train of thought, he sat opposite me, crossing one leg over the other, his arms relaxed. "May I ask, who was it you were expecting to see when you opened that door?"

Lowering my gaze demurely, I fluttered my eyelashes before giving him a sidelong glance. "Only my family and the monks who inhabit this place know I am here, Signore. Apparently, however, someone led you here to me."

"Yes, the Maestro was kind enough to show me the way. He seemed in quite a hurry. He spoke of a new composition he was working on."

"Mmm. Yes." I kept my voice noncommittal, not wanting to reveal any reaction with regard to Mozart and the fact that he had a hand in leading Casanova to my door. "Do you know him well? Wolfgang, I mean."

"Indeed," he said, one eyebrow raised. "Has he never spoken about me?"

Shaking my head, I looked back at him with a furrowed brow. "No, I am afraid not."

"Odd. We were once so close. Musicians. They can be so jealous, don't you find?"

"I am afraid I don't follow. What does his work have to do with it?"

He smiled, leaning slightly forward in his seat. "Why, my dear, I wrote the libretto for Don Giovanni. Didn't you know? Even the name was derived from mine, and certain elements of the plot are directly related to my own life. That drunkard, Da Ponte left the thing unfinished. Wolfgang begged me to complete it. The deadline for completion was running out, and he couldn't delay any longer. He had debts, you know. Someone had to step in, and it ended up being me. I didn't ask for credit for my work, you understand. Instead, he and I struck a different sort of bargain."

"Bargain? But I thought he didn't have any money."

"He didn't. But I was already vampire by then. I took my payment in blood. I didn't realize he was so ill until it was too late. If I had known, I would never have asked for such a thing. It seems, however, he got the better end of the deal. When I discovered how near death he was, I felt obligated to save him. A genius should not be left to die in a pauper's grave."

Casanova was Mozart's maker? He'd never said a word about it, and the deliberate omission felt like a betrayal somehow, though not on Casanova's part.

Not wanting to let on how hurt I felt, I kept my expression impassive, commenting only on what he'd said. "I thought that was precisely what happened. An unmarked grave."

He shrugged. "Wolfgang was furious with me for a while for having spread that rumor, but I couldn't very well have his widow following after us, demanding money, could I? She was a notoriously money grubbing woman."

I stared at him, unblinking for several moments, then swallowed hard. "I suppose not."

"No, he said, then after a brief pause, he smiled once more. "At any rate, surely you did not ask me into your bedchamber to discuss Herr Mozart."

Smoothing down my robe across my knees distractedly, I shook my head and smiled. "No. You said you came on urgent business. How can I be of assistance?"

"I am afraid, your majesty, it is I who should be asking you that question. When last we met, I told you of my suspicions of a spy in the coven. I now have reason to believe there may be several, in fact. I fear for your safety, and I could not in good conscience allow you to remain unaware of the danger."

This news had me jolting up to sit on the edge of my seat in alarm. "Who? Don't leave me in suspense."

"I am afraid I don't yet know, but my assistant Jenny is loyal and trustworthy, and she will be discreet as well as thorough in her investigation."

"Is it someone here with me? Or are you suspicions of some of the coven members?"

"Perhaps both," he said. "Jenny and I are examining all possibilities, I assure you. We believe that the coven may have been infiltrated as well, though we cannot say for certain yet."

Struggling to maintain my composure, I shifted forward in my seat. "How do you know this information is true? Where did this suspicion come from?"

"A coded message was intercepted by my intelligence personnel. We are still tracking down the source, but we have reason to suspect someone, perhaps even one of the monks, may be responsible."

A rush of anxiety shivered through me, and I leapt to my feet to fight my rising panic. "What do I do?"

Rising from his chair, he stepped in close, touching my shoulder gently. "Change nothing. Until we know who the perpetrator is, we don't want to raise any alarms. You must continue to behave as though you know nothing. Can you do that?"

"Well, it's a bit late to be asking me that question, isn't it?" Gazing up into his eyes, it was difficult not to feel an echo of the fear I had felt all those years ago when we were under siege at Versailles. How many times had I gone over those events and wished I had done things differently, and yet here I was again being asked to wait. "If we aren't safe, shouldn't I leave here? Go away and find another place that is more secluded?"

"And if the spy is still in your midst, who will help you then?"

He was right. I knew he was. Yet the helplessness of the situation was overwhelming. "Signore, what am I going to do?"

"You will continue being strong. You will get through this, your majesty, and one day, you and I will sit together and tell this story and laugh." Cupping my cheek in his palm, he gazed down at me with a tender smile.

"I am frightened." It took all my strength to admit it, but Casanova made me feel safe to be vulnerable in his presence.

Pulling me into his embrace, he held me close kissing my forehead. "So am I. We are survivors, you and I. We have lived through worse. This time, though, we have one another. I like those odds."

I clung to him, my face pressed into his shirt, breathing in the scent of his cologne, letting him comfort me. "Thank you," I murmured.

"There is no need for thanks, your majesty. It is an honor to serve you."

"I don't know what I would do without you."

To this, he said nothing, only kissed my brow again.

At last, I pulled back to look up at him, touching his chest with my palms. "Raul. I still don't know how I am going to rescue him. What if…"

My voice trailed off tremulously, and he reached up to push a lock of hair behind my ear. "Shh. No what ifs. We will find him and get him away from that madman. You must keep believing this with your whole heart. He needs you to be strong."

"What if that is not enough?"

Smiling, he touched my nose with his finger teasingly. "What did I say? No giving in to those fears. Trust in him and in yourself."

"You are a good man, Signore."

He laughed at that, stepping book, giving me a wink. "That is not what they used to say about me."

"Well, then the historians got it all wrong. You are the best of men."

"Ah, now that is a gross exaggeration, I am afraid. But say it again all the same." Just like that, he had me laughing once more, and for that I would always be grateful. "I am afraid I really must be going. Coven business, unfortunately, seems never ending."

I followed him to the door, feeling like a shy young girl again. "Will I see you again soon?"

"Would you like to?" His hand on the door knob, he paused there, one eyebrow raised, studying my expression.

Nodding, I bit my lip and smiled. "Yes, I would. Very much."

"Then I shall do my utmost to make you happy." Once more, he took my hand and brought it to his lips, kissing it, and this time he kept his eyes firmly fixed on my own. "Good night, your majesty."

"Good night Signore. And thank you."

"My pleasure," he said, bowing his head, and then with a wink and a smile, he left me there.

I pressed a palm to the closed door and stood there pondering all he had said. What he had told me was frightening, and yet coming as it did alongside his reassurances, I had to believe that things would work out all right in the end. I didn't know if I could pretend not to be worried or not, but I trusted him to do everything he could to keep me safe and aid me in whatever way he was able. That had to be reassurance enough.

The Winter of our Discontent

Ernestine

My Master told me he was making a pet of Marie's favorite, and he wanted me to try and bring him over to our way of thinking. I am not the warm and fuzzy type, as I tried to remind him, but the Master is insistent when he has his mind made up, and I can never disobey him, even when I disagree.

Thus, reluctantly, I made my way to the rooms where Raul, as I apparently was to call him, was being housed.

I didn't bother knocking. He had not yet earned pleasantries from me. Instead, I strode in with confidence, my high heels clicking on the floor with each step. The door hit the wall behind as I walked through, then shut with a click in my wake.

He was sitting on the bed, and as I entered the room, I saw him flinch and draw back as though expecting a blow.

"So, are you enjoying your freedoms?" My eyes narrowed as I turned to face him, crossing my arms over my chest. "Everything to your liking?"

"You," he spluttered in alarm. "What are you doing here?"

"I live here," I said flatly, not caring if this information caused him distress or discomfort. "You're in my domain. I assume you've met my father, yes?"

"Your father? The Marquis is your father?"

With a tired sigh, I nodded, rolling my eyes at his incredulity. "Adopted father, yes. I should have thought that was obvious. Just as you were adopted by...that woman."

"We are nothing alike, you and me." The words came out in a snarl, his lip curled with rancor.

"No? Hmm. Well, if that is the case, I suppose I'm wasting my time. I'd better tell him you said so. I'd be all too happy to put you back in a hole again. Leave you there in an oubliette to starve alone."

Turning on my heel, I shrugged and began walking toward the door again.

"No!"

His words were a broken plea, and I couldn't help my split second smile before I stopped and turned back to face him. "Good. I see you do have some sense of self-preservation after all. You might turn out to be less useless than I thought. If you're through with your tantrum, perhaps we can get down to a serious conversation, eh?"

He pushed his hair back from his face, revealing those startling blue eyes of his gazing back at me dubiously. I could see he thought this was a trap or a test of some sort, and if I didn't think it would undermine our potential rapport, I'd have laughed.

"Is that a yes, or a no? I can still send you back down below if you prefer."

"What do you want?" His jaw set defiantly, I saw his body tense, fight or flight instinct settling into his muscles.

This time, I did laugh. I couldn't help it. "Me? I don't want anything. I'd just as soon cut off your head and be done with you, but my father sees potential in you, so I am here at his behest because I trust his judgment.

You can behave civilly and agree to this, or you can go back to slowly going mad before you die alongside the rats. Your choice."

"Just talk?"

I laughed, mocking his question, parroting it back with a sneer. "'Just talk?' Did I stutter? Living with her has made you paranoid."

"It's not paranoia when someone is really out to get you."

Glaring, I narrowed my gaze and smiled menacingly, taking a step toward him. "Newsflash, pretty boy. If I tell him you aren't compliant, it's over for you. No reprieve. No more talking. You die. No one but father and I will know where you are. So make up your mind right now. Tick tock. You won't get a second offer."

The muscle in his jaw pulsed as he ground his teeth, mulling over what I said. In his eyes, I saw a flash of pure hatred. Good. Emotion. I could work with that. I kept my gaze steady, meeting his eyes unwaveringly with a cool disinterest.

"Fine," he said. "Talk, goddammit."

"So polite. You kiss your mother with that mouth?" My voice dripped with sarcasm. "You wouldn't be the first. She seduces everyone. That's how she works. You know it as well as I."

First, he gave a puzzled look, forehead furrowed, then it transformed into a scowl.

"We weren't like that." The tension in his voice told a different story.

"Is that so. Ever? Or only recently?" I couldn't help the knowing smirk that crossed my face as I saw plainly I'd hit home again. "Oh, now don't feel bad. She tires of everyone in the end. At least she hadn't discarded you completely. Not yet, anyway."

"You don't know what you're talking about," he snapped. "If all you plan to do is insult me, there are surely better uses for your time."

A bitter laugh spilled from my lips. "I'm not insulting you. Insulting her, yes, but not you."

I saw him flinch, though only for a moment before he sneered and rolled his eyes. "Whatever. Just get to your point."

"Tsk. Touchy, touchy. Just giving you some food for thought. You didn't think you were the only one, did you, Raul? Her chosen one? Marie's special baby boy? Is that what you thought? Hmm? I'm sorry to be the one to tell you, but you are far from the first son she's abandoned."

His hands balled into fists, and his nostrils flared. "She didn't abandon me. You abducted me!"

"Or perhaps I saved you," I said, raising a finger with a quirk of my brow. "Did you ever consider that possibility? Surely you've realized by now she's not some perfect queen to be adored. What's the reason for your loyalty to her, eh? What has she ever done but kept you as her lap dog, a toy, locked away from everyone else, expected to entertain her whenever she was bored or lonely? Or maybe she liked to play the damsel in distress for you? Did she beg for your help? 'Save me, you big strong man.' Did she cry and say she needed you? Was that her game?"

He didn't speak, but I saw a hesitation in his eyes. My words had finally found a sore spot. He'd thought about it. Maybe even been angry with her for reasons similar to what I'd described. It was written on his face plainly, and he wasn't bothering to deny it anymore.

I softened my tone and my expression, allowing him a little sympathy. "I have seen what she does. She betrays everyone in the end. You haven't been around long enough to know, but there is a trail of heartbreak in her past that would shock you."

He clenched his jaw defiantly. "I suppose you speak from experience."

With a soft laugh, I shook my head and waved a dismissive hand. "We aren't talking about me. Where was she when I captured that human woman for questioning? Don't think she would shed one tear for her. She knew I would be coming and did nothing to protect her. Left her ignorant, defenseless, and alone to pay the price for her misdeeds."

Talking about that woman had hit a raw nerve, and he twitched visibly, his voice dropping to a growl. "You didn't have to kill Crystal. She didn't know anything. You could have just let her go."

I scoffed. "Not a chance. She was going to die from the moment we found her. Marie knew it would happen."

"She's not like that. She wouldn't…"

"Tell a story to make herself look like a martyr? I know her better than you ever will. I saw what she did. I was there. I know every bit of it. Did she tell you how she escaped? Hmm? How she got out of prison in the first place?" Tilting my head to catch his furtive glances, I moved a little closer, pushing him as much as I dared without breaking him. The defensive look he gave me answered that question without him saying a word. "Of course not. Before you get all weepy for poor misunderstood Marie, think about the people she let starve outside the castle gates while she wasted millions of louis on frivolous trifles. I'll bet she told you everything they said about her was propaganda. Lies to justify killing her. Didn't she? That old saw. Answer me this. If so, why am I still pursuing her after all this time? Why does she have so many enemies? And if she didn't die on that scaffold, whose head went rolling under the snick of Madame Guillotine? That blood was real. Someone died in her place, and I'll bet she has never given her a moment's thought. Just like your dead friend."

He sat there, dumbstruck, still as stone. I'd found my target, all right. He felt betrayed. Lied to. Used.

"It's a lot to think about," I said. "I know. Makes you wonder, doesn't it? Why did she choose you? She wasn't in love. I'll wager you hadn't met before that day. So why you? And once she'd gotten you with her, why do you think she stayed with you? Was it love? Duty? Or did she just dread being alone? Did she simply need a servant? Someone to tell her how great she was and to sympathize with her? Someone she knew wouldn't question her lies? You think about that for a while. I'll come back later for another chat."

I was halfway to the door before he spoke at last.

"What about Sybill?" His voice trembled with emotion as he asked the question.

Turning back, head tilted to one side, I puzzled for a moment before I realized who he meant, and then I grinned, baring my fangs. "Your girlfriend? Oh, she killed her long before I got there."

He froze in place, unblinking, staring at me as if he'd been struck with an axe between the eyes.

"You're thinking I must be lying. I assure you, I'm not. Your lover is no longer breathing, and I had nothing to do with it." I smiled a little more, savoring his horror. "Think on that. Maybe when I come back, you'll have a different tune for me."

He made no movement, only stared at me in stunned silence as I turned and made my way toward the door, grim horror written on his features so plainly, I almost felt guilty for having shattered his view of her. Those haunted eyes of his stayed trained on me until the door separated us once more, and I walked away down the corridor with my head held high. The Master would be so pleased with me.

A Heart for Every Fate

Sybill

I took Byron at his word when he said he would like some company. In need of a distraction from all my worries, I gathered my sketchpad and my drawing pencils and returned to the library the next evening. True to his word, there was a second desk waiting for me right next to his own. As I approached, he looked up from his work and smiled, then stood to pull out the chair for me.

"You made it," he said. "I wasn't sure you really were coming."

I placed my things in a pile on top of the desk and then took a seat. "I won't be bothering you, will I? I promise, I'll stay quiet."

He shook his head, sitting back on his stool. "I'm happy for the company. The silent kind, that is. Let me know if you get bored."

Arranging my pencils so they were in easy reach, I grinned at him. "I'm pretty sure you couldn't bore anyone, even if you tried."

"All right then." He winked at me, settling back to his work.

For an hour or two we sat together working quietly in the library. He kept at his translations while I did some sketches just to keep in practice.

Though the only sound was the scratching of his pen and the sweep of my pencil on the paper, there was no awkwardness in the silence. No emptiness we needed to fill with idle talk.

After a long time, he turned and caught me drawing a portrait of him in my little notebook. "Is that really how you see me?"

When I looked up I saw a huge smile on his face. Though his voice was slightly mocking, I thought from his expression he seemed truly touched. "It's just a sketch. Not much more than a doodle, really."

"Well, you must be talented, then. You have me in only a few strokes." His eye was on the paper, but the double meaning in his tone would have made me blush if I could.

I decided to ignore his implication, pretending my own thoughts were innocent. "You can have it when I'm through, if you'd like. It's not much, and I'll do a better one later, if you want."

"I would like that. Should I pose for you?"

I laughed, catching a teasing gleam in his eye. "I think I would rather have it be candid, thank you."

"You are the artist. I am putty in your hands."

That last statement made it impossible for me to keep pretending not to understand his implications, but I couldn't help but laugh again just the same. "Naughty!"

He chuckled. "Why Sybill, whatever do you mean?"

"Don't even try that, Mister Innuendo." And I poked him on the shoulder playfully.

"Me? I would never."

"You so would. Don't lie. You are a very bad man."

"Interesting. I may have implied another meaning, but your mind went there all on its own, lass."

"Oh, just stop." I shook my finger at him, and he laughed.

"Very well," he said, trying to compose his face. "Back to work again, then, is it?"

"A world of yes."

Though he smirked at my expense, he did as I asked, and turned to his writing again. We kept on that way, and eventually the tension between us relaxed once more into an easy quiet. My mind was drifting, however, and I found myself brooding about the situation with Raul. I was trying to stay distracted to avoid facing the possibility I had lost him, maybe forever. Byron must have sensed my change in mood, because he stopped work to look at me. "You are thinking awfully loudly. Why don't you tell me what's wrong?"

Pausing in my drawing, I gave a deep sigh. "It's Raul. There's so much I don't know about him and vice versa. I guess I'm starting to worry what happens if we find him"

"Once we find him, you mean." Byron turned on his stool to face me. "Want my advice? Don't push yourself too hard to know exactly what you want. We don't even know how long it will take. You can't spend all that time in-between in limbo, and you can't let yourself feel guilty for what happened to him. There's no changing the past. Just focus on now. Let the future take care of itself."

Tapping my pencil on my sketchpad, I frowned thoughtfully. "I know. Still, it's frustrating I can't help him or even find out enough about what happened to even try. I was taught love means loyalty, but honestly, I don't even know what I feel for him. We were just starting to get to know one another. It's hard not to get bogged down in what-ifs, you know?"

"Sybill."

"No really. Maybe he doesn't want me anymore. Maybe he never did, and I've just been fooling myself all that time."

His voice softened, and he reached to take my hand, giving it a squeeze. "Don't do this to yourself, lass."

Tears prickled my eyes, and I sighed heavily to gather my strength. Our fingers laced together, I found myself clinging to him for dear life. "I'm just being honest. I can't keep pretending I'm okay with what happened to him or with the way Marie is just acting like I'm his fiancée and this is some romance novel. I'm so angry, and I don't know what I can do."

"Of course you are," he said, gently. "You have every night to be."

I nearly burst into tears right there. "Thank god, at least you're still talking to me. I swear, without you, I'd have gone crazy long ago."

"Oh come now, lass," he said with a laugh.

"I'm serious." I didn't speak aloud my deepest fear that even if we did pull off a rescue, Raul might not recover from what happened to him. I could hardly let myself think about that possibility, much less verbalize it.

Byron shook his head, his forehead furrowed with worry. "It'll be all right."

"I don't know. And what about Polidori?"

"Polly?" He blinked as he spoke his name. "Why are you worried about him?"

"I haven't seen him in ages. Isn't he supposed to be helping us? How is that possible if he never comes out of his lab?"

"He's just frustrated about the serum. He's always like that when he's working."

I sighed, looking down again. "I hope you're right. I mean, I understand his reluctance to let us use the serum. I do. I think he blames me for bringing it up during our discussion and putting all this pressure on him to get it ready in time."

Byron reached out to lift my chin, shaking his head. "That's not true, lass."

"Oh yes it is. I was impulsive and rude to him. I know it."

"If Polidori can get over all the things he's been angry at me for over the years, he will get over being angry with you."

I shook my head. "He's not over it. The two of you are always fighting. Where is he, anyway?"

"Polidori has been in his cellar all evening like a little rat, scurrying about. I have half a mind to go see what he is up to, but then I would have to listen to him going on and on with that scientific drivel of his. I'm stuck with him, predictable as tides."

I laughed. "Maybe."

He grinned and nodded. "Fate."

"Like us." I said this last softly, then bit my lip.

"Well, not exactly like us." He smiled at me, then gave my hand another squeeze. "Listen, why don't we get out of here this weekend?"

I raised my eyebrows, full of curiosity. "Where would we go?"

"We could do a little shopping in the city. We've been cooped up here for days. Getting out would do us both good."

"That sounds fun."

Grinning, he paused thoughtfully for a moment, then squeezed my hand again. "Carnival is coming up. Would you like to go?"

"What is it?"

He looked taken aback by my question. "Carnival? Have you never heard of it? It's similar to Mardi Gras in New Orleans. It's the celebration before Lent. Every year, there's a masquerade ball. The biggest party of the year. We should go. We can dress up in costumes and dance all night."

I laughed. "You want me to be like Cinderella or something?"

Chuckling, he bowed in his seat. "I would be honored to be your escort for the night. You need to get out and meet more of our kind. The Venice coven hosts the event. We could do our part to smooth things over with them and still have some fun for a change."

"All right. I'm in. Marie's not going to like it, though."

He shrugged. "It's easier to ask forgiveness than get permission."

"My daddy used to say that."

"Your daddy was right in this case. Anyway, we aren't in immediate danger. At least, not right now. And the Marquis doesn't know who we are or how to find us. We'll be in disguise. It'll be perfectly safe."

"Famous last words," I said, but I was laughing.

"You'll see. It'll be unforgettable."

"I already said yes."

He gave me a smile so warm, the last of my worries disappeared from my conscious thoughts again. "So you did."

I finished the portrait, and as payment he read a section of his poetry out loud to me. I had expected to be bored with it, but he had such an expressive way of talking, I found myself laughing out loud, completely at ease in his company.

The novelty of a masquerade ball was exciting to me, and when I went to bed at last, dreamed of us dancing together like something out of a fairy tale. Since I had never bought into the dream of being a Disney princess, I woke myself laughing at the irony.

"Stupid," I said to myself, punching my pillow down and rolling over. "It's just for fun. Don't get weird about it."

A Touch of Evil

Raul

Atop the battlements of the castle, I gazed back at the Marquis' daughter, laughing softly. "Do you know, I still have no idea what your name is? Hardly seems fair. You know all about me, or at least so you've said."

I was stalling, and she knew it. A little game between the two of us to see which one would break first. She had been meeting with me every day, per request of the Marquis, or the Master as she chose to call him. Interrupting her with non-sequiturs was a tactic I had tried to varying success with her, hoping to break her concentration and get her to slip up.

Of course it never worked. Not really. I might gain a momentary flicker in her expression to indicate she was startled, but the mask quickly dropped, and we were back to our usual routine.

I knew exactly what she was doing. He had told her to try and win me over, gain my trust, hoping I would divulge information about Marie. Funny thing was, I didn't have any information to give them. I didn't know where she kept her money or where she might go in search of help. I didn't know much about her past before she met me, aside from the obvious. She kept everything to herself, acting as though nothing existed except the moment she was in. I didn't dare tell them the truth, fearing once they realized I couldn't give them what they wanted, they would decide I was useless and kill me.

If I knew where Marie was, I would gladly reveal the information in exchange for my life. A part of me felt guilty to admit that fact, even to myself, but then I thought about all those things Marie kept hidden or secret from me, and about Sybill, and suddenly my guilt vanished.

That was one thing the Marquis and I agreed on. Marie kept secrets from me, and the more he and his daughter talked to me, the more I began to question my trust and loyalty to someone who didn't reciprocate the feeling. Why should I retain such faith in her when her every action kept me in the dark and betrayed my trust?

"Ernestine," said the Marquis' daughter. "My name is Ernestine."

Her straightforward reply took me aback. I blinked several times, one eyebrow raised, tucking my hair behind my ear.

"I know," she went on, "it's not a popular name. But you have to admit, neither is yours."

"I didn't choose it," I said simply.

"I thought all you actors used stage names." She put an accent on the word 'actors' as though it meant something dirty, and I glared back at her, crossing my arms over my chest.

"Some do, I guess. Not me."

I paced away from her in annoyance, gazing away over the ramparts to the city below, its twinkling lights obscuring part of the night sky.

"Did she make you change your name?" Again, she emphasized the word 'she,' obviously she meant Marie.

"We were hiding from you. What do you think? Of course. Duh." My reply sounded testy, and I knew it, but I couldn't seem to keep my anger from surfacing in spite of my best efforts.

Changing my name and giving up my whole life was a bone of contention between me and Marie. How many times had she insisted it was too risky to be seen? I had spent years in seclusion before she finally let me out, and even longer before she trusted me to go anywhere on my own. I remembered all her arguments. Anyone might see me. All it would take was one fan with a camera and our whole existence would be revealed. Plus, she was sure I would lose control and kill someone, and she didn't want to risk the possibility of our kind being exposed. Over and over I heard it, like a song on repeat, and I couldn't shake the annoyance I felt even now as a result.

"Sounds like it bothered you," She said.

"What are you? My shrink?" Squinting, I met her gaze, my lip curled in a sneer.

Her voice was annoyingly clinical. "You just seem upset. I'm not judging you for it."

"No? Well, that's a relief. Thanks for that. Really." Again, I slipped my hand into my hair raking it back from my face. "You got any cigarettes in this place? Even prisoners get cigarettes."

"You are not a prisoner," she said. "And no, I don't. It's a filthy habit anyway."

I scoffed, shaking my head with a sardonic smile. "You're health conscious now? It's not like it's going to kill me, sweetheart."

"I am stink-conscious, and don't call me sweetheart."

"Yeah. Whatever, Ernestine." Dark laughter spilled from my lips, and I turned my back on her.

Just then, another voice interrupted our conversation.

"Well, isn't this delightful?" I turned to find the Marquis, clasping his hands and grinning as he gazed at us both. "Splendid. Aren't you cozy? The two of you, getting along so well."

I looked over at Ernestine. For a moment my eyes met hers, and I saw there a kindred expression of disbelief and an instinct, like mine, to disagree with him vehemently, yet neither of us spoke it aloud. Instead, there was a quiet understanding and tacit agreement to keep our thoughts to ourselves, and we both simply turned back mutely to face the Marquis.

"What a glorious evening. I'm famished. What do you say to a bit of our native French cuisine, eh?" His eyes fixed on me, a devilish smile on his face, and god help me, but I felt my fangs descend on their own.

Nearly all of my experience of feeding from the vein had been very closely monitored and controlled by Marie. Only people who wished for death or who wouldn't be missed or who were dark of heart would do, but I had a feeling the Marquis did not have the same scruples.

Clearly, he didn't keep a supply of blood on hand in his refrigerator. I was also certain the girl he had brought to my cell the day he released me, the one he'd not only watched but relished in seeing me kill, was someone who had a family and people who would miss her. At the time, I was too desperate and starved to comprehend her thoughts and feelings, but worry dogged my steps ever since. How many dreams had I shattered in taking her life? Would anyone come looking for her? What were the long term costs for what I had done? So much anxiety, and I realized with startling clarity Marie was the reason for most of it.

She made me ashamed and fearful of what she turned me into without my consent. How hypocritical. The Marquis was right. My guilt and shame were her doing, he said, and the more I thought, the more I realized the truth of it.

The Marquis had told me there was no shame in embracing what I was. He seemed to revel in it. Perhaps he was right. Maybe it was time to let go of my grip on humanity to accept the change in me. I had fought it for so long, and for what? To be hunted? Fearful? Hating myself for something I couldn't help? Vampires had these urges for blood for a reason. We couldn't help it. Deny it all I might, the craving would remain. I had held onto the last shreds of my humanity for Sybill's sake, but knowing she was gone,

I had no reason to keep fighting. Resisting was exhausting, and in the end self-defeating and futile.

That's why, when he asked me to dine with him, I smiled, letting him see the fangs I normally kept hidden. "I could eat."

Ernestine tilted her head, eyes narrowing distrustfully at my agreement, but I simply raised an eyebrow, daring her to challenge me. She didn't. Instead, she mirrored my expression back at me. "Very well."

Grinning, the Marquis put his arms over our shoulders, leading us to the rampart's edge, and with a wink in my direction, he leaped, disappearing into the darkness below with a flutter of his coat. Ernestine smirked at me. "Try to keep up."

Before I could reply, she jumped from the edge as well, leaving me there alone, my hair blown back in the updraft.

My ingrained habits kicked in for a half second and tried to make me hesitate, but I stuffed those behavior patterns to the side and without over-thinking things, I jumped.

The fall was exhilarating, and I laughed as my vampire instincts took over for the first time, feeling free of guilt and shame. Landing on my feet, catlike, knees bent to brace for impact, I then rose and followed after the Marquis and Ernestine toward the city in the valley below.

In a cluster, we descended the winding narrow road into the village. Most of the shops were closed for the night, but as we passed the local bus station, I paused, hearing the sound of French hip-hop pulsing from somewhere within. One glance revealed two backpackers, a college age couple, peering down at the glowing screen of an iPad. Beyond, a janitor was sweeping the waiting area. The ticket booth was closed for the day, and no one else was around.

The Marquis, sensing I had stopped, halted and followed my gaze, moving in close to put an arm over my shoulder before leaning in to whisper conspiratorially, "Which one shall it be, my young friend?"

With a low chuckle, I gave in to my deepest secret desires, whispering back, "One?"

My reply must have surprised him, for he glanced over at Ernestine with a smirk. Then he slapped my shoulder as though we had shared a good joke and began laughing. "Initiative. How delightful. Very well, son. Show us what you can do."

Permission to follow my instincts was something I never experienced before. Marie always treated those predatory urges as a transgression, something unforgivably evil I had to resist at all costs.

The Marquis said such notions were absurd. Denying our vampire urges was a form of abuse. After all, would I deny a predatory animal its right to feed? Would I condemn the lion for killing a gazelle when killing is in its nature? We were predators, he said, and he invited me to embrace my nature fully without shame or recrimination.

Seven seconds. That was how long it took me to cross the street and enter the bus stop. One more to rip the camera from its housing and smash it to pieces on the wall beyond. Before either of the students could react, I sank my fangs into the jugular of the male, gripping him tight against me and swallowing down great gulping mouthfuls of blood as it spurted from the vein. The female began to scream, but I clamped a hand over her mouth, fingers tightening like iron, and I saw her eyes go wide with silent horror as her lover gurgled in my grasp and then went silent and limp. Discarding his now useless carcass, I tore into her throat next, groaning with gluttonous delight as I drained her dry. Her heart soon went still, and I rose then, dripping with crimson gore on my face, my chin, my hands, my shirt drenched in it and sticking to my chest. Their bodies lay in a widening pool of blood, already darkening and going tacky on the tiles.

I wiped my chin with my fingers, then licked them, even as I turned to face the janitor.

He wore a set of headphones and was absorbed in his work, so he had no time to react or to run before I was on him in the blink of an eye. The broom clattered to the floor, and his fingers scrabbled to loosen my grip futilely. He began to scream, but I ripped out his vocal cords, blood spraying in an arch as I did so, and he stared right into my eyes as I moved in and latched onto his neck.

Death dealing was what I was made to do. There was an artistry in it, and with every mouthful, I felt stronger, more alive, like my body was just waking up.

The man died with a surprising grace, and as I dropped his corpse at my feet, I let out a roar like no sound I had ever made before, the cry of a caged animal finally set free.

The Marquis and his daughter stood in the doorway looking on, and as I gave an involuntary shudder of delight, he laughed. That laugh was the most beautiful thing I had ever heard, signaling approval and shared excitement.

As I wiped my lips, he smiled and said, "Now you know. You feel it. The power. You understand. Yes, my son. That is what it means to be a vampire. You are death personified. No shame. No guilt. This is what you were always meant to be. A hunter. Isn't it marvelous?"

He had called me his son, and he smiled with a fatherly expression of pride and love greater than any my own human father ever showed. I was shaken to my very foundations.

Returning to his side, I got down on one knee and bowed my head. For the first time, I understood Ernestine's reverence, and with a mixture of awe and wonder, I whispered, "Yes, Master."

Be the Flame, Not the Moth

Marie

Again, at dusk, there was a monk at the door with a note. This time, it read only a few words.

Signore Casanova requests the honor of your presence for a private event this evening at nine. A boat will be waiting at the quay.

Private event? My mind whirled at the meaning of the message. However, without a cell phone to ask for clarification, I was left wondering.

Turning over the paper, I saw scrawled on the back, "Dress for cocktails." The post script made me laugh out loud. Casanova was certainly full of surprises. Perhaps he was simply passing the time as we waited for information about the spy. Or perhaps he hoped to seduce me. Whatever his intentions, I was intrigued, just as he, no doubt, expected.

The wary part of me gave a momentary pause of caution, wondering if this was a trap. However, as the note was clearly in Casanova's own hand, and I had come to trust he was firmly in my corner, I dismissed this idea from my mind altogether.

Thanking my good sense for having brought along a little black dress and some new Manolo Blahnik pumps to match, I dressed quickly, twisted my hair into a knot, and arrived just in time to find Jenny waiting patiently for me aboard the same motorboat.

"Oh hey, there," she called, looking up from her cell phone. "Right on time."

"I don't suppose you know what he has planned?" I stepped carefully aboard and took my seat.

She laughed, starting the motor. "No way. I'm not spoiling his surprise. Hang on tight!"

We took off across the water, and before long, we reached the Piazza San Marco. As she pulled up to the mooring, I saw Casanova himself standing by the water's edge. He was smiling in the moonlight, watching our approach, and I could see a bouquet of flowers in his hand.

"Hey, Gio," said Jenny, tying off the lines so I could disembark. "Brought her just like you asked."

"Thank you, Jenny." He grinned, but never took his eyes off me, reaching for my hand to help me onto the shore.

"Need anything else?" From the corner of my eye, I could see her watching us both curiously as I took the flowers from him.

"No thank you, my dear. I will see the lady home myself."

She shrugged and laughed. "I bet. All right. I'm off, then. Have fun, you two. And don't do anything I wouldn't do."

Without replying, he held out his arm to me and led me away toward the square.

"You look lovely, madame." The catch in his voice told me his words were sincere, and I gave his arm a little squeeze.

"So do you," I said, and I meant it.

He was wearing a well tailored double-breasted black suit with a purple silk tie and pocket handkerchief to match. His hair was slicked back, though one rogue strand fell across his forehead, making him seem even more handsome for that tiny perfect flaw. I couldn't help but be impressed with the effort he had made, though it made me even more curious to understand just what this secret event might be.

We crossed the square in front of the cathedral, and I realized all eyes were on us. It was strange not worrying about their notice. I realized I had let go some of my fear of capture for the first time in two centuries. I wondered what we must look like to the tourists snapping pictures under the moon drenched tower. They stared as though we were movie stars. Their gaze was flattering, and I found myself carrying my head a little higher, putting on that practiced regal bearing that was at one time such second nature to me.

"You look every inch a queen, madame." He turned to look at me, and his eyes glittered like stars in the night. "You honor me with your trust and with your legendary beauty."

I laughed softly. "You Italians. You always know just what to say to a lady."

"We have a reputation to uphold, of course," he said, and his voice was teasing. "Me most of all. Indeed, it would be a shame to waste such a lovely evening without attempting to fulfill your expectations."

"Of course." And I laughed again. "I appreciate your sense of duty, signore."

"And am I living up to my reputation thus far?" As he asked the question, we walked across a little bridge over one of the narrow canals, and he took my hand in his to lead me on.

"I expected masks and a clandestine rendezvous, but you have kept me in sufficient suspense and flattery to be a delightful surprise."

We stopped abruptly in front of an unimposing and rather simple church building. He smiled and bowed his head. "I am your humble servant in these matters, my lady. I do hope by the end of the evening, you will be satisfied."

Before I could reply, a man stepped out of the main doors of the church and looked directly at us. "They are ready for you, signore."

I raised one eyebrow, but Casanova simply looked back at the man and nodded. "Excellent," he said, and with that he led me forward toward the large wooden doors.

"Are we going to church, Signore Casanova?"

"Something like that."

He laughed, but led me inside without any more information. Painted frescoes covered the walls and ceilings, sweeping arches rising high above. As the door closed behind us, the air was practically humming with energy. Several humans sat at the front of the room by the altar, all with musical instruments at the ready. One man was seated at an antique harpsichord, while the others held violins or violas. The entire church was bathed in the golden glow of hundreds of candles all around the place.

Mouth agape in astonishment, I whispered, "What is this?"

"Your surprise, your majesty." He led me forward to take a seat in one of the pews in front. "In this church in seventeen twenty five, Maestro Antonio Vivaldi's Four Seasons was first performed. Tonight, these gentlemen will repeat the performance just for you."

Eyes wide in wonder, I gasped, truly stunned. "Oh, Gio. I don't know what to say."

It was the first time I'd used his first name, and he smiled, pulling my hand to his lips and kissing it gently. "Then listen."

Without looking away, he gave the musicians a nod, and they began.

The acoustics of the building were astounding. As the strings worked in a frenzy, I could feel the sound reverberating in my chest, making my hollow heart ache as though it were almost beating once again. Every breath of the musicians sounded in my ears, their heartbeats adding an extra rhythm to the notes.

I leaned my head on Casanova's shoulder, and for that golden hour, nothing in the world existed outside of the whirling notes. The first movement, Spring, had been one of Louis' favorites, and the musicians played, I was transported back to the gardens of Versailles. I could almost feel the breeze through the hedge maze, the sound of water splashing in the fountains, the flutter of my fan, and the warmth of sunlight on my skin Most of all, I could remember my children playing at my feet. That day was one of my last before I was turned, and the memories brought me to tears.

Next came summer, then fall, and finally winter with its bittersweet denouement. Sitting in that church beside Casanova, his hand in mine, was one of the most magical and breathtaking experiences of my long life. Enthralled by the performance, I felt my whole body relax, and when at last the music ended, I cried with joy and gratitude.

"Thank you" was all I could choke out as the musicians bowed and filed out, but the words felt inadequate for the gift I had been given.

Casanova handed me his pocket handkerchief. "Has it been so long since someone gave you a nice surprise?"

It had, though until he asked the question, the thought had not occurred to me. I simply nodded and dabbed at my eyes.

"My lady, you have been in hiding for so long, you have forgotten what makes living worthwhile. Why fight so hard to survive if you cannot enjoy your immortality? Is it such a burden to get from one day to the next? We need art and nature and companionship and love to feed our soul, do we not?" He lifted my chin so I was looking directly into his eyes. "A woman like you should never be unappreciated or hidden away."

"Signore, I cannot repay you for this kindness."

His eyes softened. "I did not do it for payment, my lady. I did it because I wanted to share it with you. That is payment enough."

"How did you know what this would mean to me?"

Raising my fingers to his lips, he brushed a light kiss over them and smiled. "Madame, you arrived at my door as the lover of Herr Mozart. Knowing your heart was not difficult for a man like me. Forgive me, but you obviously did not love the man for his looks."

It was my turn to laugh. "No, that is true. Though he can be charming."

"All the more so because of his genius, yes? That ethereal music that stirs the soul."

"You do understand me," I said.

"I am learning to." His penetrating gaze was guileless and intoxicating, and I was mesmerized, unable to look away or move. "I would like to know you better. Once all of this is over, of course."

Still staring at him, I froze. It was one thing to flirt with a man like Casanova. Flirting was a game we had both learned long ago. But I could see from his expression he was not playing a game with me. He was sincere, not at all what I had expected from a man who had made a reputation with his conquests. "Signore, my life is very complicated. I am flattered and moved, but I don't want to bring my messy problems to your door."

"Madame, I am well aware of the...complexities of your situation." He smiled, kissing my fingers again. "I can offer you protection and a sincere affection. I don't expect you to answer now. All I hope for is that you will keep your heart open when the time is right and you are ready."

"I will remember and consider what you have said, signore."

"Please, do me the honor of calling me Gio. I like the way my name sounds on your tongue. I hope we are good enough friends for first names by now. At least in private." And he flashed a smile so charming, it was impossible for me to refuse.

"Very well. Gio. And you may call me Marie."

He bowed his head courteously. "Your name is safe upon my lips, Marie. It will never be spoken with dishonor or to bring danger to you and yours. You have my word."

When he looked back up, I leaned in and kissed him lightly on the cheek. "And yours is safe with me."

Given his reputation, I expected him to make more of an advance, but Casanova was a perfect gentleman. He knew the value of delayed gratification, and he clearly meant what he said about waiting until my situation was less complicated. Rather than move in for a more ardent embrace, he rose from his seat, held out his hand to me, and bowed deeply. "Allow me the honor of escorting you home, Marie."

"Of course." I placed my small hand in his larger one, and he helped me to my feet. He stopped at the door and whispered to the man who was still waiting at the door, presumably about arranging payment for the performance, and both men shook hands and smiled at one another before Casanova turned back to me and led me back out into the avenue. Our walk back to the boat was leisurely, and we did not speak, but I held his arm and smiled contentedly. I did not think about Raul or the Marquis or any of the other worries praying on my mind. It was enough to be present in the moment with him at my side and the silvery moon above. For the first time since leaving Saint Louis, I was not afraid.

When we arrived back at San Lazzaro, he helped me out onto the steps and walked me to the gate. There, he paused holding both my hands. "The annual Carnival masquerade ball takes place this week. I would be honored if you would be at my side. No one need know you are my guest."
I blinked. "You have managed to surprise me three times in a week."

"I hope you are pleased," he said, his eye crinkling at the corners good naturally.

"I had forgotten how it felt to be treated so well." I looked down at our clasped hands and then back up at his face. "I would be delighted. I can't remember the last time I went to a ball."

"With your dainty feet and light step, you should always be dancing."

He said this last without missing a beat, and I laughed at his easy flattery. "You have such a way with words, dear Gio. I fear I am half in love with you already."

Stepping closer, he lifted one hand to touch my cheek. "Is that a yes, then, Marie?"

I kept my eyes on his and whispered, "Yes," letting layers of meaning settle around that one word.

He kissed my lips with the delicacy of a butterfly's wings. "Jenny will bring a costume for you. Until then, goodnight, Marie."

And just like that, he pulled away and walked back to his boat, turning only when he reached the mooring to give me a small wave. I returned it, then watched as he sped away out of sight across the water.

The gate creaked a little as I opened it, and I couldn't help smiling. He made me feel like a young girl with a suitor again, and I was drunk with happiness.

The Night was Made for Loving

Sybill

"So explain again about this masquerade ball thing?"

Our gondolier was pulling up in front of the Piazza San Marco, and Byron gave me a sharp look of concern as he paid our fare. "Do you not want to go?"

"No, it's not that. Really. I'm excited about it." I took his hand and let me help me out onto the pier. "I just don't know the details, and I don't want to say or do something stupid, that's all."

Laughing, he shook his head, wrapping my arm in his as he led me away. "All right, lass. Let's start at the beginning. The masquerade ball is a centuries-old annual event. During Carnival every year, the vampire coven holds it here in the Doge's Palace."

He gestured to his right toward an imposing facade, indicating the building in question. I peered up, taking in the architecture. "Doge?"

"The Venetians call it the Palazzo Ducale."

"Oh. Duke's Palace. Got it."

"Yes. Because it's an event steeped in tradition, the humans believe it's put on by an exclusive club. In a way, I guess they're right." He flashed a smile at me. "Tourists like to take photos of the guests, and since we are all wearing masks, we allow it. But entrance is by invitation only."

We passed the cathedral where the bronze horses watched over us imposingly. I shivered, looking away and clutching his arm a little tighter. "And you were invited?"

"Of course."

I raised an eyebrow with alarm, stopping in the center of the piazza to look at him face-to-face. "Wait. Is there going to be a problem for me at this shindig since I don't have an invitation of my own? Will they kick me out?"

Chuckling at my wording, he shook his head. "My invitation includes a guest of my choosing. I usually take Polidori, but this time I want you by my side."

"Won't he be mad?"

"He gripes every year at having to leave his work. I think he will enjoy the solitude."

"Hmm." I raised a dubious brow, but he laughed softly and said nothing more on the subject.

We began walking again, and we passed by an outdoor cafe with people drinking coffee at little tables under the colonnade. The air was chilly, but the women were dressed in fur coats and looking elegant in the moonlight. Several waiters in tuxes attended on them, and one of them gave me a saucy wink as we passed. He was handsome, and I was flattered. I looked down with a little smile, and I heard him whisper, "Ai, Madonna."

I couldn't help but laugh at his outburst, but Byron turned to look at the man, scowling territorially. The waiter, backed away, bowing and touching his chest apologetically. I swear, I heard Byron growl before he turned to look down the alleyway ahead.

"He wasn't hurting anyone," I said. "I think he meant it as a complement."

"Complement, my ass." Byron sniffed. "Sorry. You should not have to tolerate the attentions of ruffians."

"Ruffians?" I laughed at the old-fashioned word. "I don't think it's fair to call him that."

"There are words I could use, but not in the company of a lady." He kept his eyes straight ahead, and though his tone was self-mocking, I could tell he meant every word.

"You worry too much. He wasn't bothering me."

"Perhaps not. But he bothered me very much." I saw his jaw twitch, and I wondered if I'd see a demonstration of the dangerous part of his 'mad, bad, and dangerous' self shortly.

I nearly said something else on the subject, but then I decided doing so would only keep the issue fresh in his mind. Changing the subject was a better option, so I did just that, deliberately keeping my tone light. "How do you know your way around here so well? Every twist and turn looks the same to me, especially in the dark. This city is a labyrinth."

His ruffled feathers settled down at the question, and he managed a smile. "I have lived in this city off and on for the last two hundred years. Live anywhere long enough, and you could walk it blindfolded."

I blinked contemplating the enormity of that prospect. What must living so long be like? I couldn't imagine all the changes he saw in all that time. The United States was a fairly new idea when he was born. He lived through the defeat of Napoleon, the American Civil War, the rise of industry, the invention of electric lights, railways, indoor plumbing, gas engines, airplanes, telephones, televisions, computers...heck, even most breeds of dog weren't even been thought of when he was a kid. How is it possible for someone to adapt to so much change? Then I realized it happened just as it had with everything. Gradually. There were no cell phones when I was little unless you were rich. Now, every two year old could use one. Our brains are remarkably flexible and able to adopt new technology until it becomes second nature. Whether you've lived twenty or two hundred and twenty years, change happens at the same speed. What would the world be like two hundred years in the future? I realized eventually I would find out. That thought was enough to have me reeling.

"You all right in there?" he said after I hadn't spoken for several minutes.

"Oh, yes. Sorry. I was just thinking."

"Never apologize for that, lass. I admire a woman with a sharp mind."

I gave his arm a squeeze. "Thanks."

He pulled me a little closer to his side, and we crossed a little bridge over a canal. I felt safe with him, and I leaned my head over onto his shoulder affectionately, dropping my voice to an intimate whisper. "Is this costume shop of yours very far?"

"It's just ahead," he said, pointing casually forward. In the middle of the darkened alleyway was a buttery glow of light streaming through antique glass windows onto the pavement below. A wooden sign hung over the door hidden in shadow, but I could see as we grew closer, an array of masks on display inside. "These are the best mask makers in the city. Here, we will find everything we need for the ball."

We stepped inside, and the sound of a merry little bell announced our entrance.

A round faced happy little man with a beard came forward to greet us, arms raised in greeting. "Welcome, my friends. Welcome. Please, make yourselves at home. If you do not see something you like, you have only to ask, and I will make you something special."

The array of choices was staggering. My eyes bugged out and my mouth opened wide as I stared around the room at all the colors and styles, looking every inch the tourist.

My obvious admiration pleased the little shop owner, and he grinned from ear to ear. "Take your time. The right mask will speak to you. Perhaps you would like to look at my book of costume photos?"

He led us to a large spiral bound photo album lying on the counter near the front of the shop to peruse. I stared down at the pages, amazed by the detail and inventiveness. The artist in me was fascinated to learn the creative process the little man used to complete his creations. Some masks were painted porcelain or papier mâché, while others seemed made of gold or silver. He had beautiful masks with festoons of feathers, seductive half masks, and still others covering the entire face and incorporating a cloak, hat, or wig to complete the disguise. Some looked like the face of a painted china doll, while others were strange and almost monstrous. One in particular had round circular glass eyes and an elongated shape like an antique gas mask.

"Creepy," I muttered, pointing a finger and wrinkling my nose.

Byron laughed. "That's a plague mask. Doctors used to wear them during the time of the Black Death. Polidori loves that one."

Shaking my head, I flipped the page only to find photos of a costume so beautiful I gasped. The dress was a soft purple with a swirling light gray embroidered pattern on the fabric and a tight corseted top. The mask was silver with black lace, and there was a stunning eighteenth century wig like something from a movie. I reached out to stroke the magical image longingly.

"You would look like a princess in that, lass," Byron said, leaning in close to whisper. He kissed my cheek affectionately, putting his arm around my waist. "We'll take it."

"Excellent!" said the little man, rubbing his hands together in a way that made me sure the costume must be extremely expensive.

Shaking my head, I reached to stop him. "Wait. Albé. That's too much."

"Nonsense," Byron said, waving his hand dismissively. "It's perfect for you. Just what I would have chosen myself."

I laughed. "It's so not me. Not at all."

"That's the point. A masquerade is all about being someone else. It's a fantasy. That is what makes it so perfect for you."

"I never fantasized about looking like that," I said, closing the book.

Byron curled his lip in a smirk. "No? Because I swear I heard your jaw hit the floor the moment you turned that page. Well, maybe I should cancel then."

He moved toward the register, and I reached out my hand to stop him. "Oh cut it out. Of course I want it."

With a deep laugh, he looked back at me, grinning. "There. Now was that so hard to admit?"

The shopkeeper reached into a pocket and pulled out a measuring tape, then began wrapping it around me in some shockingly intimate ways, making some quick notes. When he was done, he nodded and stepped back, tapping the pencil on the notepad. "And for you, signore?"

"I have my own, thank you." Byron smiled at him and handed over a credit card, not even asking the price.

The little man swiped the card, then brought him a clip board with a pen for Byron to sign. In a flourish, he signed "Noel Baron" and handed it back to the shop keeper. "I will send someone to collect the costume tomorrow."

The little man nodded, his jowls wobbling with his excitement. "Very good, signore. Very good."

We walked back out into the darkened street, the door bell jingling behind us as the door swung shut.

"You didn't have to go to all this trouble," I said, running price estimates in my head and feeling guilty about how much he spent on my account.

He stopped and turned to face me. "Let's get something straight. It's trouble I looked for. I want to go. You want to go. Costumes cost money. Stop thinking of yourself as an imposition. You are not."

"I feel like I'm in the way." I looked down at the stones. "I can't help Marie. I can't help Raul. I've pissed off Polidori. And you're being so sweet. I just…I can't pay you back or make it worth it."

His hands gripped my shoulders and he gave me a little shake. "Worth it? I enjoy your company. Is that so hard to believe?"

I paused for a moment, looking up into his deep blue eyes, and I felt my chin begin to tremble. "Yes. Sometimes."

"Well, stop it!"

The absurdity of that made me laugh, but I could feel the tears welling up, though I fought them back. He frowned at the pain he saw in my eyes. "Stop it, or I'll be forced to do something drastic."

"Like what?"

"Like this." And suddenly his lips were on mine, kissing me hard, his hands in my hair. He shoved me back against the stone wall of a building and pinned me there, parting my lips with overwhelming passion. The shock of it made me freeze for a moment, but I quickly found myself melting against him, kissing back with an urgency I hadn't anticipated. I lost myself in it, forgetting everything in the heat of that moment. Raul had kissed me tenderly, as though he thought I was a fragile thing he might break, but this kiss was far from that. This was a claiming. He knew how to kiss a woman and leave her breathless, tingling, and desperate with animalistic need. My body responded instinctively before my mind could process what was happening, my fingers clutching his shirt.

Just as abruptly, he stepped back, breaking the kiss and closing his eyes. My lips were swollen, and I gasped with shock at what we had done. "Oh," was all I said.

He moved away from me, leaving several feet between us and licking his lips with a darting tongue. "Better?" he said, the sardonic wit back in his voice.

I stared at him, back still against the cold damp stones, stammering. "Wha…uh…"

Shaking his head, he laughed, and the sound was brittle and cold in the wintry air. "I can't stand seeing a woman cry. You left me no choice."

"Uh..." I said, blinking and stumbling forward.

"Steady, lass. You'd think no one had kissed you before." He caught me by the shoulder to keep me from falling, but he still held me at arm's length.

"We...we should go."

"Mmm. Yes, I suppose so. Have you recovered yet?"

Unsure whether he was asking about my tears or the kiss, I nodded, pulling away from his grip. "I'm fine."

"Right then. Any other shopping you'd like to do while we're here? I had thought of getting one of those laptops you mentioned. Maybe you're right. I should try to become more modern."

I stared at him, trying to keep my knees from buckling. He was going to try to pretend everything was normal again, that nothing had happened between us. I felt as if I was in the bottom of a well, and I nodded dumbly as I struggled to recover my senses. "Sounds good."

My voice sounded hollow, but he ignored it, giving me a curt nod, gesturing on down the path ahead. "This way, then."

We both turned and began walking once more, maintaining a little distance between us, heading for another area of the city. I followed his lead, having no idea how to navigate in this winding maze of passageways and waterway bridges, all the while trying to wrap my head around the echoes of the kiss still lingering on my lips, his taste on my tongue.

As we rounded a corner, we entered a large square courtyard with several shops and cafes still open. Some small children kicked a soccer ball around in the corner, laughing and pushing one another. We strolled past the lighted windows, gazing in at the people inside. One of the shops had a window display full of musical instruments, and I stopped in my tracks, gazing up at them. Beside several violins and cellos stood a guitar. The frets had inlaid mother of pearl, and the delicate carving on the front showed it must be handmade, not something from a factory.

Byron was several yards ahead before he realized I wasn't next to him anymore. He turned back, raising one eyebrow. "Do you play?"

I shook my head, still looking through the window. "No. But Raul does."

Striding back to stand next to me, his hands stuffed down in his pockets, he gazed up at the guitar with me. "I see."

"He's very good."

"Is he?"

"That's how we met." I didn't dare turn to look at his expression, afraid I would see jealousy there in his eyes.

"Ah." He shifted his feet.

"He doesn't have a guitar anymore, I guess. It was left behind along with everything else when we ran from Saint Louis."

"That's a pity." I could tell he was straining to make his voice sound unemotional.

"Maybe it would help him once we find him if he could play. You know, remind him who he is." I turned to look at Byron, hoping for his understanding.

He shrugged, still not looking at me. "Would that make you happy?"

"It would make him happy, I think. I hope so, anyway. Do you think we could get it for him? Like a 'welcome home' present?" I bit my lip, looking at him intensely.

His eyes scanned the guitar again, then he turned and smiled at me. "Of course. Good idea."

Reaching out to touch his arm, I squeezed it gratefully. "Thank you. I think he'll love it."

Byron's smile tightened only for a second. "I'll be right back."

Shoulders squared, he turned and walked into the shop. A few minutes later, he came back with the guitar in a case, and he gave me a wink and a bright grin. "Done."

I reached to take it from him, but he shook his head and kept his grip on the handle. "I can carry it. Shall we?"

He held out his arm to me, and I saw a flicker of hope behind his eyes. That expression told me that he was afraid of losing my trust. I wrapped my arm around his, putting my hand in the crook of his elbow. He sighed softly as though he had been holding his breath until that moment, and I felt his shoulders relax. The awkwardness was gone, and he knew I wasn't angry over the kiss.

We passed over one more bridge into another shopping district and found an electronics store. The door showed it was nearly closing time, but the saleswoman greeted us with enthusiasm, and I guessed business had been slow that day. She spoke English with a strong Italian accent, but after a few starts and stops with Byron acting as translator, we were able to explain what we were looking for. Byron deferred completely to me in the selection, admitting freely he had no understanding of the specifications. He only knew what he wanted the laptop to do, and he made it clear he was willing to pay whatever it cost to have the right product for the job. In the end, I found one with voice recognition software built in and a keyboard wide enough to accommodate a man's fingers. We also bought a wireless printer and mouse alone with a ream of paper and some ink.

"That should do it," I said, pleased to be useful at last.

Byron paid, making arrangements for delivery to the island, and when we left, I saw the sales woman beaming happily as she locked the door.

"I think we made her quota for the week." I put my arm in Byron's again, and the two of us turned back to walk the way we had come.

He laughed. "Remind me to tell the abbot about all these deliveries. Otherwise, I'm afraid the monks will be completely baffled."

We arrived back at San Lazzaro an hour before dawn. Byron walked me to my room and put the guitar case inside near the door. "You can take care of it for him. And Sybill, I'm sure he misses you."

"I hope you're right," I said, following him back to the door.

"I'm always right. Haven't you learned that by now?" He was teasing me again.

I leaned in to kiss his cheek. "Thank you for a wonderful evening. I had fun tonight."

For a moment, he looked down at me, and I thought he was going to say something about what had happened or perhaps even kiss me again. Then just as quickly the moment was gone, and he simply patted my shoulder. "Goodnight, Sybill."

"Night," I said, but he was already walking away. I shut the door and leaned back against it with a heavy sigh.

IF THIS BE NOTHING

Mozart

In all these long years, I've learned building my life around anyone else only leads to heartbreak for us both. During my human life, I had a few dalliances with opera singers, though I never allowed anything to progress into something more serious because of my wife. Instead, I focused on the moment, enjoying it for what it was, letting it go when it had run its course.

This situation with Marie, however, was different. If things went wrong between us, the consequences for her were minimal, but for me they were dire, and I stood to lose much more than my heart. Though I could learn to accept changing the nature of our relationship into one of friendship, I got the feeling that such an alteration meant a dismissal from her company. I couldn't countenance that situation. I needed to remain with her at all costs, even if it meant sacrificing my pride.

I thought reminding her I was still the genius I had always been would rekindle her feelings. She just needed some space, I told myself. Time to recover from the events of the last few weeks. We all were under a strain, and she wasn't used to spending time in close quarters with anyone. Neither was I, if I was honest with myself.

To keep myself busy and out of her way, I buried myself in my work, the notes flowing out of me with passion and gusto, as quickly as they had when I was young. The piece was full of minor keys and somber notes, but there were moments of breathtaking beauty and light that left me almost giddy as I scrawled them from my teeming brain onto the page. Every moment was spent at my desk, writing as if the devil himself were driving me on. I didn't sleep. I barely stopped to have any blood. My one thought was of completing the piece and then playing it for Marie. I poured all of my worry, pain, and love into it, letting the music speak the feelings I did not dare to say aloud. She would hear it and know all the things I couldn't say.

At last, the composition was complete. In my mind, I heard a choir of angels singing in accompaniment, but as the pipe organ was the only instrument I had access to, I had tailored the piece to fit what was available. Without even pausing to look in a mirror to make myself presentable, I went directly to Marie's chambers to seek her out.

To my surprise, Marie wasn't there, nor was she anywhere to be found on the island, I discovered. Instead, there was a crumpled note she had left behind on her nightstand. She was meeting Casanova again.

Staring down at that handwriting I recognized so well, I remembered in vivid detail the man's conquests, and I felt my stomach drop, heart aching in my chest. My fingers closed into a fist, the note crumpling in my hand as I stood there like a fool. She had already moved on, and I mattered so little to her, she hadn't even bothered to tell me. All this time, I was afraid of treating her like a dalliance. I never realized our roles might be reversed.

Jealousy wasn't a feeling I was used to. In the past, I'd done as I pleased and walked away when a situation no longer suited me. I was confident in my genius, certain that if others did not appreciate what I had to offer, the defect was in them rather than myself.

Here, however, I had the least to offer and the most to lose, and recognizing that fact was painful to face.

Of course she would choose him over me. I had a genius, yes, but with a narrow scope and one which did not provide for her needs. I had neither rank nor power nor money, few friends and no allies to speak of. I had nothing to give her but my music and my wit, neither of which were practical in this situation. Music would not bring back her missing progeny, and as for wit, both Albé and Casanova, as men of letters, could provide a bounty of that for her.

Wordlessly, I strode over to the wastebasket and tossed the balled-up note away, gritting my teeth, my heart turning to stone. As I turned and left the room, I felt a cold calm descend into my bones.

The composition I had labored over so tirelessly as a gift to her was pointless now. Even the very idea of it made me sick. With a newfound sense of purpose, I marched to my quarters, grasped the pages from my desktop where they had been stacked awaiting her approval, and I ripped them to shreds, throwing the pieces onto the little fireplace hearth that served to heat the room, then lighting a match and watching them burn. The paper flared with brilliant flame, curling and turning to ash there on the grate. I stood watching as each note was wiped out of existence, vanishing into smoke, until nothing remained but a blackened mass upon the coals.

From this moment on, my heart would be cold to her, and I determined not to let it cause me another moment's pain. If she could discard me so easily without a word, then my own loyalties to her were at an end. No arguments. No recriminations. No remorse. I would only concern myself with self-preservation. I would work alongside her as long as it suited my needs, but my concerns were for myself alone and all the rest be damned.

Beauty Like the Night

Byron

I was kicking myself for the way I botched the evening with the kiss. Though I put on a good show for Sybill, I was shaken by the force of my emotions and devastated to think she didn't feel it too. My fingers still traced the shape of her lips on my own when I turned down the hallway to my room and ran directly into Polidori wearing his lab coat and carrying a file under his arm. As we collided, the folder fell to the floor, papers scattering everywhere across the stones.

"Dammit," I said. "Watch where you're going."

He scowled, bending to collect the pages. "I was paying attention, it was you who seem distracted. Where have you and Miss Know-it-All been all evening?"

"I thought you liked her. Careful. Your fangs are showing." I sneered at him, crossing my arms over my chest.

"I do like her. It's you I don't trust. You think you can do whatever you want? I know what you're doing." Jamming the sheets back into the folder, he stood back up, frowning at me.

I chuckled softly, rocking back on my heels. "I'm not doing anything, you insufferable git. The poor girl needed to get out, that's all. She doesn't know anyone. I'm trying to make her feel welcome."

"Pah. I know exactly what you're trying to do. I've seen it all before. You think you can make her your new plaything. Leave that girl alone. She's not for you. Marie said so." He squinted at me, shaking his finger.

"Marie said so." I put on a mocking falsetto, rolling my eyes. "Do you have any idea how ridiculous you are right now?"

"Say what you like. I know I'm right. You think you're so smart, but I see straight through you." His self-righteous smugness was unbearable.

"Do you? It must be a burden being such a pompous jackass all the time. How you manage it, I'll never know." I stepped forward and sniffed, wrinkling my nose. "Ugh. You smell like death and formaldehyde."

His lips pressed together in a line, and he glared at me without speaking, hands clenched tightly on the folder. For a moment, I felt a twinge of guilt.

Shaking my head, I laughed, putting my hands down into my pockets. "Go back to the basement, Polly. You have a job to do."

"Go to hell." Nostrils flaring, his jaw clenched, and then he pushed past me.

With those words, my guilt disappeared. Just before he turned the corner, I called after him. "By the way, I'm taking the girl to the ball this year. You understand, I'm sure."

He whirled back around, eyes twitching. "Bastard."

"My father would be very sorry to hear it, though perhaps not surprised. Scurry along." I waved him away, and he stomped off fuming without another word. I kept my eye on him until he disappeared from view, then strolled back to my room, whistling Tchaikovsky's 1812 Overture.

I passed Marie's door, but she was clearly still out. Absently, I wondered where she might be but decided she deserved her secrets just as I did.

Back in my room, I stripped off my clothes, turned out the light, and stretched myself out on the satin sheets, staring up at the canopy curtains over my head. There in the dark as I struggled for sleep, I thought of Sybill. The lines of her neck. The bones beneath her skin. That glorious skin, soft and glowing, yearning to be touched. The way her body fit perfectly to me. I could still feel the press of her lips on mine as though we had only just parted. She should be mine.

Even so, Polidori was right about one thing, though I hated to admit it. Sybill's heart was still his. My brother's. And not being able to claim those lips as my own was like a second death each time I saw her. Every room seemed small when she was in it, just large enough to hold us both together. Made to cause the closeness.

I knew I had to continue my charade of disinterest, and the thought tormented my soul. I was dying slowly with the weight of my desire. Damn my honor, I thought. And damn hers too if that was the reason she was not beside me in the dark.

The masquerade ball was my chance to make her mine. What woman could resist such a magical night? She would put her arms around me, and the night would do the rest. I held onto that tiny bit of hope as I slid into sleep at last.

Ripe for the Picking

Ernestine

"He isn't ready," I said firmly, fists clenched at my sides as I stood in the Master's chambers.

Leaning over a long table, he spread maps over its surface, and as I spoke, he barely looked up. Instead, he waved his hand dismissively and chucked disapproval at my words. "Tsk. Nonsense, girl. You saw him. That look on his face. He is one of us now. He has given himself to me. He said so himself."

"I don't trust it," I said. "What if it is a trick?"

"To what end? He had opportunity to run. Instead, he remained with us. He wants to stay. He wants to be one of us."

Frustrated, I gritted my teeth, hitting the table hard with the flat of my hand. "He doesn't know what he wants yet. We still don't know where his loyalties lie with regard to the deposed queen. If all goes to plan, we will have her here in custody. How will he react to that?"

"How will you react, my girl?" He glared right back at me in challenge. "After all these years, do you know the answer to that question for yourself?"

"I fail to see how it relates to me in any way," I said, my chin jutting out defiantly.

He snorted a laugh, shaking his finger at me with a crooked smirk. "It's as relevant as your question about his loyalties."

Nostrils flared, I stood there, shaking with rage. "Do all my years in service to you mean nothing? How can you question my loyalty now? After everything I've given up and sacrificed and done in your name?"

Sighing, he shook his head and looked back down at his maps, forehead furrowing with concentration. "Come now, child, there is no need for this childish jealousy. He is to be your brother. His success and yours are linked inextricably."

"My brother?" I spat the word, grimacing at the very thought. How could he say such a thing? Did he not understand how hurtful it was? Did he not care?

"You will teach him everything he needs to know. He will follow you now, sharing all the secrets I've given you. It's an enormous responsibility and opportunity for you."

I couldn't hide the disgust in my voice. "Me? Teach him?"

"You are not a parrot, my dear. Pray, stop sounding like one." An exasperated gasp escaped from my lips, and he looked up at me with an eyebrow quirked in question. "I believe you told me only moments ago of your loyalty, and yet here you are, questioning my direct instructions."

My mouth opened, but there was nothing I could say in response, and so I shut it again with a snap.

"You are not a fish either." He was laughing at me. I could see it in his expression even if he didn't make a sound. Smirking triumphantly, he looked back down at his plans. "The boy has been woefully neglected. You can see it as well as I. If he is to be useful to us, he will require training. I trust no one so well as you. There's a good girl. I want him to heel on command. You know what it requires."

I did know. I remembered vividly my own training. I had trained others in the past, but never with the same level of importance as in this situation. This was a new level of trust between the Master and myself, and I wanted more than ever to please him.

"The boy is ripe for the picking. Now is your moment. I have been preparing you for this your whole life."

The silence in the room was deafening for a moment while I considered what he was asking of me. "Master, haven't I always pleased you?"

At that word, he looked up and smiled. "That's my good girl."

I melted at those words, dropping to my knees before him. "If I do as you ask, what will be my reward?"

"If?" There was a warning in his tone that had me bowing my head. "Are you asking me for punishment, hmm?"

A thrill went through me, and I looked up with a crooked smile. "It has been a while."

"Will it properly motivate you to do as I say?"

"Oh yes, Master," I said, head still bent low in supplication.

"Very well," he said coolly. "Go to the dungeon and wait for me on your knees. I will be there presently. Once we have finished our business there, I will expect you to make the room ready for his training. Are we understood?"

"Yes, Master."

Saying nothing more to me, he returned to his work, clearly dismissing me, and I quietly rose, going to do as he bid me. My heart was light once more. He did still care for me. I was still worthy of his time and training. I was still his to command. Whether he made me wait half an hour or a week, I was determined to follow his instructions to the letter.

Cicero

Vincent

Back when prohibition was in full swing, I bought a warehouse in K-Town in Cicero, so when my hotel was destroyed, I moved my base of operations there to I regroup. Replacing all the poor bastards who died that day was a pain in the ass, but at least it wasn't a total loss. I had guys working security in South Side too, and they were used to taking orders.

The middle management positions were harder to fill. I brought in a bookkeeper from Detroit. The schmuck kept stuttering whenever I asked him a direct question, so I had to show him just what was going to happen to him if he fucked up. He was properly motivated after that.

By far, the worst thing about the destruction of my hotel wasn't the pain of losing my home, though I'd lived there for almost ninety years. The loss of my black-market blood production facility and all the stock I had in the pens was something I wasn't sure I'd ever get over. Not only did it mean an abrupt loss of business, but also rebuilding the operation would take years. I had some product in cold storage, but not nearly enough to fill the demand. Yeah, sure, I could spike the cost to try and make lemonade out of this sour deal, but nothing I did would cut the bitterness I felt.

Goldie turned me over for that two bit piano playing chump. Hell no, I wasn't going to forget anytime soon, and I would to make her pay for what helping her cost me. I wasn't the type to lie down and take it when someone double crossed me, and that was exactly what this was. Nobody was going to convince me otherwise. She knew what she was doing, waltzing into my joint. She never gave a shit about anyone but herself, that dame. I should have remembered that.

What is it they say? "The enemy of my enemy is my friend?" Yeah. That. I decided that would be my golden rule from then on out. And them as wasn't her enemies yet were going to change their mind or be begging for mercy. Al Capone didn't trust me with his hit list for nothing. I know how to make people see things my way.

First things first, I called in some markers. There were people in Venice who owed me. People who already didn't like the idea of helping her get what she wanted and who thought it was high time that son of a bitch Casanova got taken out.

Surprise, surprise, they told me he was doing everything he could to get that dame into his bed, and she wasn't giving him any resistance. According to them, she had forgotten all about Wolfie already and had set her cap on the head of the Venice coven. Of course she had. One more poor sap who would get what was coming to him.

Those Venetians had their old fashioned ways, always smiling in their enemies' faces while they stab them in the back. Not me. I always favored a direct approach. Stab folks in the face, preferably with an audience. People respect that. None of this cloak and dagger shit.

I gave direct orders. "Put pressure on them monks," I said. "Make them see they'd better turn her and everyone with her out on their asses. Let her see how she likes it."

"But Signore DeLuca, they're men of God. We can't threaten them," the guy tried to tell me.

"The hell you can't," I said. "They're scared of dying like anyone else. You think them monks are in a hurry to meet their maker any more than you and me? I don't care how you explain it to them, but you do it. Remind them they've got vampires living in their place. Tell them in detail what happens when vampires get hungry. Show 'em if you got to. I don't give a shit. Just do it."

"Signore, we can't just..."

"Shut the hell up," I said, cutting him off. "You can, and you will, because if you don't, you and all your buddies are going to be getting a demonstration of what happens when people tell me no. Capiche? And as for that bastard, Casanova, he's on my list. You got two choices. You work with me, or you go down with him. That's how it's going to be. There ain't no in between, you got me? I'm sending someone to clean up that mess and to take care of her while I'm at it."

Needless to say, the guy saw things my way. By the end of our conversation, he was licking my boots and saying "Yes sir" to everything I told him.

I knew exactly what my next move had to be. I'd looked at things from every angle, and it was the only option that made sense. I knew a guy who knew a guy, and in the end, I had the information I needed, the phone number for the bitch who worked for The Marquis.

Yeah, I knew she was the one who blew up my hotel. She would pay for that one day. But I reminded myself that in this case, we were stronger if we worked together. Once Marie was dealt with, then I could afford to even out the score between us. I could be patient, though. I had to be.

The phone rang several times before she finally picked up. Maybe she didn't like strangers calling her either.

"Hello?" she said, a kind of wary tension in her voice.

"I ain't no telemarketer, just so you know. We ain't friends, either, in case you're wondering that too," I said, "This is Ernestine Lambriquet, yeah? This is Vince DeLuca. I hear you got some business to discuss with me."

There was dead silence on her end for a moment while she dealt with that information.

I laughed. "Yeah, I ain't dead. I figure it's time you and me had a chat."

"Bit late for that, isn't it?" Her voice sounded sharp and tense, like a piano wire ready to snap.

"It ain't never to late to talk business."

"What is it you want, Mister DeLuca?"

"I think you and me got some mutual interests we should talk about," I said, leaning back in my office chair. I had her running scared, which was all to my liking.

"Mutual interests? I fail to see how you come to that conclusion."

Setting my feet on top of the desk and crossing my ankles, I laughed again. "You want to find Marie and make her pay. I've got my reasons for wanting it too now. Seems to me, I've got some information you want, and I'm willing to swap that, plus give you some manpower where you need it in exchange for you doing a few things for me."

"What sort of information?" I could hear the change in her tone from wariness to interest.

"Well, I ain't telling you details until you agree to give me what I want. After all, fair's fair, and you can't get something for nothing. That's just how the world works."

"And why should I trust your information is worth anything, given our last interaction?"

"Ha! Interaction? Well, if that ain't a five dollar word to describe something that ain't worth five cents. Listen, missy. Here's what I know. I can tell you where she's at. I can tell you who's helping her. And I got the muscle to help you bring her in. What I don't got is time to spend sitting around making nice. You got a guy you can send to lead my team, I'll give you all the rest."

Again, she was quiet, and I knew she was considering my offer. "All right, let's say I do this. What do you get out of it?"

I smiled. The negotiation had begun. "Same as you, I'm guessing. It's personal. I get to even a score. She screwed me over, and she's got to pay for that. Now, I don't know what she's done to you, and frankly I don't care. You can get your jollies ripping out her lungs while she's still using 'em for all of me. Hell, I'll even pay to watch that on my big screen."

"I thought you were helping her. Why should I believe your feelings toward her are changed?"

Putting my feet back down on the floor, I leaned forward, my elbows on the desktop. "Well, being blown up gives you a little perspective on things, Miss Lambriquet. Wouldn't you agree?"

This time, she was the one who laughed. "I suppose so."

"Sounds like we understand one another," I said, tapping my fingers on the desk.

"Very well," she said. "Allies."

"That's a good way to put it," I said.

"Tell me your plan," she said. "I'll send someone I know I can trust to bring her in."

"Now you're talking my language." Grinning in triumph, I gave her the location of the monastery and explained about the call I had made.

"You'll send her running," she said, a tone of irritation in her voice.

"Relax, sweetheart. I'm narrowing her options. Where do you think she's going to turn when she can't stay in that joint anymore? That island she's on is like a fortress. There's a wall and a fuckin' moat for Chrissakes, and if you think them friends of hers ain't going to fight for her, you ain't as smart as I thought. Who do you think she's going to ask for help, huh? Only person she can. Casanova. I want that guy gone too. I want him to hurt just as much as I do her, and this way, we'll catch them in one net."

"I see," she said, and her voice sounded a little calmer.

"I like efficiency, Miss Lambriquet. I've got the chance to make both of them pay for disrespecting me. I plan on making sure I don't miss that opportunity."

Again, she went quiet, and I could hear the sound of a pen scratching on a piece of paper.

"You making notes? I like that. You seem like a dame who gets things done. Too bad we didn't work together sooner."

"Yes, well, you were the one who didn't meet with me before, remember?"

With a low chuckle, I shook my head. "Yeah, hindsight is a bitch. Learned my lesson the hard way, I guess. I won't make that mistake again, believe me."

It was her turn to laugh, and I heard the pen move again. "I'll take care of things on my end. Just make sure your people are in place when I need them, understood?"

"Right back at you. And Miss Lambriquet? I want to be the first one to know when they're caught, yeah?"

"Of course, Mister DeLuca."

"Listen, you got that kid of hers? The one she came here all worried about?"

"That information isn't relevant to this conversation, Mister DeLuca. Whether he is or not is not important for you."

In refusing to tell me, I knew the answer was yes, and I smiled in the knowledge. "Isn't it? Hmm. Maybe that's something we can revisit once this business is concluded. I might have something to tell him that might make him really damn relevant. But I'll let this play out first before we get into that negotiation."

"As you say, Mister DeLuca," she said. "In the meantime, I have some calls to make."

"You do that. Keep me in the loop. You've got my number now. Use it." Without waiting for her response, I hung up. I had my own people to get in touch with, and there was no time to waste.

Lie to Me

Sybill

For weeks, I had been reading the book Byron had loaned me. Full of his poetry, it was flattering he had trusted me with a book which clearly meant so much to him. This book was one of his prized possessions, and as I read further through it, I could see why. His words, old fashioned as they seemed at first, were powerful and emotional. He told a story, but in doing so, he revealed much more about himself than a simple narrative would suggest. Through his eyes, I could see each place he visited throughout his human life, and the ways the events he lived through changed and shaped him into the man I was just getting to know.

He had not just given me a book to read. He had given me a copy of his soul and trusted me not to damage it or hurt him. Some passages were so emotionally revealing, it was almost breathtaking in their naked honesty. I felt responsible to honor the gift.

To show my understanding of what his gift meant, I decided to produce a painting that would be as revealing of my own soul. I didn't know if he would understand it in quite the same way, but I had reason to hope so after my reading.

I began work on a painting of him in secret, a mix of the way he presented himself and the inner self he had let me see through his poems. I spread out the multiple sketches I had made of him and used them as a basis for the likeness.

My painting showed him at work, which is how I pictured him. I doubted he'd ever been painted that way. He tended to enjoy working alone, and I couldn't imagine him allowing anyone near enough to observe him, despite the fact writing took up far more of his time than he even admitted to himself. Something in him resisted letting anyone think he actually worked, even though he did, and quite tirelessly at that.

Around the central figure of him shown in classical and formal style, I added swirling and increasingly fantastical images from his writing, places he had been, ideas or characters he had expressed, even bits of nature or themes from mythology, all of it seeming to spring from his teeming brain. All of this against a stark black background, heightening the imaginative quality of his creations which hovered around him like moths to a flame.

I kept the painting covered when I wasn't working on it so he wouldn't see it whenever he barged into my room to chat or to drag me off somewhere on a small adventure.

When I finally made the final brush stroke on the canvas, I felt a moment of serenity that only comes when a piece is complete. Though it may not be the best work you ever produce, you know that if you add or change anything else, you will spoil it, and as it is, the piece is the very best you are capable of in that moment.

I stood there, tilting my head, examining my work, and knew it was time to let him see it. I had never done a detailed study of someone in such a personal way, and I feared he would find it too revealing. Perhaps I had seen things he wouldn't want others to know. At last, I decided to risk his reaction anyway. I had painted him as I saw him, and to me that honest vision was beautiful and complex.

Paint stained my fingers and the heel of my hand, the shirt I had worn in place of a smock covered in flecks and streaks of color, but I was too excited to bother with more than a cursory cleaning before I went in search of Byron.

He would be in the library, I knew, and my feet flew on their way to him with urgent delight. Before I arrived there, however, I heard voices in the corridor. They were far away and whispering, but with my heightened sense of hearing, I could still make out the speakers. I froze in place and listened, excitement forgotten.

Byron was talking to a man, and his voice was agitated. "We would never put you in danger. I give you my word. You will be protected."

"Your word will not save us from these creatures." The man had an accent I couldn't place.

I heard Byron sigh audibly. "You promised to give them refuge."

"My lord, we have been most patient. But you told us this was a temporary situation. We owe you a debt, of course, but we do not have the means to take in so many and for so long. Surely you can understand that."

"It is temporary. We only need a little longer."

"We understand, my lord, but their continued presence is not one that we are equipped to manage. In the interest of our own safety, we urge you to find another place for these newcomers."

"You're kicking us out?"

"Our younger brothers are frightened, my lord. Surely you can understand their fear. They have guessed at the nature of your illness as well as that of your companions. It is too dangerous for you to remain."

In all the time we stayed in the monastery, I had not once considered what the monks thought of us. Clearly, this was not the first time Byron had been forced to plead for our continued presence here. I had taken for granted the free blood, the spartan but comfortable rooms, the garden, the library, and the safety of the island as a safe haven from our enemies. It never occurred to me these were luxuries that might be taken away.

"They are my family. You are putting us at the mercy of those who seek our death. You know as well as I this illness is not a punishment from God or the work of the devil. It is an incurable sickness. We have no safe place to go."

Hearing him beg for more time made me feel ashamed and spoiled.

"Our history is one of caring for the sick. We will give you some time, my lord, but only until the end of the month. I am afraid we must ask you to find other lodgings by then."

"I haven't finished my translations! Dammit, surely you wouldn't toss me out. You need me. I need this work. My mind without employment is apt to lead me to dangerous action. Here, I can keep my thoughts focused and avoid temptation. You understand me? I need to work."

"Until the end of the month, my lord. Any longer is impossible. Speak to the others and make plans."

I heard feet shuffle on the stones, then walk away down a distant hall.

"Damn!" Byron said, and then there was the sound of something shattering against a wall.

Panic attacks were something I used to deal with periodically as a teenager. Usually, they were brought on by something with my father. Years had passed since I had one, but the signs were unmistakable. A wave of nausea washed over me, and I bent over, clutched my stomach, closed my eyes, and took several slow, deep breaths to calm my nerves. I almost laughed at the absurdity of the idea of a vampire suffering from anxiety, but then the feeling grew even stronger, and I couldn't think at all anymore. Breathing was no longer automatic for my body, but cleansing breaths had always helped me get through the worst of my attacks in the past, and I fell back on what I knew. It took concentration to fill my lungs. Even stranger was the recognition that my heart was silent and still, though in the past the thump would have roared in my ears. Could a vampire have a heart attack? I was sure the answer was no. Whether I could keep myself from throwing up blood in the hallway was another matter entirely.

I bent myself at the waist, trying to calm my stomach and my mind. Slowly, I counted backwards from ten, and when I reached the bottom, I did it over. The fourth time through, I finally started believing I might be okay after all.

I stood there frozen in the hallway, unsure of what to do next. I realized I didn't know Byron well enough to anticipate whether he would want company in this situation or need time alone until his anger passed. I wished I had an easy answer to give, but I had no idea how to solve this problem. Being useless, I was embarrassed to show my face.

Worst of all, the reason I came looking for him in the first place seemed selfish and childish. I had wanted his approval and attention. My painting seemed stupid in comparison to this catastrophe threatening us all.

Gaining perspective on the scope of what was at stake made me realize I couldn't keep acting like an entitled princess. I needed to contribute to finding a solution or I was going to drag everyone down as they tried to carry me.

The practical part of me wondered if I should tell him to cancel our Carnival plans and return the costume. A masquerade ball seemed so trivial now. After a few moments, however, I realized choosing not to have fun would not make things any better. Byron was excited to share the evening with me, and our plans were already made. I decided the best thing I could do was make sure Byron had a good time, free from worry, and not let on I knew anything was wrong. He had been hiding the controversy with the abbot since our arrival, and I didn't want him to think I had been eavesdropping, even though I had, or make his worries worse by adding my own concerns on top of them.

I turned and walked to my room, determined to find ways to make him happy until I found a way to be useful.

As You Wish

Byron

Years ago when I first moved to San Lazzaro, I was overjoyed to discover that one of the monks had been a junior fencing champion in his youth. I hadn't had a decent sparring partner in decades. Polidori refused to participate in "that barbaric sport" as he called it. Idiot. What he really meant was he had no skill and didn't like to be bested.

Brother Julian and I practiced every Tuesday and Thursday after Vespers. He saw it as a form of exercise. As for me, however, I wanted to be ready to face my enemies.

The evening the abbot informed me we had to move, Brother Julian appeared at my door as usual, and though he never told me he knew about our eviction and I never mentioned it to him, I got the sense from his looks he was feeling nostalgic about our years together, sensing our acquaintance was drawing to a close. I welcomed his company and walked with him to the open courtyard where we habitually sparred. Just as with all friendships in my long life, I had known one day he would be gone while I would remain unchanged, but having a firm date for the ending made me feel all the more aware of how much his companionship had brought to my life.

We suited up, bowed to one another, and then... "en garde."

Fencing is like a dance, but a deadly one. The movements are made with surgical precision. Any false move or fault in equipment can mean murder to the opponent. Thus, our practice was an act of ultimate trust. A test of life.

I was better than he was. We both knew it. I always had been. After all, I had nearly two hundred years more experience. Brother Julian was also getting older, while I was not. He got in a few good hits that night, mainly because I allowed it. Still, in the end, he was defeated.

By the time we were through, he was winded and sweating, and I could feel the ache in my foot, though I knew it would fade quickly. We bowed once more, and I clapped him on the shoulder, smiling, thanking him for a good match.

Part of me wished I never had to use this skill, yet the reckless soul yearning for excitement hoped I could one day use it to crush Marie's enemies.

The real benefit to the fencing practice for me was always the opportunity to clear my busy mind. With sword in hand, I was forced to concentrate on the action and couldn't brood over my troubles. Afterward, I approached daily problems with a fresh perspective. Such was the case with our eviction from the abbey. I walked back from the courtyard, realizing there was no sense fretting over the move. Worrying would not change what must be done. We needed to make a new start and be done. That meant breaking the news to the others as soon as possible.

With that in mind, I decided to tackle the most difficult conversation first to have it over with. That meant talking to Polidori. I knew he would be upset, but waiting would only complicate matters. Thus, rather than returning to my room or going to the library, I turned in search of the doctor. It didn't take long to locate him. The scent of fresh corpses was easy for me to follow.

"We have a problem," I said without preamble, strolling into Polidori's lab.

He didn't look up from the slides he was examining under the microscope. "Only one?"

"I am being serious."

"As am I. We have many problems. To which are you referring?" Making some notes on a clipboard, he continued his work. "If you thought you might take me to the masquerade ball because your plans with the girl fell through, I made other arrangements for my evening."

"We have to move out of the abbey by the end of the month."

At this, he looked up in complete shock, eyes wide with alarm. "Move? I can't. I am just starting to make progress. I can't move all this equipment, my specimens, my test subjects. You have to tell them. It's impossible."

"The abbot insists."

He pulled off his latex gloves and threw them into the trash. "Well, insist back. I cannot relocate. Not now. I'm on the verge of a breakthrough."

"You are always on the verge of a breakthrough, Polly. I have done my best. They refused. It is over. We have no options left."

He tossed his pen across the laboratory table with frustration. "I knew bringing the three of them here to stay with us would ruin everything. Didn't I say that? These monks are not scientists. They are full of superstitions and fear of what they don't understand. We should never have let the others move in. It was too many of us. I knew it."

"Stop being so dramatic and self-centered. Where else could they have gone, you fool? They had no one."

"Women are always trouble. Always. That's your weakness. You and your urges have led us to this." He was pointing a finger at me in accusation.

I rolled my eyes. "Oh please. This has nothing to do with my urges. They are family, for Christ's sake, or have you forgotten?"

"Your family," he said, scowling.

"Ours," I said firmly.

"They brought nothing but trouble from the moment they arrived. And now they have cost us our home." He had a dejected, hangdog look as he said these words.

I slapped him on the back for encouragement. "Pack. We will find a place."

"How can I pack up my life's work?" Whining, he turned, open palmed with a sweeping gesture toward the entirety of the lab. "It took me years to set this up."

I nodded. "And you will do it again. Somewhere else."

Polidori frowned thoughtfully. "Maybe they will let me stay if the rest of you go. I am no trouble to them."

Again, I patted his shoulder. "We need you, Polly. I need you. We are your family."

He stood still, gazing back at me in silence.

With a smile, I picked up the pen from where he'd thrown it and slipped it into the pocket protector of his lab coat. "Start packing."

I turned to go, and he called out to stop me as I reached the door. "You're going to buy me a new centrifuge."

"Make a list," I said, looking over my shoulder at him. "I'll see to it that you have what you need."

"It won't be cheap." He picked up the pen and began writing in a notepad.

I chuckled as I turned away once more. "I expect not."

From there, I decided to go looking for Marie. However, she was not in her room or anywhere else to be found. After checking her usual haunts, I reasoned she must have gone out. I left a note on her door, asking her to speak with me as soon as possible, and then I decided to spend some time working on translations in the library.

However, no sooner had I entered the library than I found several boxes surrounding my desk. I smiled, knowing inside were the fruits of my shopping trip with Sybill. I smiled even more remembering my stolen kiss.

I picked up the costume box and went in search of Sybill, leaving the computer boxes behind. She would have to help me understand that machine and show me how to make it work. But the costume was something that brought me joy, and I couldn't wait to see it on her.

Her door was open when I arrived, and as I peeked my head in the door, I saw her lying on her stomach on her bed, reading the copy of Don Juan she had borrowed. She was over halfway through and so immersed in the reading she didn't notice me in the doorway until I spoke.

"Knock, knock."

She looked up and smiled as soon as she saw me and what I was carrying. "Is that what I think it is?" Shutting the book, she put it down on the bed and rolled off onto her feet.

"Well, it isn't a new car. Sorry." I laughed, handing the box over into her outstretched hands.

"Can't drive a car here anyway." Chuckling, she carried the box over to the bed and opened it carefully. The costume was wrapped in tissue paper, and when she peeled it back and got her first glimpse of the fabric, she squealed with excitement. "Oh my god, it's even prettier than I thought!"

I watched her pull the dress from the box and hold it up against her body. Grinning, she looked down and swished the skirts. My heart squeezed with happiness to see her so clearly delighted. "It will be beautiful on you, lass."

"Oh, Albé. I love it!" Her eyes lifted to meet mine, full of joy.

I smiled back at her. "You'll need to try it on to be sure the measurements were correct."

"Okay. Turn around for a minute."

The thought of her undressing in my presence made my body react in ways that were uncomfortable, so I was only too happy to face away from her with hopes she would be too preoccupied to notice while I adjusted my trousers.

I heard her take off her shirt and toss it on the bed. Then she unzipped her jeans and began pulling them down. I squeezed my eyes closed and tried to think about anything else besides the knowledge she was stripped to her underwear just behind me. Fabric rustled, and I heard her squirming against it. I bit my lip.

Then she tapped me on the shoulder. I opened my eyes and turned to face her. "Can you lace this thing up in back? This is a two-person job."

I swallowed hard and nodded slowly. She smiled and turned, revealing her back. The dress was open from her shoulders to below her waist. Her back was covered in a stunningly beautiful tattoo of a dragon, tail entwining her ribs and body circling up to her shoulder. Around the dragon were branches full of cherry blossoms. I had never seen anything so striking. My fingers were aching to trace the design on her skin, and I wanted to see the rest of it. I pressed my lips together, then I reached out and began working the laces, hoping my fingers wouldn't tremble. I forced myself to keep my mind on the task, pulling and tightening the strings against her spine. She stood very still, hands on hips, patiently waiting as I continued my work.

"How tight do you want this?"

"Well, since I don't have to breathe, let's see how tight it can be without becoming uncomfortable. I'll tell you when to stop."

"All right. You might want to hold onto something."

She turned her head to look at me over her shoulder, raising an eyebrow. "You seem to know what you're doing back there."

I laughed. "I've had some practice in my day."

"I so don't want to know."

"I was married, you know," I said, pulling tighter. "But after the divorce, I had more experience loosening corsets than tightening them."

"La la la la la!" She poked her fingers in her ears and shut her eyes, laughing. I gave the strings a hard yank, and she fell back against me. "Oh!"

She smelled like cinnamon. I closed my eyes and breathed in the scent of her hair. "Sorry. I did tell you to hold on."

"I thought you were joking." She laughed, stepping forward and out of my arms. "I think that's tight enough."

"Let me tie it, then." I moved closer again and finished it off with a bow. When I was done, I put my hands on her shoulders lightly, daring to touch her bare skin. "There. All done."

She turned to face me, grinning from ear to ear. "How do I look?"

I looked her up and down, my eyes following every curve. Finally, I licked my lips. "Breathtaking. You'll be the most beautiful woman there."

Twirling experimentally on her toes, she lifted her arms and spun gracefully. "You think so?"

"Without question." I stepped forward and bowed. "May I have this dance?"

She stopped and stared at me. "Oh god. I don't know how."

I blinked. "Have you never waltzed before?"

"Well, only at my sweet sixteen party with my father. I don't think that counts."

"I'm not much of a dancer either," I admitted. "This foot of mine can be a bit of a problem. Still, as long as the music is slow enough and we can take our time, I'm sure we will do an admirable enough job of it. They'll be too dazzled by your looks to notice a few missteps, and we can always blame it on my error rather than yours."

I winked at her and she nodded, smiling once more. "Deal. And anyway, I really just want to wear the costume. I don't really go for stuffed shirt dancing."

"Stuffed shirt?" I chuckled at her phrasing.

"You know, old fashioned. No offense."

"None taken." I said, shaking my head.

"I'd better take this off before it wrinkles, don't you think?" She looked down at the dress admiringly once more. "Help me out of it?"

"As you wish." I shrugged.

She turned her back to me and I began loosening the laces. I was forced to touch her skin this time, and each brush of my fingers sent a thrill through me like a jolt of electricity. When it was done, I moved away quickly as though I had been burned. "There." I turned my back, trying to steady myself. I heard the skirt whispering against her body as it slid to the floor, then she stepped out of the dress. Though my eyes were closed, I knew she put the dress back into the box. I tried to send my mind far away as she put her clothes back on.

Finally, she said, "Done! You can turn around again now."

I breathed a sigh of relief before I looked back toward her.

She slipped on her shoes and then looked up, stuffing her hands in her pockets. "Cool. Well, it definitely fits. I can hardly wait."

All I could do was nod.

"Oh, hey, did the laptop get here? I can help you set it up, if you want."

"That is an excellent idea," I said. "They brought it to the library, but I have no idea how to even turn the thing on."

"Hoo boy. Seriously?" She raised her eyebrows in surprise. "We'll have our work cut out for ourselves then, huh?"

"You mean it won't be 'boom,' done?" I was teasing her, and she smiled back at me as we started for the door.

"You're going to have to put in some work, mister. There's kind of a learning curve." She shut the door behind us, then we started down the hallway for the library.

Playfully, I poked her elbow with my own. "Excellent. Good thing I have forever to learn it."

She shook her head. "It had better not take that long."

"I will do my best to be a good pupil."

"You'd better, mister." She winked at me, and I grinned.

I knew soon I would have to tell her about the move. I would have to tell the others as well. But I couldn't bring myself to talk about anything unpleasant and spoil the easy camaraderie between us. No sense in ruining her fun. There would be time enough to discuss troubles and difficulties afterward. In the meantime, I wanted her to focus on happy things. Too much of her time had been spent worrying about all the things that had gone wrong since she had met Marie. I wanted to be the one thing that went right.

We decided the best placement for the laptop was on my desk, with the printer on the corner of hers. She spent what seemed like hours registering the machine and installing software. The entire time, she became absorbed in her work and non-communicative. I was of no use at all, so I took a seat at her desk with a book to wait.

She began muttering to herself, urging it to hurry up and cursing under her breath.

I looked up and chuckled, raising one eyebrow inquisitively. "Are you absolutely sure this equipment was a good idea? Seems like an awful lot of work for something that is supposed to make my life simpler."

"You're going to love it. You'll see. This is just the setup. It won't take long." Her face was lit by the glow of the computer screen. She scowled at what she saw there and tapped some of the keys. "Come on, dammit. Work."

Shutting the book, I sat up straighter, pushing back my chair. "You seem to be experiencing a great deal of frustration. Can I assist you in some way?"

She waved her hand. "Shh. Don't distract me."

I laughed at the ludicrousness of being shushed so summarily. "You know, there was a time when I might have taken great offense to that."

"Yeah yeah." Clearly not paying attention to me at all, she pushed a few more buttons, and the computer made a musical sound and the screen changed. She sat up grinning with an expression of triumph. "There. Okay. What do you want your password to be?"

"I beg your pardon?"

"Your password. So no one can hack your stuff. You need one to log onto the machine." Apparently, she saw something dubious in the way I looked at her because she rolled her eyes and sighed. "Look, I'm not going to hack you. You can just tell me what you want and I'll set it."

I crossed my arms over my chest. Though I hadn't understood half of what she'd said, I got the general gist, anyway, and I wasn't about to admit just how foreign all the terms she used seemed to me. "What sort of password, exactly?"

"Something you'll remember. It shouldn't be left lying around on a piece of paper where anyone can find it. It ought to be something that matters to you, but not something that's easy to guess."

I frowned. "What do people usually choose?"

"Pet's names, birth dates, favorite TV shows. Something personal, but not obvious. The best include a combination of both letters and numbers."

"Hmm." I sat in silence for a moment, thinking. "Ada1815."

She stared at me strangely. "I thought you didn't know anything about computers."

"I don't."

"You just gave me the name of a programming language used by the United States Department of Defense. How did you know it if you're not a hacker?" Her eyes pierced through me as she struggled to understand.

Softly, I said, "It's the name and birth date of my daughter."

She blinked. "Well, that's a hell of a coincidence."

"I doubt it very much," I said, looking down at the desk, folding my hands in front of me.

"You had a daughter?"

"Clearly."

"Named Ada. Born in 1815."

I spread my hands upon the wooden desk. "Yes."

"Wait. Ada Lovelace?"

Sighing, I shrugged, crossing my arms over my chest again. "Why do Americans always insist on confusing surnames and titles? She married that idiot, William King, Earl of Lovelace. My ex-wife's idea."

"Your daughter was Ada Lovelace? The Ada Lovelace. First computer programmer, like ever?"

I rolled my eyes. "She got all her mathematical skills from her mother. Insufferable woman. Love was like algebra with her. Painful. Boring. Absolute. Unforgiving."

"You just blew my mind."

I laughed. "Do I need to choose a different password?"

"No." She shook her head and began typing. "That's fine. Just..."

Sitting back, I sighed softly. "I know. I didn't tell you I had a daughter. I'm sorry. It was a long time ago."

She stopped what she was doing and turned back to face me. "I'm sorry. I was really insensitive."

"You live long enough, and you lose everyone you ever knew. That's how it works."

"You must miss her."

"I miss all my daughters," I said. Until I said it out loud, I hadn't realized how much it still made my heart ache. "Even after all this time."

She raised her eyebrows, tilting her head to one side, regarding me with curiosity. "You have others?"

"Had. They're all gone now."

There must have been something sadder than I intended to show in my tone because her voice softened, and she whispered. "I'm sorry."

I shook my head. "It was a long time ago. No sense in being sorry."

She reached out and touched my hand, giving it a squeeze.

"I'm fine." The words came automatically to my lips, but they rang hollow. I cleared my throat. "Anyway, let's talk about something less morbid, shall we?"

"You don't have to pretend for me," she said.

"No," I said. "But I do prefer to pretend for myself. Someday, I'll tell you all about them. Just not today."

She nodded and squeezed my hand once more. "Okay."

Our eyes met for a wordless conversation, and I saw from her look she understood me in a way no one had in ages. I smiled and swallowed the lump in my throat. "Right then. How do I use this contraption of yours?"

Laughing, she proceeded to launch into a complicated explanation of the software. She opened the writing program and showed me a few of the features. We tested the voice recognition software and demonstrated it would, indeed, type what I told it to. By that time, it was growing late, and we both agreed since the ball was on the following evening, any further use of the laptop would need to wait until we had more time later in the week. I walked her back to her room and kissed her cheek, thanking her for her help.

"I appreciate you trying to bring me into the modern world," I said. "You're right. I probably will get a good deal of use from that machine once I understand it."

She beamed up at me happily. "I think you will too. And you're welcome. I'm glad you like it."

With that, she stretched up on tiptoe and kissed my cheek tenderly, then touched back down again, gazing into my eyes.

"Goodnight," I said quietly, reaching out to brush a stray lock of hair from her cheek.

"Night, Albé."

She backed away and closed the door, leaving me in the hall alone. My hand stretched up to touch my cheek where her lips had been, and I smiled to myself, walking back to my room in silence.

Under the Arm of the Madman

Raul

A knock woke me the next evening. I opened the door to find the Marquis standing outside, an excited gleam in his eye. "Come, boy. I have wonders to show you."

I paused, running my hand through my hair to brush it away from my face. "Wonders? What are you talking about?"

"Come and see!" he said, and he laughed in a manic way that made me slightly uncomfortable. Putting his hand on my shoulder, he pulled me out into the hallway. "I have much to show you."

His arm hung around my shoulder as though we were old friends, but something in his behavior made my skin crawl. I didn't dare pull away for fear of offending him and being sent back to the dungeons, so I forced myself to smile and go with him, hiding my uncertainty but reminding myself to keep my eyes open in case of a trap.

We walked down two flights of steps, and I had a momentary panic my fears of re-imprisonment were coming true. However, when we came to the doorway I knew led down to that horrible place, he passed it by completely and instead walked to the left and out into a courtyard. Crossing that open space bathed in moonlight, I thought perhaps he intended to give me a continued tour of the property.

On the far side of the courtyard, stood a wall with a large door in the middle. It led not to the outside but into another enclosed set of large rooms with bare stone walls. No furniture decorated the space at all, and I thought perhaps we had reached an area still under construction. Only when we passed through another set of doors did I discover his true intent.

We stopped in the center of a large windowless chamber. Around the perimeter of the room were a series of glass walled cages.

"Wait here, my boy," he said, stepping away from me, and I stood silently, fearful after everything I had experienced since I was taken hostage. Dancing a funny little jig-like step, he made his way over to a panel of switches and flipped them one by one with a dramatic flair. Lights came on all the way down the row, and what I saw inside filled me with horror.

Hundreds of walking corpses in various states of decay thrust themselves against the glass, jostling one another, eyes bulging, fingers like bloody talons, their lips pulled back in grimaces of death, revealing long and terrifying fangs. They seemed to have no rational thought, and not one of them spoke human words in any language. Instead, there came a terrifying inhuman roar as all of them clamored with only one desire, blood.

I stood, frozen with fear, and the Marquis returned to my side with a skip and a jump, clapping with delight. "Aren't they lovely? My beauties."

He snapped his fingers and a loud buzzing came from above. The creatures all stopped, turning to look up with expectation. Then, blood began to pour from fixtures in the ceiling, raining down as they stood open-mouthed and moaning with hunger. I wanted to run from that place, but I couldn't make my feet move.

"I have them trained, you see? Like Pavlov with his dogs. They see me, then hear that buzzing, and they know its time to eat. Soon, they will be ready." He grinned, beaming with pride.

"Ready for what?" I asked, dreading the answer.

"Why, they are my army, of course."

How anyone could look on those wretched things and see an army was more than my mind could comprehend.

"W-what are they?" I couldn't help the shaking in my voice. "Those things. They're not human. Are they...are they zombies?"

The Marquis laughed, and this time it filled me with cold dread. "They are no different from you or me, my boy. I have shaped and molded them to become as you see. My army of killing machines. Fast, deadly, and unstoppable. They associate my presence with attaining what they want most. Isn't it marvelous? You can be at my side, dear boy, when the world changes."

I nodded, hoping he couldn't see my terror. Not human. Not vampire. These were true monsters, and he thought to use and control them. This man was insane, more so than I could ever have believed. Worst of all, I could not stop him. He threw his arm around me and began to talk of his great plans for the end of mankind. All the while, I stared at the creatures in their cages and fought the urge to scream.

"The beauty of it, dear boy, is this facility is one of many. I have been growing my army slowly over many years. At last, they are nearly ready. Shall we test them on the town? I have been waiting so long to revenge for the destruction of my home."

While I had hunted and killed people in the town, it was true, the thought of releasing these creatures for en masse extermination was a level of violence beyond my imagination. Everything in me balked as I contemplated what this man was suggesting in the name of vengeance.

"But they weren't the people who tore things down," I said. "Their ancestors did."

He shook his head and smiled. "No matter. Do you think humans have changed so much in the years since? Cattle is what they are. The sooner you recognize that fact, the better, for in letting go of your attachment to the human coil, you come to see your own place above them and your right to take control of the world and rule it as you see fit. We are the ultimate predators, my boy. Don't you see? All this restraint and caution, what has it gotten you? Hiding in the shadows, afraid of how the humans might react to your superiority? That is nonsense. What do you care about their reaction? Why should you? You are not one of them any longer, and you are not beholden to their rules or laws. We should strike, subjugate them, show them just how weak they really are."

"Then what?" I asked.

"Then we will be free! It will be a world ruled by vampires, now and forever! Glorious! You will stand at my side and say you were there at the beginning."

"And these poor creatures?" I said, gesturing down at the mindless army he had created. "Will they be free? Did they agree to this?"

He smiled, an expression void of any mirth or emotion, and it chilled me to the core. "Do you wish to join them and find out?"

Shaking my head, I took a step back, staring at him in wide eyed horror. He was not making an idle threat.

All this time, I believed he was a man of reason. I underestimated him completely. With sudden shock, I remembered I was standing next to a man who was kept in prison for the criminally insane. He protested his innocence to me, and his philosophical arguments had seemed so reasonable, but in this place, witnessing the extent of his plans, I could see why he was deemed so dangerous.

Something in my reaction made him laugh, then. "Relax, dear boy. I was only joking. You are far too sensitive. Do you fancy these creatures before us as my prisoners? Nothing could be farther from the case. I found each of them wandering lost and alone, and I brought them here to care for them. Who would do so if I did not?"

He gestured down at the mass of monsters below, still drinking in the blood that rained down on them. "They were once no different from you or I, but the disease that changed us both had a much more sinister effect on those you see before you. How can you blame them for what they are? I helped them in the only way I can. Without me, every one of them would have been killed by those who misunderstand their suffering. I understand. I give their suffering meaning. Separated and alone, they are vulnerable and weak, but together under my protection and guidance, I can ensure no one else need suffer as they have. Our kind need never hide in the shadows in fear and doubt again. I cannot save these wretches, you are right, but I can make their sacrifice fulfill a purpose."

For several moments, I gazed around at the monstrous walking corpses pressing against the glass and looking at me with mindless hunger in their soulless eyes. That could have been me in there. It was a fate I would not wish on anyone. Was this the future I had to look forward to? Is this what we all would become in time? My horror turned to pity, and I knew he was right. They needed him. I needed him.

With a shudder, I turned and looked back at the Marquis, and in that moment I saw again the father figure I had longed for. His reasoning held a sudden clarity of meaning for me, and all my doubts and fears fell away. I had been wrong to question. What he was suggesting was a necessity for all our kind. He offered self-acceptance, purpose, freedom from judgment and a pardon for our sins. He offered salvation.

Bowing my head with respect, I dropped to my knees before him to submit to his command. "What do you need me to do, Master? I am your instrument."

Carnival

Marie

Casanova made arrangements for everything regarding our attendance at the masquerade ball. When I awoke, I found a box had been delivered with a costume for me. The dress was a beautiful white and gold brocade, and it came with a mask that covered my face and a cloak with a hood. He thought of everything to ensure we were not recognized together. I was taken with a sense of giddy delight at flirting with danger.

Once I was dressed, I left my room to meet Casanova. I carried the mask, planning to put it on once I was safely aboard his motorboat. As I walked past Byron's door, however, he popped out of it and nearly ran into me. I was almost as surprised by his appearance in knee breeches, a ruffled shirt, embroidered jacket, cloak, and Carnival mask as I was by his sudden startling entrance.

"Oh!" I gasped, looking him up and down. "You're like a well dressed Jack-in-the-box. I didn't know you were going to the ball."

He took in my appearance, and I could see his eyes widen behind his mask. "I didn't know you were going either. Did you get my note last night?"

"Note?" Then I remembered what he was talking about. "Oh, yes. I was so busy, I had forgotten about it. Everything all right?"

He shook his head. "Well, no. Not really."

I held up my hand. "Don't tell me about it right now, please. Wait until after the ball. I don't want to spoil the evening."

"But…"

"No, darling. I must insist. I am late as it is."

"All right. But when it's over, I would like to talk with your friend Casanova about the matter as well."

"Casanova?" I laughed, hoping I sounded casual. "Oh, we are just acquaintances, that's all. I hardly know the man."

I knew beneath his mask, Byron was raising an eyebrow. "I see," he said. "So it's just business between you."

"Darling, of course. What else would it be? Do you honestly think a man like that would appeal to me? Or I to him, for that matter? You should know better. I need his help and he needs mine. It's that simple."

He nodded. "If you say so. I'm sorry I jumped to conclusions. Still, we will need his help. Once I've explained the situation to you, then you will understand why."

"Oh very well, darling. Just go and have fun tonight, won't you? You're always so serious these days. You need to relax a little. Don't be so tedious."

"Tedious?" He laughed a little. "I see. That is an indictment. And one I intend to remedy."

"Good." I patted him on the shoulder. "Now I must run. Have a good time."

"You too," he said, tipping his three-cornered hat to me. "And be careful."

"I am always careful, darling." And giving a little wave, I walked away quickly, heading for the waiting boat.

True to his word, Casanova was waiting for me in his beautiful wooden boat. As I approached, he raised his mask, and I saw his starlit eyes take in the whole of me. He smiled and reached a hand to help me step aboard. "Marie, you are breathtaking this evening. A vision. That dress suits you perfectly. Even better than I dreamed." He kissed my hand as he led me to my seat. "I am honored to have you by my side tonight."

I laughed, opening my fan to cover my smile. "Oh Gio, your way with words is delightful. And you look very handsome yourself. The clothes suit you."

He bowed. "I thank you, my lady."

Taking his seat, he started the motor, and we headed out across the lagoon. The stars were bright up above, and as we approached the city, it seemed for a moment like another constellation, beckoning us toward heaven.

Knowing we had to avoid being recognized, I put on my mask as we approached, and he pulled his own down to cover his face down to his chin. Despite the crowds on shore, he pulled up directly in front of the Palazzo Ducale and found an open slip waiting for him. "Do you have a reserved spot?" I said, watching him tie off the lines.

"Being coven leader does have its perks," he said.

He helped me out onto the shore, then tucked my arm around his own and led me away toward the swarming crowds.

As we approached the Piazza San Marco, I saw acrobats and men on stilts and torches flickering, and it felt as though we had stepped back in time. At least until we got closer, that is. In the midst of the traditionally dressed revelers were thoroughly modern tourists with cameras snapping away. They swarmed around us like insects, photographing us we walked toward the Palazzo Ducale. They shouted at us to wave or pose, but Casanova didn't pause until we were near the front of the building. Once there and behind velvet ropes with the other costumed guests waiting to enter, he turned and put his arm around me, whispering, "Let's give them just a little of what they want, shall we?"

The flashes from their cameras was momentarily blinding,

but we stayed still for several minutes, waving to the throng. At last, in spite of complaints from the onlookers, we turned away and walked forward toward the doors that led to the ball. I breathed a little sigh of relief, and he laughed privately to me. "Don't worry. They aren't allowed inside."

Reaching into his pocket, he pulled out a gilded invitation and when we arrived at the door, he showed the card to the security personnel. "Welcome, Signore Casanova. May we have the name of your guest, please?"

"Claire Marie Hapsburg," I said, speaking before I thought. I was supposed to be leaving that name behind in Saint Louis. But surely, I thought, the name couldn't harm me now. After all, no one from Venice would know me by that name.

The guard nodded and wrote down the name on a clipboard, then waved us on through.

"Claire Marie, eh?" Casanova said with amusement.

"It's what I was called in Saint Louis before I...before I came here."

"I see. It suits you," he said.

The Palazzo was festooned with flowers and lit with candles throughout. I could hear music from a farther room as we pressed in among the costumed guests. Everywhere I looked, there were men in knee breeches and buckled shoes wearing masks, and the women were all outdoing one another for elegance, mystery, and whimsy. I saw one woman wearing a wig with a gigantic swan on top, and I laughed remembering some of the fanciful dresses I used to wear years ago in Versailles. Casanova and I blended in among the others, appearing elegant but not in a way that attracted too much attention.

Casanova led me through the crowd toward the ballroom. As we entered, I could see an orchestra arranged at the far end of the room. Dancers whirled around in pairs, the women's dresses fanning out around them. Candles flickered in tall candelabras around the periphery of the room, lending a glow of romance and intrigue to the revelers.

"May I have this dance, my lady?" said Casanova, turning and bowing slightly to me.

"Of course," I said, and he led me out onto the floor.

We enjoyed several dances and waltzes together, and my heart felt lighter than it had in ages. All my fears left aside, I lost myself in the joy of simply being there with him and feeling adored and appreciated. Across the room, I caught sight of Byron, dancing with another woman. They looked beautiful together, and I smiled behind my mask, glad to see that he too was able to take pleasure in the moment. I hoped that after all these years, he could find a measure of happiness all his own.

In the midst of a waltz, a man in a cloak tapped Casanova's shoulder, as if to cut in. We stopped, and Casanova turned to look at the person who interrupted us. As politely as he could muster, Casanova shook his head and said, "I apologize, sir, but the lady is with me."

"May I ask to whom I have the honor of addressing," the man said, his voice disarmingly sharp.

Though I expected him to refuse, Casanova removed his mask and smiled. "Gioccomo Casanova, at your service."

"And your lady friend?"

I shook my head, and Casanova hastily answered for me. "She would prefer not to reveal herself, sir. After all, it is a masquerade. But since I have shown you my face, will you not do the same?"

Without warning, two hands came from behind me and grabbed my arms, pulling me abruptly away from Casanova. I kicked and squirmed, but the man who held me had a firm grip. Casanova himself stepped forward to protest, but suddenly there were people on either side of him, holding him back, keeping him from struggling. The man who had approached us walked up to face me and with one swift gesture removed my mask, throwing it on the floor where it broke in half. I cried out in shock and anger.

There was a collective gasp and the music stopped.

"Voila. Madame Deficit. Quelle surprise."

The man's French accent made my blood run cold. "Who are you?"

With a dramatic flair, the man removed his mask. I knew his face instantly, and I gasped in horror.

"Monsieur Robespierre!"

He gave me a predatory grin that shook my soul with fear. It was the same face that had brought my husband and all his supporters to the guillotine. It was the face that had worked with the Marquis to topple my nation and cost me my crown. "You have not forgotten me. I am glad to know it."

"I thought you were dead."

"The feeling was mutual, I assure you."

"What do you want, you monster?" I was terrified of what the man might do if he managed to get me out of sight of the audience surrounding us. Not daring to take my eyes off him, I racked my brain for possible ways we might escape. My ideas came up short, and I struggled to keep my desperation from showing on my face.

Robespierre laughed. "Why to prove once and for all what a lying, manipulative, dangerous woman you are. I am sure Signore Casanova had no idea what sort of trouble you were bringing to him. Pity." He turned to look at Casanova who was still trying unsuccessfully to wrench his arms free. "You made my job far too easy, I'm afraid." With a nod to Casanova's captors, Robespierre said, "Take him away."

"On what charge?" I said, a quaver of fear in my voice betraying my emotions.

"Conspiracy with foreign dignitaries to deceive his fellow coven members. A vote of no confidence regarding his compromised leadership of this coven. And treason against the state."

I gasped, but Casanova shook his head at me not to argue. The men began dragging him through the crowd toward the outer doors, and the people parted the way, staring in shock.

"He will have a fair trial, of course," said Robespierre, turning a fanged smile toward me. "As will you, madame. Before you are executed."

Fighting against the hands that held me tight, I glared at Robespierre, helpless as Casanova disappeared from view. "You seem to be judge and jury all in one, monsieur. Some things never change."

He laughed coldly, but before he could reply, a sword swung through the air and cut off his head.

His mouth opened with a soundless scream, eyes still moving for a few moments before going still. From the neck, blood spurted everywhere, in great jetting arcs, spraying my dress and those of the onlookers who gaped and shrieked in horror.

As the body toppled and the head rolled across the marble floor to rest somewhere in the vicinity of my feet, I saw the hand holding that sword belonged to Byron. He had taken off his mask and pulled the sword from his cane to defend me. At his side, Sybill stood, holding up her skirts, eyes wide with shock as she stared at the growing pool of livid crimson which poured over the stone floor from the neck of the still twitching body.

Screams ensued as revelers scrambled in all directions.

Byron slashed toward my captor, and the man pushed me away in order to avoid the blade. I slipped on the blood and fell, staining the front of my dress a brilliant red. Sybill sprang forward, gripping my arm to help me up, and as I struggled to my feet, dripping, I saw Byron thrust the blade again. He stabbed the man in the chest, piercing his heart, and he went down heavily to his knees, clutching the wound. Before he could recover, Byron cut off his head and kicked the body beside the other one.

"Run," he said, swirling to see if there were other attackers on their way.

Three men came from the doorway toward us, but Sybill and I ran the opposite direction through the scattering crowd, out a side door. Though I heard crashes and shouting behind us, I kept running, hoping to find an exit in the midst of the mayhem. Fortunately for us, tourism in the city meant every exit was clearly marked. We found one marked as a fire door, but we pushed through, hearing the sound of a fire alarm as we ran from the building.

We found ourselves out in the square, surrounded by crowds of people all looking up to see the fireworks over the city. I stopped to see where we should run, and Sybill slammed into me.

"Which way?" she said, her eyes wide with fear.

I shook my head uncertainly, looking around in helpless dismay. No matter which direction we chose, neither of us knew the city, and our pursuers would capture us easily. I had never felt so frightened or vulnerable.

Just as I was beginning to speak, however, a hand grasped my shoulder, and I shrieked in terror, whirling to strike my captor.

It was Byron. His face and shirt were spattered with blood, and his hair was wild from running. With a cry, Sybill threw her arms around him, but he pushed her quickly away.

"No time. This way." Holding his sword in front of him, he led us off into the night and away from the crowds.

There were so many twists and turns, I lost my sense of direction completely, but Byron seemed to know exactly where he was going. He kept to the shadows where we could, but we never stopped moving. The narrow passageways were crowded with people celebrating, but they finally began to thin out as we got away from the main tourist centers of the city.

Finally, we crossed a bridge and he turned to descend some steps that led down to a waterside cafe. Out front, a motorboat was tied to a cleat on the canal. The owner was nowhere to be seen. Byron looked both ways before pointing at the boat. "Get in."

I hesitated for a moment, but Sybill pulled me on board. Byron let loose the lines, then followed us into the open boat. The key was still in the ignition, and the engine quickly roared to life. A man stood up at the cafe, waving and shouting, but he was too late. We were gone before he could reach the water's edge.

"Do you know where you're going?" Sybill said as Byron wove past gondolas full of drunken tourists.

"Away," was all he said.

We held on tight as he guided the boat as fast as he dared, turning down narrow canals just wide enough for the hull to fit between the buildings.

At last, we came out onto open water, and he pushed the throttle forward and pointed us out away from the city toward the sea. I knew returning to San Lazzaro was out of the question. Too many people knew how to find us there. We would have to find another place to hide before dawn.

With no safe place to turn and knowing my one champion among the coven was imprisoned and likely to be killed, I had lost not only Casanova but also any chance of finding the traitor and saving Raul along with him. Overwhelmed with loss, I sank down with my head in my hands and wept.

Turncoat

Mozart

Times like these made me miss getting drunk.

My bag sat on my bed, ready to be packed, but I hadn't quite gotten myself ready to put anything in it yet.

I had gone over everything in my mind a million times. I even made a side by side list of reasons to stay versus reasons to go. Though my list of reasons for leaving was long, there were still a few reasons left to stay.

Sybill and Albé were kind to me. I liked them. Even my anger with Marie didn't alter that fact. They were innocent of all her scheming and didn't deserve to be lumped in alongside her when her past caught up with her at last.

Doctor Polidori and I had barely interacted, so I had no way to judge his character, but I suspected he too was a victim of circumstance as far as Marie was concerned. From what I had observed, he kept himself separate from her as much as possible. He could hardly therefore, be held to blame. If I left, he would likely become collateral damage, and I would regret being responsible for that.

The problem was the Marquis owned me. He had for years. Escaping his grasp was impossible. I long ago accepted that. Once you give yourself over to a man like that, there is no escape, no matter how far you run.

Gambling was always a weakness of mine. Even as a human, I could never resist a wager or a game of cards. In life, I ran up debts I could never hope to repay. That was part of the reason I let Casanova turn me. Creditors can't get money from you if you're dead. So much for my assumptions. Once I thought Casanova was dead, I was on my own to make my way in the world, and I fell into bad habits all over again.

The Marquis preyed upon my weakness and loaned me money. At that time, I didn't know what he was like. I thought he was a friend to me. I was foolish. He was simply buying a pawn, and when my luck went sour, he used that as leverage to make me do his bidding. For years, he kept me with him, a prisoner in all but name, working with that bitch of a daughter of his, letting her make me her errand boy.

I thought when I finally escaped to the United States I would be free of them both. I believed working for Vincent DeLuca would insulate me from their influence. Foolishly, I thought it was all in my past. As soon as they suspected Marie was in America, however, I learned it would never be over.

That first call I had gotten from Ernestine last fall had left me feeling broken and hopeless. She grilled me for an hour and made threats to bring me in if I didn't cooperate. I didn't know anything. I told her that. It didn't matter. She insisted I try to learn what I could from Vincent, and then share that information with her.

Getting a man like Vincent to talk about secrets was a suicide mission. I knew it. Still there had to be something I could glean from him to get the Marquis off my back.

The only thing I managed to learn was he had known Marie back during Prohibition. Probably nothing Ernestine didn't already know, but I contacted her and gave her that information anyway, hoping that would be an end to my dealings with the matter.

Imagine my surprise when Marie turned up at Vincent's hotel a few weeks later. This was a chance for me to barter for my freedom. I never expected to care for her. I never expected to be taken with her to Venice. And I never expected she would break my heart.

In the time since Marie arrived at the hotel, I tried my best to stall with Ernestine. I fed her just enough information to keep her off my back but not enough to get us caught.

Even when Marie threw me over for Casanova, I resisted the temptation to act out of vindictive rage, tempting as it was. I couldn't stand thinking the others who were caught up in Marie's mess through no fault of their own would be punished for it because of me.

Standing there looking down at my bag, I debated with my-self what to do. I could hardly stay and remain with them without helping the Marquis. Things had gone too far, and Marie no longer wanted me with her. If, on the other hand, I stayed and betrayed them, I would bear that on my conscience forever. The only other option was to run, but where could I go? The Marquis found me in Chicago. No matter where I went, he would eventually track me down, and when that happened, I would be severely punished. I was out of options.

By now, I thought, she would be dancing with Casanova. They would smile and laugh together and pretend people weren't dying on her account. The very thought of it made me sick. Still, I couldn't make myself give their position away, even after everything. Let Marie have one last dance, I thought. For old time's sake and the love I felt for her.

Laughing at my stupid sentimentality, I moved to the closet, intent on gathering my clothes and making an attempt to escape, despite every good reason I had to betray her.

My phone rang. I considered letting it go unanswered. After several minutes, the ringing stopped. I breathed a sigh of relief. Then the phone rang again. No escape.

With a sigh, I picked up the phone. "Yes?"

"Wolfgang, you have to go in to the city right now."

It was Ernestine. No prelude. No requests. Just instructions. As though I was her dog to command. She expected me to roll over and heel like a good boy.

I couldn't keep the exhausted tone out of my voice. "Hello to you too. Which city might that be?"

"Don't play dumb. I don't have time for games. Get a boat. Go now. I need you at the Palazzo Ducale now."

"And I need a million dollars. We all have our crosses to bear. Tell me why I care what you want."

Her voice dropped to a cold whisper. "Because your contact, Robespierre, is dead. Casanova is imprisoned. Marie and two others are on the loose. And if you don't do as I say right now to help contain the situation, I will make it my personal mission to have you drawn and quartered alive. Is that enough reason for you?"

She could do it. Of that I had no doubt. I had seen her torture others at the Marquis' behest, and I knew the creative ways she could inflict pain.

I winced. I had no more cards to play. Sighing heavily, I closed my eyes, trying to squash the image of her turning my entrails into extrails.

"You win," I said flatly. "You win."

With that, I hung up the phone, then began packing my bag in a hurry. I would be leaving, all right, but not escaping. There would be no escape for any of us.

This ends

Out For Blood
Book Two Of The Blood Royal Saga

Keep reading for a

Sneak Peek of

Trial By Blood
Book Three Of The Blood Royal Saga

And An

Afterward
By The Author

SNEAK PEEK INSIDE THE UPCOMING SEQUEL,

Trial By Blood

The Tomb by the Pounding Sea

Byron

"You have got to be kidding me." Sybill was goggling at the view of the gravestones beyond the open gates as they slowly creaked open.

"Well, I didn't have much choice given the circumstances, did I?" I shook my head, but my tone softened when I saw Marie struggling out of the boat onto the shore of the cemetery island of San Michele. The entire front of her white dress was soaked in blood, and her hands were shaking. "Help her, would you? I think she's in shock."

Sybill looked back and then hurried to her side, speaking softly to Marie and wrapping an arm around her waist to help steady her. "Hey, it's okay. We're safe."

"We will never be safe. And they have him. They'll kill him, you know. They'll kill him. It's all my fault. I ruined his life." Stumbling, Marie clung to Sybill with white knuckles as though if she let go she might collapse completely. "I'm a disaster to you and everyone else."

"Hush. Don't talk like that. This isn't your fault."

I cleared my throat, and Sybill looked up at me with a sour expression. "Get inside. I'll get rid of the boat."

As soon as they were safely behind the high walls, I started the boat engine, lashed the wheel so the prow headed out toward the lagoon, and I loosed the lines. The boat headed off unmanned out across the water, and I prayed it wouldn't be found too near us.

"Wasn't that our ride?" Sybill said.

I entered the gates and swung them shut behind us with a loud clank. "That was going to lead them straight to us. Now come on and let me get you both settled someplace safe."

"Does it get any more cliché than this? A graveyard? Seriously, you're not really expecting us to stay here, are you?" Her eyes were distressed and panicky, but there was nothing for it.

"I expect you to have survival instincts. You want to go on living? Well, this is the best I've got. I'm sorry I didn't have time to book you a room at the Ritz. I was a little busy saving our asses."

Marie began crying softly, and she went limp in Sybill's arms. "Oh Jeez." Sybill lost her grip and Marie slipped down onto the stones in a heap. "Help me with her, would you?"

I hurried over and picked Marie up. She rested her head on my shoulder, arms around my neck like a child. Though she was not heavy, the extra weight made my foot ache, but I kept silent about it, trying not to let the pain show on my face. There was nothing else for it. Marie was in no shape to walk. "Hurry. We need to get out of sight."

We made our way out of the entrance and into the first high walled enclosure. There was a semicircular wall of open doors that led into family crypts, and paths fanned out toward them like spokes in a wheel. Sybill wrinkled her nose. "You're not going to put us in one of those, are you? They stink."

I shook my head, walking straight up the paved center walkway toward an archway. "This is too close. We need to go further in."

The narrow avenue of stone pavement continued on to the center of the second enclosure, but smaller gravel paths made a grid of walkways between row upon row of gravestones. The paths were flanked by pointed and fragrant cypress trees, drenching the whole place in long patches of deep shadow. I could see the dome of the church to my left, its spires gleaming in the moonlight. Stopping beneath the arch, Sybill gaped open-mouthed, then whispered as she hurried to catch up to me. "This is creepy. I don't want to stay here."

I snorted and kept walking. "Creepy is the least of our worries. You're a vampire. What do you think is going to hurt you here?"

"Ghosts?" She looked around with wide eyes.

"Tsk. No such thing."

"How do you know?"

"Two hundred years of experience. Now stop talking and let me think." I paused by a dry stone fountain, the water having been shut off until spring. Nothing moved besides us, and the only sound was of the wind in the trees and our feet on the gravel. I turned slowly, looking at our options. Many of the crypts were designed to hold cremated remains in tiny vaults on the wall. No good. There were no fresh graves in the ground, and I knew that even if that were an option, Sybill would never agree to lie buried in a box until I returned. That left only one choice. I walked over to a nearby bench and set Marie down carefully. "Just wait here a moment."

Sybill came to sit beside her, eyeing me with uncertainty.

Ignoring her, I turned away and walked over to the door of one of the four large family tombs that stood facing one another across the intersection of paths. The door was padlocked to keep out vandals and tourists. I swore under my breath, then turned back to look at Sybill. "Do you have any hairpins?"

"What?"

"Hairpins. This door is locked."

She smiled in surprise. "You're a regular James Bond, aren't you?"

"I don't know what that means." I shook my head, holding out my hand toward her. "Just tell me if you have any or not. I would rather not break this lock if I don't have to."

"I don't," she said, taking off her wig to reveal her startling blonde spiky hair, so in contrast with her gown, "but I'm sure Marie does."

And without saying anything to Marie who was sitting still, staring out vacantly across the graveyard, Sybill reached up and pulled two hairpins out of Marie's wig. Marie blinked, but didn't say anything. "Here," said Sybill, bringing them over and placing them into my palm. "You sure you know what you're doing?"

"Watch and learn," I said.

It didn't take long before the lock clicked and the hasp slid open. I pocketed the lock, then pushed the door back, revealing the interior of the crypt. The air was close and musty inside. Clearly, no one had entered in quite some time. The flowers on the tomb had mummified, and there was a fine layer of dust over everything. Still, as I looked around, I could see that it was light tight. "This will do."

Sybill peeked in. "No way. It's not big enough for all three of us."

"I won't be inside."

"What? Where are you going?" Her eyes were wildly searching mine and full of fear.

"Someone has to get word to Polidori and Mozart. They need to get out of there before the coven arrives. Marie needs you. That means me."

"But...how? You got rid of the boat."

I laughed. "You really don't know anything about me, do you? I'm a strong swimmer. I can make it there before dawn."

"Swimming?" She gripped my arm tightly. "But it's so far."

I patted her hand reassuringly. "First of all, I swam across the Hellespont almost two hundred years ago. I've had centuries of practice since then. And secondly, do you really think I could drown? We don't have to breathe, remember? I'll be fine. Trust me."

"But what if they're already at San Lazarro?"

"Then Mozart and Polidori will need rescuing, won't they?" I smiled and leaned in to kiss her forehead. "I'm sorry things went so wrong tonight. This was not how I pictured our date ending."

She stared up at me. "This wasn't how I pictured it either."

"Oh? What did you think would happen?" I stepped in closer, brushing back a lock of hair from her forehead.

Biting her lip, she shook her head. "I don't know. I guess I hadn't thought it through that far. I just wanted to have a good time, really."

I nodded. "So did I."

"Rotten timing."

"That it is."

Just then a clock rang out four times. "Speaking of time, I'm running out of it. I have to hurry if I'm going to be there before dawn."

She reached a hand up and touched my cheek. "Thank you for saving us. You were amazing. Like Zorro or something."

"I'll teach you sometime, just like I said. In the meantime, let's get you both inside."

And like that, we parted, focusing on the task at hand. We got on either side of Marie and hoisted her to her feet, then walked her into the tomb together. Sybill helped me lower her down onto the floor, brushing away the patina of grime and spiderwebs that covered the stone slabs.

"I'll be back as soon as I can," I said, kissing Marie on the forehead. Then I turned and stroked Sybill's hair one time. "Take care of yourselves."

She nodded, and I backed away before I wasted any more precious time. I pulled the door shut, then pulled the padlock out of my pocket.

I knew that the caretakers would notice if the crypt appeared to have been tampered with. I couldn't risk exposing Sybill and Marie to the sun because of a careless mistake. I had to trust that I would be back the following night to free them. Silently so Sybill wouldn't become alarmed, I slid the lock into the hasp on the door and clicked it shut.

Afterward by the Author

This book was full of surprise as I was writing. I know it's something of a cliché to say that the characters tell the author what to do, but in this case, they really did.

I knew going into it I was going to include Lord Byron as a character. I've had him in mind for a book for what seems like forever. My first attempt at writing a novel about him was an historical fiction I began writing when I was still an undergrad English major. That book will likely never see the light of day, or at least not in the form in which it was originally written, but as a character, he has always fascinated me. Larger than life, he was the first real "rock star" of literary figures, attracting groupies wherever he went. His life was the basis for the first vampire novel written in English, ***The Vampyre*** by none other than Doctor John Polidori. I felt if I was going to write a vampire novel which featured real historical figures, I couldn't miss the opportunity to include him. I hope he is as fun to read as he has been to write. I look forward to telling a lot more of his story as the series continues.

Another new character that goes hand in hand with Byron is Polidori. I couldn't have the one without the other. Their real life connection was so twisted, and given that Polidori wrote **The Vampyre** as a form of revenge against his former employer, an attempt that backfired, I just could not resist bringing him into the tale. As you can tell already, he has a bit of a dark side, and there will be more of that revealed in the next book. I can't say more than that because I hate to give spoilers. Sorry!

Casanova was simply a delightful surprise. I'd intended him to be a cameo appearance only, but clearly he had other ideas, and I am thrilled with the way he burst into my imagination in such vivid detail. I'd love to explore more of the city with him, especially his nightclub, and I wish I could tell you what's going to happen with him, but quite honestly he hasn't told me yet. Whatever happens, I can promise it'll be exciting and full of flair.

His assistant, Jenny, is based on a friend of mine. I'm not sure yet just what part she will have to play in the books to come, but she is an utter delight to write and a wonderful contrast to all the other characters we've seen so far.

Those who told me how much they loved Wolfie in **In The Blood** may be surprised by the turns his story has taken. I hope, however, they will forgive me and hang in there for where his tale leads.

Sybill really seemed to come into her own more in this second book. She is much more confident and strong, and her voice is clearer in my head now that she is learning how to deal with the changes in her life.

As for Raul, well...I'm not going to say anything about him until the end of the next book. I really can't discuss him at all without giving too much away. All I can tell you is that his story isn't over yet. The same goes for the people he's with now. There will be more of them in the future, but beyond that, I'm keeping my mouth shut.

Finally, Marie has really become like an old friend to me. She's my constant companion on my book tours, and nearly everyone who comes to the table to talk to me about the series wants to talk to me about her and what's in store. I love her more with each passing chapter. I could not have chosen a more amazing leading lady, as far as I'm concerned.

I hope with this second installment, I've given you surprises and thrills and I've delivered on my promise to keep you coming back for more. Trial By Blood will round out this part of the story arch of the series, but I have ideas for at least five more books depending on reader interest.

Want the series to continue? There are a few ways you can help me make that happen.

Write a review on Goodreads, Amazon, Barnes & Noble or wherever you think people will see your recommendation. Reviews help other readers decide what to try, and every little bit helps.

Talk to your friends. Word of mouth works! I cannot afford big budget ad campaigns, so if you want me to afford to keep going on these stories, help get the word out.

If you see my posts on social media, boost the signal.

Whenever I've got an event happening in your area, come out and see me! I'd love to sign your book or just hear your thoughts about the series. I may even have some of Marie's cupcakes with me, and you're welcome to come eat cake.

And finally, just keep reading! As long as people are reading, I will keep on writing.

About the Press

Eagle Heights Press, a division of *Eagle Heights LLC.*, publishes thriller, fantasy, science fiction, historical fiction, paranormal romance, speculative fiction, young adult, non-fiction, and more.

Find us on the web at eagleheightspress.com.

www.ingramcontent.com/pod-product-compliance
Lightning Source LLC
Chambersburg PA
CBHW050606190726
48283CB00007B/2305